Bix's Trumpet and other stories

Bix's Trumpet and other stories

Dave Margoshes

NeWest Press

Library and Archives Canada Cataloguing in Publication
Margoshes, Dave, 1941–
Bix's trumpet and other stories / Dave Margoshes

ISBN 978-1-897126-18-9
I. Title.

PS8576.A647B59 2007 C813'.54 C2007-902158-1

Editor for the Board: Lynne Van Luven
Cover and interior design: Virginia Penny
Cover image: Alex Colville, *Pacific,* 1967, acrylic on hardboard,
copyright © A.C.Fine Art Inc.
Author photo: Bryan Schlosser

NeWest Press acknowledges the support of the Canada Council for the Arts and the Alberta Foundation for the Arts, and the Edmonton Arts Council for our publishing program. We also acknowledge the financial support of the Government of Canada through the Book Publishing Industry Development Program (BPIDP) for our publishing activities.

NeWest Press
201-8540-109 Street
Edmonton, Alberta T6G 1E6

(780) 432-9427

www.newestpress.com

NeWest Press is committed to protecting the environment and to the responsible use of natural resources. This book is printed on recycled and ancient-forest-friendly paper. For more information, please visit www.oldgrowthfree.com

1 2 3 4 5 10 09 08 07

printed and bound in Canada

For Ilya, who helps me to see

Acknowledgements

My thanks to the editors of the following publications, in which some of these stories appeared, in earlier versions:

"Bix's Trumpet" in *Grain* and in *06: Best Canadian Stories* (Oberon, 2006)

"Careless" in *Alberta Views*

"Comfort" in *Windsor Review*

"The Gift" in *The Antigonish Review*

"A Love Story" in *sub-Terrain*

"Last Words" in *Ars Medica*

"A Man of Distinction" in *Windsor Review*

"Party Girls" in *Grain*

"Pornography" in *03: Best Canadian Stories* (Oberon, 2003)

"Promises" in *Windsor Review*

"Scars" in *Quarry*

"A Lake Named for Daddy" was broadcast on CBC's *Ambience* in Saskatchewan in an abridged form.

Bix's Trumpet and other stories, under a different title, was a winner of the 2001 John V. Hicks Award presented by the Saskatchewan Writers Guild for a full-length manuscript. The judges were Austin Clarke and Helen Humphreys. My thanks to them.

My thanks also to these friends and acquaintances whose stories inspired or enriched my own: Sharon Butala, Anne Boody, Melanie Collison, Barbara Murdoch, Bob Parkins, Mari-Lou Rowley, Betsy Rosenwald, Sybil Shaw-Hamm, and the late Sylvia Haltrecht, Kit Stratton and Ted White.

Dave Margoshes

The Stories

Bix's Trumpet

THE WAY THE STORY WENT, Bix pawned it, the real Bix, I mean, the great Beiderbecke, out of work for a week, broke, trading shining brass bulbs and valves for five bucks for booze, meaning to redeem it, of course, but a gig came up out of town, short notice, and the pawnshop was closed, someone lent him a horn, and when he came back to the city, weeks later, the trumpet was gone. Bix's father—*my* Bix's father, who, years later, sober for the first time in ages, would fall from the roof of their Highland Park house, breaking his back and leaving a stain on Bix somehow, almost as if it had been *his* bones breaking under the weight of his father's fatal fall—Bix's father, the story went, won it in a crap game, took it in lieu of a fifty dollar marker, not that he could play it but, shit, man, Beiderbecke's trumpet, the great man's own horn, that was something. That was the story.

I thought of it a few years later, that desperate fiver, in Chicago, the sun beating down on us in Bix's open Pontiac convertible, stopped at a light on Diversey, the hooker's question hanging in the air above us like static after heat lightning. She was high yellow, gorgeous but faded, cheekbones of a model, mini pasted on, afro—this was the late sixties—no more than twenty-two, probably, but looking thirty or more, the vein of one eyelid jerking like a plucked bass string. "I gotta have five bucks real bad," she'd said. "One a you cats wanna blow job?"

I gave her the five and waved her off, but Bix was grinning. "Hey, man . . ." He was grinning, but I wasn't sure what exactly
he meant.

I thought of it again when Cathy's letter came, Beiderbecke's trumpet, where the hell was it now, now that Bix, *my* Bix, was dead? And I thought of it again today, looking out at fresh snow falling, the way I always do when snow is deep and new.

"You take a good man off the sauce, this is what happens," Bix said his father whispered to him as they were loading him into the ambulance after that Chaplinesque fall from the roof, the last view he ever had of his old man alive. I thought of that too. Bix had been at a clinic, Cathy wrote. He was sober, doing well. Thirty-three! Already five years older than the other Bix had been. It didn't make any sense for him to do it now, she said, but it did, of course. Hadn't seen each other for years, but I still knew him better than she did.

⊗

We'd become friends out in Iowa, undergrads but older and wiser than our years, or so we thought. Bix had been kicked out of some fancyass school down east for running amuck one night, taking a snowplow someone had parked on a city street and carving his initials and more in the snow all over the campus. What had happened was he'd overheard something that drove him way over the top, he took a dive into a swimming pool filled with booze and didn't pull himself out till half past the following night, staggering home from whatever bar he'd crashed in till they turfed his sorry, sodden ass, zigzagging through freshly fallen snow, so drunk he didn't feel the cold, falling down and lying there, arms and legs splayed, making snow angels—yellow ones, some of them, he was that drunk—then making it back onto his feet and suddenly there was the snowplow, just sitting there, the engine cold but the key in the ignition.

We met one night when Bix was strolling back to his room from the john and stuck his head in my partly open door. "Miles," he said. "*Birth of the Cool.* Dig it."

That's what was on my hi fi, Miles Davis with that great sextet from the fifties, but I didn't think anyone but me would know that, not in the dorm, not in fucking Iowa. I had transferred in my third year, got to Iowa City late, and all I'd been able to find was an awful rat trap downtown. I'd put myself on the waiting list for a dorm and now, right after the Christmas break, a room came open, someone flunking out, I guess, and I'd moved in just that day. Boxes of my books and painting stuff were still stacked on the floor.

The head bopping up and down in my doorway was crewcut, the first one of those I'd seen for a while, and the pan handsome in a WASPy way, but his expression was so dreamy, the heavy lids over Paul Newman-blue eyes so romantic, I waved him in and onto the foot of my bed. We sat in silence, digging the music, until the side ended and my visitor reached over to lift off the needle, which usually stuck in the slick alley at the centre. He was wearing a checked sports shirt with a button-down collar, had a crease in his chino pants. He looked shiny, but dissipated somehow, but how dissipated could a twenty-year-old be? "Hey, hope you don't mind me butting in, man. I heard Miles and..."

"No, that's cool," I said. "You've got a good ear."

"Fuckin' A, babe. But Miles is easy. I *do* have Sherlock Holmes senses, though. You put a dozen shot glasses of bourbon in front of me, different brands, and I'll pick out the Jack Daniel's every time, the green label *and* the black."

I laughed. "Sorry, man, I can't put you to that test. I've got some Jim Beam, though, you don't mind slumming."

"Hell, no." He grinned an incredible, wide-open, shit-eating grin and extended a hand with an almost painful grip. "Bix Stone."

"Leo Singer," I said, getting up to get the bottle. "Bix? As in ..."

"Fuckin' A. My old man hung that on me, a mistaken case of hero worship. I don't mind, though. The old man had good taste. Did you know he was born in Davenport? Right here in Iowa? Beiderbecke, I mean, not my dad. Over by the river?"

The next thing I knew, we were down the hall in his room, Bix proudly showing off Beiderbecke's trumpet hanging on the wall, explaining that it was a cornet, actually, pointing out the differences, listening to *Live at the Blackhawk,* which had just come out and had some incredible Coltrane solos. Then we were struggling into our coats and boots, braving the cold and snow to get downtown before they ran out of beer. The story of the snowplow came tumbling out with the first pitcher and bag of beernuts.

We were at a table in this little bar Bix knew, in the basement of the Jefferson Hotel, the Hubbub Room, a leering, slope-shouldered barman called Stanley, with a neat, Clark Gable moustache, presiding. Bix had been screwing this skirt named Cathy at the Eastern school, popping her ears, or so he thought, he told me. "I mean, the sex was great, but it was more than that," he said. "Can a cat like me, boozer son of a boozer, heart like a shotglass, can a cat like me fall in love? I don't know, man." He shook the crewcut head and I felt out of my depth. I thought I knew something about love, but it was considerably chaster, more sober. He was tossing the beer back like water, twice as fast as me, maybe three times, the blue of his eyes darkening just a shade. "But the sex, at least, was great.

"Then I was at this party, man, crowded, dark, smoky, you know, a jumble of faces and voices. I *may* have had a bit too much to drink. I was on the floor, well, behind a sofa, actually, staring up at this great water spot on the ceiling. It kept changing, getting bigger, smaller, pulsing like an amoeba or something you see under a fucking microscope. Gradually, I start tuning in to these voices, a conversation, a couple of chicks, sitting on the sofa. One of the voices is a little familiar. She's saying how she's balling this guy, nice guy and all, he tries hard enough, but she hasn't come once and she's getting tired of faking it, though it's *easy* to fake it, the poor slob is so eager to please. I'm thinking, that poor dumb bastard, then all of a sudden it hits me, this is Cathy's voice I'm hearing, man, Cathy's voice, nailing me down to the floor, fucking nails right through the heart."

I took a deep breath. "Through the balls, you mean."

"I'm hip, babe." Bix looked at me for a second, the heavy lids lowering to make slits of his eyes. "Then I'm hearing the voice saying, 'I just don't have the heart to tell him. He's a real sweet kid called Bix.' 'Oh, I know him,' the other chick says, 'I didn't come either.' Hey, Stanley," he suddenly called, twisting his head around, "whadda we have to do to get another pitcher?"

We closed the Hub and shifted the base of our operations to the Campus Grease, my name for the Campus Grill, the bus depot cafe, where I initiated him into the mystery of the fifty-nine-cent Number 3: eggs over easy, toast dripping with butter, battery-acid coffee, and what they called American fries, which were hash browns, real ones. Before the dorm room came open, I'd been living in one of the bedbug rooms upstairs, so I knew the Grease well. Crossing the wind-battered bridge on the way back to the dorm, we got the giggles as we contemplated the creamy mounds of fresh snow blanketing the iced-over river.

"I wanted to spell out f-f-f-fuck C-C-C-Cathy," Bix hiccuped, "but I couldn't get the fucking snowplow to spell properly."

He was through with women, he'd said at the bar, had been celibate since leaving Maryland, all those winter and spring months back home in Highland Park, the arid summer, all these fall and winter months in Iowa, almost a year. "I could die, you know, man? I mean, all that jizz backed up, I could blow one day, take out half of downtown Iowa City, seventeen innocent pedestrians torn to pieces. But it's worth the risk, man, to lead a chaste life. Purity, man. That fucking Dhali Lama's no fucking fool. Nor the Pope. Gonna lie down now, man, gonna lie down in the snow and take a little nap."

"Come on, man, don't do that." I grabbed him before he was actually down, pulled him back up from his knees, the bottoms of his chinos covered with snow.

"Just for a minute, man. Just for a minute."

But I lured him on with visions of Miles and Coltrane on the turntable and the half full bottle of Jim Beam in my room. Soon as we got back, we both crashed.

We kept on that way all semester, long after the snow had melted and the river was running: down to the Hub after dinner every evening, beer till Stanley folded his hands, rolled his eyes, and announced, "You don't have to go home, folks, but you have to leave here," then to the Grease for eggs, then back to the dorm for jazz, always pausing on the bridge to invoke the memory of the snowplow. I couldn't afford this kind of life but Bix subsidized me, "for the company, man, I can't live like this on my *own*." He'd dropped out of school the third week of the semester, just in time to get most of his tuition back, though he somehow talked them into letting him stay on at the dorm. It was that money we pissed away, that and the monthly allowance his mother sent him, every fucking cent.

Daytimes, I managed to keep up with my classes, but just, and I didn't even unpack my brushes or paints for months. Bix slept in, the prick, and spent the day lying on his unmade bed, reading paperbacks, Salinger or Hellman or Burroughs, whom he liked to read over and over again, in rotation, or working on his own novel or blowing riffs on his horn, not the Bix cornet—a valve was broken and he didn't play that—but a good Conn trumpet he'd had since high school. One Saturday, he rented a car and we drove to Davenport, tried to find the house where Beiderbecke was born but couldn't, torn down, I suppose, or any other trace of him. We wound up at a whorehouse, Bix treating again. "Thank God the pressure's off, man," he yelled afterwards, "the good burghers of Iowa City can relax now. Too bad about the girl, though. Blew the back of her head clean off."

He fell in with a good sax player, a grad student in English, and a professional drummer with the tight mouth and closed-in look of a junkie; what he was doing in Iowa City I never did figure out. Somehow, they scraped up a bass player, a young cat so green he could barely hold his instrument up, though over the months he got noticeably better, and they formed the nucleus of a jam session every Sunday afternoon at the student union, drawing big crowds to hear them play the Miles songbook and other standards. Bix was good, though he sounded more like Nat Adderley than Miles, and nothing at all like Beiderbecke. The sax player wasn't bad either. After they got into a groove, which the drummer effortlessly led them to, they could really cook, Bix and the sax trading solos as crisp and cool as anything you'd hear on most records, Bix's cheeks puffing out Dizzy-style, his eyes popping. When the sax was soloing, he'd lay back, the trumpet and his other hand crossed over his chest, eyes closed, looking serene. It was the only time I ever saw him really relaxed. I was jealous of those guys he gigged with, not just taking up Bix's time on Sunday, but for speaking his language in a way I never could. I would hang out, digging the music and endlessly sketching them, a couple of those sketches turning themselves into paintings that spring when I finally got back to work. Bix would come over to cop a look when they took a break, but I always was on the outside and I knew it.

At the end of the school year, I went to Pennsylvania to a waiting job at a hotel I'd had for three summers, Bix home to Chicago, and it didn't seem likely he'd be back in the fall. "What's the fucking point, man?" His mother would go through the roof when his marks didn't come in the mail and wouldn't underwrite him again, he was certain, and his father's old boss at Burnett Johnson had promised him a tryout if he ever wanted to take a crack at writing ad copy. As it turned out, I hooked up with Terry in the fall, my last year, and I wouldn't have had much time for Bix if he had been around. Actually, I've wondered sometimes if Terry and I would have come to anything if he'd been there, the lure of the Hub pulling me away evenings. I don't know if you can have a love affair and a friendship as intense as ours had been at the same time. Maybe Bix knew that; that was part of why he didn't want to come back. Like a lovers' fling, we'd had our time, burned ourselves out.

Over the next few years, though, we kept in touch, sporadically sometimes. My last year in Iowa, I'd get into Chicago for a weekend now and then. Bix would lead us on a crawl along Sixty-third Street, where the best blues clubs were, or to the Sutherland Lounge to hear Miles or Trane or some other hot band, driving through the black and blue streets in his open Pontiac like there was never any chance of rain or anything else falling on us. This was before King went down, before Watts, and we had no fear of where our passion for the music took us, me because I was too dumb to realize the danger, Bix because he had that fearlessness people develop like a second skin when they feel they've got nothing to lose.

He'd discovered grass, and had given up beer permanently for martinis at lunch, bourbon at night. "Beer's okay for *you,* man, you're still a *schoolboy,*" he said, that grin lighting up his face. He still shone, but there was a haze around it, like a smudge. "I'm a grown-up, I got responsibilities." He swirled the amber poison in his glass and held it up to the twirling light from the bandstand, laughing. "Got a lot of catching up to do. A role model like I got, it's a heavy weight, man, a *heavyweight.*"

I didn't really know if he meant his father or Beiderbecke, both of whom had come to bad ends. I didn't know a lot about Bix's father, just that he'd been some kind of an advertising genius, owned a month's worth of fresh-daily button-down Oxfords which Bix's mother, The Wicked Witch of the West, kept starched—and, of course, that booze killed him eventually even though he'd quit it, by sneaking up behind him and pushing him off that suburban roof, where he was adjusting the TV antenna, right in front of Bix's eyes. You'd think that would have scared Bix dry as a desert, but it didn't work that way. "After the funeral, the Wicked Witch took all the bottles in the den and hauled them out to the garbage," he'd told me one beery night at the Hub. "Why the hell didn't she pour it down the drain, like they do in the movies? No, she had to go for the dramatic gesture. I just went out and hauled them back in, to my room. I hadn't even tasted the stuff before that day." He grinned and rolled his eyes, doing a good imitation of Stanley at closing time. "Dad was strict about that." He'd been thirteen then.

Now he was following in his father's footsteps, making great bread supervising a campaign for potato chips, of all things, and trying to convince himself the work was important; sitting in occasionally with a combo at a bar in Old Town; sharing a cool pad on the upper north side with an icy blonde who called herself Jade. He was still working on the novel, but it didn't sound like it had progressed much.

Terry and I got really serious, and we headed out to San Francisco after I graduated, did the starving artist routine. Bix's agency had an office there and he would get out occasionally. He'd come over to our little studio in the Haight for Terry's famous spaghetti and tomato sauce made with wine and mushrooms. Afterwards, she'd stay home and Bix and I would crawl the jazz spots, starting at the Blackhawk, till they closed, then do the after-hours clubs where you could get mixers but had to provide your own juice, preferably in a brown paper bag. One night we wound up just before closing at Fenocchio's, the female impersonator club, and wandered with some of the regulars to an up-the-stairs, down-the-hall joint where the performers went to relax. Bix was completely out of his head by this point and tried to get on the stage, singing, "I wanna be loved by you, boo boop be-doo," in a scratchy falsetto and pulling up the cuffs of his chinos.

We never wrote to each other; neither of us could punch our way out of an envelope, but he would phone once in a while, usually late at night, regaling me with tales of his adventures in the skin trade, as he called it. He had a big brewery account now, one of the national brands, and he recited some of the jingles they'd thought of that didn't make the grade or were too dirty to be taken seriously. Most of them were funnier than the one they wound up using. The agency had done some work for the White House, and Bix was offered a gig writing speeches for LBJ, tagging along on Air Force One to write, literally, on the fly. "I told that honky to shove it, man," he said. "I mean, I may be a whore, but I ain't no *Texas* whore. I got *some* standards." One night he called at 4 AM and I was still on the phone when Terry, who had a waitressing job then and got up early, wandered into the kitchen to make coffee.

An amazing thing had happened, he told me: "The great love of my youth has come back into my life." This was Cathy, the girl who'd driven him over the edge back in Maryland the year before we met. She'd graduated, married, moved to Chicago, divorced. They'd bumped into each other, literally, in the record section at Marshall Fields, dissolved into laughter in each other's arms. They dated, getting to know each other all over again, and this time, Bix told me, "There ain't no fucking faking, man. I mean, no faking, period. This is it, man, in every sense of the word."

"Yeah, but can a cat like you, a cat with a flugelhorn for a heart, fall in love?" I reproached him.

"I'm hip, babe. I don't know, just don't know. The road to purity is a twisted one."

Terry and I didn't have the bread to get to Chicago for the wedding, but Bix sent me one of the special lighters he'd had made for the wedding party, my name inscribed on one side, his and Cathy's initials, the date, and the outline of a trumpet on the other. Maybe it's a cornet.

By the time he was transferred to Frisco, Terry and I were living outside the city, up near Petaluma, where I had a studio and was really trying to get some work done after having my first one-man show light a fire under me. It didn't occur to me then, really only did after he was dead, that he may have been pursuing me, trying to get me back in his life the way he had Cathy. But we didn't get to see that much of each other, us out of town, him busy at his job when we did get in. There were some dinners, usually out on the town but one time at their place, a three-storey on Russian Hill, decorated to the nines by Cathy, who had a good touch. Bix's trumpet—the great man's, I mean—was hung on the wall over the fireplace, alongside one of my paintings, but Bix—*my* Bix—wasn't playing anymore; he'd finally decided he wasn't really that good, he said. It had been a long time since he'd mentioned the novel.

And there was one great winter weekend we all spent together at Lake Tahoe, once again Bix footing the bill, although I was a lot less comfortable with this than I used to be.

We shared a condo, a two-storey thing with a lot of glass and open beams and slanting rooflines, two bedrooms, a fireplace in the main room, a hot tub outside on the deck.

We went skiing, gambled in the casino—Bix did, that is, winning enough at twenty-one, where his nerve was impressive, to pay for the weekend—and generally having as wild a time as we thought we could at our advanced age, pushing thirty as we were. In the bar at Harrah's, Bix demonstrated the Amazing Bourbon Challenge, as he called it, actually having the bartender pour out a dozen shots of different brands, paying with a fifty-dollar bill.

"Bix, you'll kill yourself if you drink all those," Terry said. "Leo, make him stop."

"At least that'll shut him up," Cathy said, rolling her eyes.

"If I do, at least my estate will save on the embalming charges," Bix said, flashing his shit-eater. He had taken off his cashmere jacket and was rolling up the sleeves of his blue Oxford, making a show of it.

"It's okay, I've seen him do this before," I told the girls. Cathy was frowning but didn't look worried, so I guessed she'd seen the trick before too.

Actually, there was no trick, just the law of averages and a sharp sense of smell. Bix bent over the bar and delicately sniffed, moving his head slowly down the row of glasses spaced two inches apart on the glossy oak. He picked up one glass, put it down, reached for another, sniffed it, put it down. "A drum roll would be nice."

"That only comes after you've drunk half of them," I said.

"Forget about drums, then." He picked up the first glass and tossed it back. "I believe that's the green label."

"Dead on," the bartender said. He was a big, beefy guy with a deep tan, looked more like a bouncer than a barman, nothing like Stanley. "Pretty good."

"Fuckin' A," Bix said. He bowed and made a slight self-deprecating gesture with his hands as he bent over the bar again.

"The black'll be a little harder," I whispered to Terry. "The first shot tilts his senses a bit and every one after tilts them even more."

Just the same, he got the black on the fourth try. "That's amazing," the bartender said, nodding his head.

"I'm hip." He turned to Cathy. "Sorry, babe, the rumours of my death are greatly exaggerated." He threw his arm over her shoulder and she shrugged it off effortlessly, with a smile. She put her hand on his bicep and squeezed.

"What should I do with these shots?" the bartender asked.

"I'm drinking this one," I said. "I'm not so fussy."

"Fuckin' A," Bix said, picking one up too.

Ahmad Jamal was playing in the showbar, but Bix wanted to gamble more. Later, we went for breakfast but the hash browns were just chunky fried potatoes and Bix started to make a fuss till Cathy cooled him down. Eventually, we wound up back at the condo, the Beatles playing loudly on a fancy tape player Bix had brought along, "All You Need Is Love" and "Hey, Jude" over and over again. Bix must have been the last man in America to tip to the Beatles—he never had much use for the radio—but I'd finally convinced him to give them a good listen and he'd fallen hard. Terry and Cathy were inside changing and Bix and I were in the hot tub, a glass of JD and ice in his hand, a green bottle of Heineken in mine, passing a big thick joint back and forth. "This is the fucking life," Bix said, taking an exaggerated inhale. "This is the life my mother warned me about, but, hey, did I listen?"

He started to tell a story, something riotous at the agency, but I was half asleep, the back of my head submerged, gazing up at the stars, trying to make out the dippers, and I wasn't really paying attention. "An incredible girl," I heard him say. "Right on the desk, man, and she's taking dictation ten minutes later like nothing happened."

I sat up and took a swallow of beer to rouse myself. "Whoa, Bix. I missed the beginning of this. You talking about balling your secretary?"

"Not just balling," he said. The shit-eating grin was plastered over his face. Puffs of white steam were rising from his mouth, and his hair, longer than I'd ever seen him wear it, lay damp on his forehead. "Anything you can imagine, we've done it, man."

"Does Cathy know?"

"What, I look like I have a death wish?"

"How long has this been going on?"

"Like the song says? Couple months. It should burn itself out soon. Just an itch."

I didn't say anything right away and in the silence I became aware that the music had stopped. I looked to my left, through the open sliding glass door. The girls were standing there in their swimsuits, Terry in a black two-piece I liked, her hair tied back in a ponytail, Cathy in a flowered bikini, towels over their shoulders. Cathy was leaning over the player, changing the tape, so I couldn't see her face, but the expression on Terry's was clear enough. Bix caught the expression on *my* face and twisted his head around. "Oh, shit," he said quietly. "I think maybe I'll just go lie down in the snow for a while."

⊗

We only saw each other one more time after that, martinis and beer in some joint on Market Street, just Bix and me, before he and Cathy went back to Chicago. I remember I asked him about Cathy, but only obliquely—"You two Okay?"—and he replied with a shrug and an off-centre grin. The subject of Tahoe and what had happened there didn't come up, nor anything that might have come of it. Maybe nothing did. Over the years, he kept up with the late night calls, long, rambling conversations—monologues, really—and Terry and Cathy kept up the Christmas card exchange. We have a photo in our album of Bix holding up their baby, a day or two after he was born—Leo, they called him. Bix's hair is short again, the crew, but he has a moustache, and he's looking down, so you can't see the Paul Newmans. It's the only photo I have of him. Bix scrawled on the back, "Don't worry, man, he's not named after *you.*"

And then Cathy's letter. He'd left Burnett Johnson years ago and been through a series of smaller agencies; I knew all that. I didn't know he'd been out of work the last year, or about the clinic, of course. He had prospects, she wrote; that's what made it so hard for her to accept. I meant to call her afterwards, but it was hard to pick up the phone and by the time I did, she'd moved and I wasn't able to trace her. I still think about Bix's trumpet, Beiderbecke's, I mean. Cornet, I mean. I think about the great man coming back to the pawn shop, the instrument he loved gone.

* * *

Pornography

THE FIRST TIME I EVER saw a woman's breast, other than my mother's or one of my aunts', was in the snow, smiling up at me like the first crocus of spring. This was in Chopin, Saskatchewan, in 1963, when I was a giddy schoolgirl of eleven. I knew I was going to have breasts myself soon—or so I hoped—so I was intensely interested. I would have liked to have gotten down on my knees to scoop away the snow with my mittened hands and pick up the photo and the others around it to take a closer look, but the ribbing from the other kids would have been too much to bear. As it was, Jimmy Macleod did kneel down, and got pushed into the snow for his efforts by my older brother Tom, always the jerk.

The photos—there were hundreds of them under the snow, revealing themselves shyly as the thaw peeled away their insulation—had belonged to Brick-Shy Bob, who lived in a plywood and tarpaper shack in the bush outside of town. Everyone who lived in Chopin in the sixties had been there a long time, so we kids never got the admonition children do today about not taking candy or rides from strangers, but we were warned to stay clear of Bob, whose nickname seemed to say everything necessary about him: there was something about him that just wasn't right. He had been known to sometimes talk to a young girl, to offer a photo to a boy, but nothing had ever happened. He wouldn't have still been walking around loose if it had, my father always said when my mother went on about Bob. She and some of the other women of the town would have liked to have had him sent to the mental at Weyburn, or thrown in jail or just rousted from town, but Daddy and some of the other men, without exactly taking Bob's side, argued that having a loose screw or two wasn't enough to have a man committed, and smelling bad, talking to himself, and keeping a pile of dirty magazines were no grounds for either jail or being driven from his home.

I don't think I ever heard the word "pornography" applied to Brick-Shy Bob. "Dirty pictures," "dirty magazines," that's what we kids would say Bob kept in that smelly old shack of his, the boys laughing and bragging that they'd seen some of them, the girls blushing and turning away with screams when the boys would start to describe what the people in the pictures were doing. The magazines apparently arrived from time to time in plain brown envelopes that Bob would pick up at the post office; along with his monthly pension cheque from the Veterans and the annual Christmas card from a cousin in Ontario, they were all the mail he ever received. He didn't open the packages till he got back to his shack, and nobody believed the boys who bragged they'd seen the magazines anyway, so they didn't do any harm, that's what Daddy said.

Eventually Bob did say something to someone's daughter that got the town riled up, enough so that some of the women, my mother among them, stormed down to Baylik's hardware store to insist that Ron Baylik, who was mayor that year, do something. Calls were made to the RCMP detachment at Carlyle, and something might actually have happened to Bob except that, as my mother put it, God took a hand.

It was late October. There was a terrible wind that night; it blew sparks from Bob's woodstove chimney back onto the tar roof of his shack and set it ablaze. The plywood walls burst into smelly, sooty flames so fast Bob barely got out with his own skin and the ratty long underwear he had on. Before they could be consumed by the fire, thousands of photos he had scissored from magazines and stacked on a table were caught up in the wind and blown into the trees. Hundreds of them gusted into town, settling on the grass around the United Church and in the lane behind the hardware store, near the school, all over. Then rain came bucketing out of the sky, dousing the flames and soaking my father and other volunteer firemen who were standing by to make sure the fire didn't spread. During the night, the temperature dropped, freezing the sodden photos into place. And before dawn, the sleet turned to snow, the first of the season, covering the pictures, wiping away all trace of them before anyone even knew they were there.

No one would have Bob in their homes, so he slept in the church that night, in the first clean clothes he'd worn in years, my mother said. The next morning, he was gone, no one knew where, and was never seen in Chopin again. No one knew about the photos until spring, when the snow melted and they blossomed all around us, breasts and thighs and bums erupting out of the slush like landmines from some all-but-forgotten war, ambushing us.

⊗

My father died a few years later, when I was fourteen, and my mother eventually married again, to a man who wrote pornography. I didn't know anything about that side of my stepfather, a quiet, dignified man, until she told me, years later, soon after he died, and I didn't see any of it until last week, after my mother's funeral.

My real father's death came as naturally and as unexpectedly as the fire that had driven Brick-Shy Bob from Chopin, in an accident at the grain elevator where he worked. After a suitable period of mourning, my mother took my brothers and sister and me to Regina, where she enrolled in a secretarial course. She wound up working at the university, in the engineering faculty, which was where she met Armin.

He was a prematurely bald, very well-mannered man, so tall he towered over my petite mother. He liked to joke that he was a *civil* engineer, apparently something of a rarity in the profession, who frowned on the students' traditional pranks, which some years involved hiring a stripper to play Lady Godiva. Like my mother, he'd been unexpectedly widowed, the cancer that began in his wife's breasts streaking through her body, and left with children. Two of them had grown and already left home, as had my brother Tom, by the time Armin and my mother got together, but the two younger ones were still with him. We became a large family, living in Armin's sprawling ranch-style house in University Park, which in those days was at the farthest reaches of Regina. Life in the city, in University Park, in Armin's house, with Armin's family, with *Armin*—who was as unlike my own father as could be imagined, although he was always kind to me—was entirely different from anything I'd experienced before, and my teenaged years were troubled and turbulent. I did some of the usual stupid things certain girls do, and it's a miracle I never wound up pregnant or in jail. I left home as soon as I could, and went as far away as was reasonable, enrolling at the University of British Columbia, where I settled down. One by one, the other children in the family—both Armin's and my mother's—grew of age and left home, leaving them eventually with only each other. "This is where most people *begin* their married lives," my mother wrote to me, "where your Daddy and I began our lives together. It sounds funny to say this, after being married almost eight years, but Armin and I can finally get to know each other."

My mother was in her mid-fifties then, Armin a few years older, and it was funny to think of them as newlyweds, but whenever I talked to her on the phone and the few times I came home to Regina, she always seemed happy. Armin too seemed content—he'd been desperately unhappy after his first wife died, my mother believed, and was still in the dumps when she'd come on the scene, although I'd been too young and self-absorbed to be aware of it then. After he died, she showed me a leather-bound volume of poems he'd written in the year after his wife's death; a preface indicated that he'd written one a day, in a ritualistic way, almost as if he'd been saying prayers, though he'd selected just what he considered the best of them for the book he put together and had printed locally. They were formal poems, many of them sonnets, with precise rhythms and natural sounding, often clever rhymes, filled with classic allusions, very much like Armin, who always sounded like an encyclopedia and liked to show off his knowledge of the constellations on starry nights. Some of them, I thought, were good, filled with unexpected bursts of feeling, and I said so.

"It's hard to believe the hand that wrote those poems could also write filth," my mother said. She looked more fragile, older than I'd ever seen her, her hair closer to white now than grey.

We were at the house in Indiana that had turned out to be their retirement home, although Armin's death came too soon for them to enjoy his unplanned retirement.

"What sort of filth?" I asked, looking up from the poems. "What do you mean?"

"Real filth, pornography of the vilest sort. Men doing horrible things to women, women doing horrible things to men, all of them having a jolly old time, though. Fondling and thrusting and drooling..." Her voice trailed off. "You know. Well, actually, I hope you don't, but I'm sure you can imagine."

"More than Danielle Steel, you mean."

"Oh, my, way, way more. I mean the real stuff. Every filthy word you've ever heard and dozens more you never heard. Every bodily function and fluid. I've never seen any other kind so I can't compare, but I imagine it was fairly standard of that type. Not much plot to speak of." My mother forced a smile here. She had been a reader all her life and was a particularly voracious consumer of mysteries, so, as far as a layman can, she knew something of the mechanics of plot. And, with Armin's encouragement, she had taken classes at the university, almost finishing a degree in English. "But he had a way with words." She gestured toward the volume I held in my hand. "As you can see."

"And you read this stuff?" I put the book of poems down, glancing at it skeptically. I have to admit I was shocked.

"Some. There is a certain fascination."

"I still don't really understand what you're saying, though, Mom. Armin *wrote* pornography? You mean novels? Published books?"

"Oh, no, nothing that ambitious. Novels, yes, I guess they were. Are. I have some of them. They're in a box in that closet." She lifted her head, pointing with her chin, still firm though the skin on her neck was loose. "Scribblers, like you used when you were a girl. Remember? But he would lose interest, so none of them ever finish properly. They just stop. But, no, I'm sure he had no idea of publishing them or had any idea how you'd even go about doing that. It was just something he did for relaxation."

"A pretty weird hobby." I really couldn't believe what I was hearing.

"I wouldn't have called it that, but, yes, I suppose so. It was just something he did when he was tense, like some people will doodle pictures."

"*I* doodle pictures, Mom."

"As I say."

"But I do it on napkins or on the backs of envelopes and I throw them away afterwards. I don't keep them in a box in the den closet."

There was a silence, and, after a moment or two, I realized that my mother was glaring at me. Gradually, the glare softened. "And in his desk drawer," she said presently. "And *on* his desk."

When my mother met and married Armin, he'd been an associate professor. Before I left home, he'd been promoted to full professor, and, during the time I was at UBC, I had the small satisfaction, whenever I had to deal with a professor of mine, of knowing that my stepfather likely outranked him, and had become chairman of his department. But then, for reasons that were never clear to me, he'd left the university and he and my mother moved to Montreal, where he worked for a year or two at a community college, and then to a small college in Indiana. He had no intention of retiring that I knew of, but, after three or four years, again, for reasons that weren't spelled out in my mother's weekly letters, he suddenly changed his plans. Barely a year later, he had the heart attack that killed him.

I thought of all this as I considered what my mother was telling me and waited for her to go on. I thought I knew what was coming.

"You know, we had to leave Regina."

"I was just guessing that, Mom." I got up and moved to the sofa, sitting next to her and taking her hand, which was small even in mine and seemed very cool.

"He left some of that... material on his desk where his secretary saw it. The next thing we knew, he had to resign."

"But... he didn't *do* anything, did he?"

"Do?" My mother smiled wanly. "No, of course not. Your... father loved me," she said, hesitating just a moment before the word "father." Gradually, over the years, that word had replaced "stepfather" in my mother's letters and conversation. "As far as I know, he was always faithful. No, that's not fair. He *was* faithful. No, he didn't do anything. He didn't chase his secretary around the desk." She paused to laugh, and, even though I didn't see anything funny, it was nice to hear my mother laugh, the first time she had in the three days I'd been with her, since the day after Armin's death and through the funeral. "He didn't goose her—is that the word?—or do *anything* inappropriate. Oh, you know Armin, always a perfect gentleman. But he was stupid or careless—or, I don't know, maybe deliberate and desperate, like these people who shoplift hoping to get caught—and she saw some of his scribbling and word flew around the department. She wouldn't work for him—none of the secretaries would. Then his colleagues stopped talking to him."

She lowered her head. "It was an awful time, honey, simply awful. People can be so... cruel." She paused again, then added: "The same thing happened here."

I tightened my hand around hers and put my arm around her shoulder, which seemed painfully thin. As far as I knew, she hadn't cried yet, but she did now. I held her, rocking her, the way I remember her holding me years before, back in Chopin, before Daddy died and everything changed.

"I'm all right, dear," she said, blowing her nose into a Kleenex. "It's stupid to talk about this. I was just remembering the last time I had a really good cry. It was the night Armin's mother died. She was old and had been sick; it was a relief when she finally went, you remember. Well, you were at UBC then, but you'd been to visit her at Christmas that year, remember? We came back from the nursing home late and I had a bath and went right to bed. Armin stayed up. In the middle of the night, I woke up and he still hadn't come to bed. I went downstairs and found him in the den, scribbling away. He was so intent he didn't hear me come in. 'What's that you're writing?' I asked. That was the first time I found out about... what did you call it? His hobby? I ran right back to the bedroom, eyes streaming... well, you can imagine. After awhile, he came in and sat on the bed and rubbed my back, which I always liked. 'It doesn't have anything to do with us,' he said."

"And you believed him?" I was, if anything, more shocked by this then anything else I'd heard in the last twenty minutes.

My mother looked at me, sniffing, and blew her nose. "Of course I believed him."

⊗

Although she had nothing to keep her there, my mother stayed on in Indiana for a couple of years after Armin's death. Then she moved back to Regina and bought a very comfortable condo. I visited her there only twice. My own marriage fell apart during this period, and I was annoyed with her for ... what? Not supporting me enough? Siding with Peter? I don't know, there were other things between us, too, but I don't want to get into that—this isn't about me.

What *is* it about, though? I've thought about that, many times. When things were going wrong between Peter and me, I would sometimes lie in bed, sometimes crying, maybe by myself, maybe with him next to me, sleeping and in a different world, and think of what she said Armin had told her: *"It doesn't have anything to do with us."* Was that what Peter would say if I told him I knew he was seeing another woman? Is that what *I'd* tell him when he threw at me again that one time with another man? I poked my finger against the soft flesh of my upper arm, gingerly at first, as if there were a sore there, then harder and harder, until it started to hurt, wondering if nothing we did as individuals, he or I, had anything to do with *us*. But I kept coming back to our bed, him on his side, me on mine, the empty room down the hall I'd hoped would be a nursery, all the other slights and hurts and misunderstandings of the years that, while each one on its own didn't amount to much, taken together, added up to more than 100 per cent.

My mother had as happy an old age as one can expect, I think, considering she'd been widowed twice. I wasn't the most dutiful of daughters, and my older brother is a heel who dropped out of touch with everyone, but the younger kids and even Armin's youngest, who she'd helped to raise, stayed close to her, gave her grandchildren and company and comfort. I have things to work out about my relationship with her, but, like they say, that's my problem.

When she died, it was more or less without warning, although we knew she'd had heart trouble. "But why should we be surprised?" my sister Liz asked. "Our parents keep dying on us." Even though I had the furthest to come, it somehow fell to me to take charge of things, maybe because I'm the eldest, not counting Tom, who no one knew how to contact. At any rate, after the funeral, when we started cleaning out the condo, I delegated the selling of furniture to my younger brother, the clothes and jewelry to Liz, and kept the sorting of papers for myself.

My mother had been a packrat. There were filing cabinets filled with correspondence, tax forms, bank statements, paid bills, birth certificates, marriage licences, photocopies of everything even remotely important. In closets were boxes stuffed with circulars, pamphlets, manila envelopes thick with unsorted photos and negatives. Desk and table drawers yielded loose photos and letters, cheques that had been written and signed but never sent. I emptied the many bookcases, finding more loose papers on top of books and between them, in the pages of some.

There was much of Armin's presence among these papers, surprisingly so, I thought, considering he'd been dead for over four years. Many of the documents were his, even some dating back to his first marriage, birth certificates for his children, memos he'd received and copies of ones he'd sent, papers he'd delivered at conferences, even a box overflowing with marked exam papers. Finally, in the back of a closet I thought I'd already emptied, I found an oversized shoebox with what I'd been looking for, the scribblers, along with the volume of poetry, its handsome brown leather binding still new and inviting, and a sheaf of letters held together by a ribbon.

I poured a cup of coffee and moved piles of sorted papers to clear a spot for myself on the sofa. I didn't read all the poems, but browsed long enough to let Armin's voice come back to me, clear and precise. It had been several years since I'd heard that voice, but it filled my head as I read the poems, poems about Artemis aiming an arrow into an achingly empty sky, Orpheus searching the underworld for Eurydice, the wax melting on Daedalus's wings as he soared too high, all of them filled not just with the ghost of his wife but this palpable sense of longing, his dread of being alone.

I turned to the scribblers. I remembered what my mother had said about the same hand having written them and the poems, but the poems were typed, and the stories, if that's what you could call them, handwritten, so there wasn't even a visual similarity. Nor was there any form or elegance in what I was reading now, no Greek myth, no attempt at art or artifice—no attempt at anything more than what was there, push and shove. I had no trouble with my stepfather's careful, precise hand, the looping blue script unravelling itself before my eyes like a hawk lazily inscribing a pattern against the sky.

My mother had been right, there *was* a certain fascination, and I read on, long past curiosity. I've been without a man for some time, and I have to admit I found a few passages stirring, others amusing, some disgusting, but most of it was merely tedious, an endless repetition of expected gestures and motions, an exercise in hunger that went way beyond appetite. Very little of it, I realized, had as much to do with release as it did with touching.

The sunlight streaming through the living room windows faded, and I turned on the three-way lamp on the end table before turning to the letters. I had already glanced at them and knew that they were from Armin to my mother. Looking at them more closely, the postmarks on the envelopes and the date in the salutations, I could see some had been written before their marriage, others after, during absences related to his teaching when he was away at conferences. These *were* in the same hand as the dreadful stuff in the scribblers, the same precise script, the same faded blue ink. I arranged the letters in chronological order, best I could, hesitating before beginning to read only for a moment. Armin and my mother, sender and receiver, were both dead, so privacy didn't strike me as an issue.

"My dearest Alma," they all began, and they were filled with the dearest, most tender messages, everything he had attempted to say, years earlier, in the poems for his first wife, but stripped of form, artifice, pretension, and metaphor. *I love you, I miss you, you are everything to me,* that's what the letters said, in a variety of ways, but often as simply and directly as just that: "I love you . . . I miss you . . . you are everything to me."

Outside the living room window, the last remnant of light was snuffed out of the sky. A wind lifted the naked hand of the lilac bush and tapped it against the glass. Snow began to fall, more messages of tenderness, these from the heavens. I folded the letter I'd been reading and put it back in its envelope. The volume of poems, I'd decided, should go to Armin's children, my stepbrothers and stepsisters, for them to deal with as they wished, but the rest I took to the fireplace. Armin and my mother had both become ashes, so should these. I knelt and lit the gas. I began to tear pages from the scribblers and fed them into the flames, alternating with the letters, still in their envelopes. The burning paper gave off a strange smell, poison of the heart and perfume of the heart blending into one liquor, a heady mixture racing up the flue.

* * *

Music by Rodgers, Lyrics by Hart

THESE DAYS, ENVELOPES come to my house almost weekly, offering to make me a millionaire. All I have to do is open them and look inside; I may already be a winner. I never am, and I've largely stopped looking, but these letters remind me of a time when my mother and her friend Moishe Cahan entered magazine and grocery store contests with a vengeance, the same sort of grim determination that drives a gambler to the slot machines and card tables.

My father took a dim view of these pursuits. "This is foolishness, Bertie," he would complain to my mother, sitting at the chipped Formica kitchen table in his undershirt, perhaps with the first of his several evening glasses of sherry in front of him, a hand-rolled cigarette burning in the ashtray. My mother, still in her housedress and apron, sat across from him, the dark curls that adorned her head falling over her brow as she scribbled furiously in a steno pad, making rhymes. "Flour, hour, our, scour, dour, power," she was writing in the light blue ink she favoured, using the silver-tipped pen she'd won in college for high marks in French. In my father's moral lexicon, *foolishness* was one of the worst sins a person could fall prey to, even worse than larceny, which could perhaps be explained by need—hungry children, for example. Foolishness was a moral failure for which its author could have only himself to blame. He would never have thought of my mother as a fool, but he did believe some of her actions were foolish, and was always quick to say so. The contests she pursued, the jingles and slogans she composed, clearly fell into that category in his view.

"But what does it hurt?" my mother asked absently, brushing away a lock of chestnut hair as she looked up. She gave my father a crooked little smile, half innocence, half impudence.

"Is my jingle any more foolish than your sherry? Now really."

My father, who was a newspaper reporter, was employed all through the Depression, actually made a good wage, and had no desperate need for instant riches; neither, of course, did my mother, but, as a young mother with first one, then two small children at home, and my father gone all day and often into the evening, she did have a craving for diversion.

Their friend Moishe, on the other hand, was in conspicuously dire straits. The Crash had come during his final year of architecture school, forcing him to drop out. He worked sporadically as a draftsman—an occupation he would sourly continue with when times got better—but mostly he was unemployed, disappointed, and at loose ends, in need of something to do with his restless, birdlike hands. His wife, Rachel, who had been my mother's best friend since high school, also had two young children to look after, but her poetic, abstract mind didn't lend itself to the riddles, puzzles, and other concrete challenges of the magazine and radio contests that attracted her husband and my mother, though she didn't frown on them the way my father did.

There were certain expenses involved, which, because my parents had money and the Cahans didn't, my mother undertook to cover. These were postage, of course, but also the purchasing of certain products: labels had to be scissored from cereal boxes and flour sacks, protective seals gingerly snipped from beneath the lids of peanut butter, jam, and pickle jars. My mother could rationalize these purchases easily enough—she had to shop anyway, and most of the products were ones she might well have bought, contest or no, though not always in such large numbers. But it wasn't the money my father begrudged, or even, since he wasn't the jealous sort, the growing intensity of the relationship between my mother and her friend's husband, the two of them sitting at the kitchen table in the Cahans' cramped apartment in the Bronx, near the Grand Concourse, or at my parents' only slightly larger place in Coney Island, their heads close together as they pored over pencil and paper or some reference book, or falling helplessly together on the carpeted living room floor in bursts of giggles as they laboured over a limerick or a jingle while my father and Rachel, who had been attempting to carry on a conversation, looked on with slightly amused expressions. No, it was the wasted time he thought was foolishness, especially since, in his view, the chance of them actually winning anything was highly unlikely, the contests being either rigged or impossible. Testimonials in the magazines from previous winners he always dismissed as "cock and bull stories." Earlier in his career in the Yiddish press, he had written the *bintel briefs,* the advice to the lovelorn column, at *The Day,* and no one knew better than he how little one could rely on what one read.

"But it's *my* time," my mother responded when my father complained of the hours she spent thumbing through dictionaries, encyclopedias, and the thesaurus, out of which the answers to puzzles and the rhymes for jingles emerged. Although it seemed frustratingly impossible that he might actually sell any, Moishe had even taken on a commission job as an encyclopedia salesman to give them access to more reference books. Many of these works were stacked on the coffee table in the living room and on the kitchen counter of my parents' apartment, just as they must have been in the Cahans'. "And what *else* should I be doing with my time, Harry? I can't wash and fold diapers *all* day long."

My mother had spent two years at Hunter College before she married; her education was one thing my father, who had only gone as far as the fifth grade and was largely self-taught, *was* jealous of. It was a matter of great pride to him that he had come so far, that he made his living writing, with so little schooling, and it irritated him that she didn't take more advantage of what she had. Never mind that her education, and Moishe's even greater one, were great assets in their pursuit of the contests, where knowledge of things as trivial as the states' capitals and as arcane as Greek myth and European history could be invaluable; he would have liked to have seen her writing poetry, which Rachel Cahan did, or reading serious books, like the Freud and Shakespeare he himself was partial to, to improve her mind, not reference works in hopes of winning some money—"filthy lucre," he sneered—or a new stove or living room ensemble.

In fact, my mother *did* write poems, and after her death my sisters and I found some of them, folded and bound with a blue velvet ribbon along with love letters she and my father had written to each other during their occasional separations in their early years together, when my father, who covered the labour beat, would travel out of town on stories.

As it happened, he was away on just such a trip when my mother and Moishe Cahan finally won a contest.

⊗

As he did every summer, my father went to Atlantic City that year, 1936, to cover the ladies garment workers union convention. He was gone for barely more than a week, but in the six letters my mother wrote to him (four mailed, including two which came back after his return, marked "addressee no longer here," and two left unmailed for him to read on his return), she expressed such longing that it might have been a month, or a year. She felt, she wrote on the third day, "like the wife of a seafarer, one of those whaling men or merchant marines who would be at sea for years on end, while their families lived their own closeted lives in Liverpool or New Bedford. It's only the boardwalk at Coney Island, and I know your feet are walking on a similar boardwalk no more than a hundred miles from here, but I feel like I'm on one of those legendary widow's walks, my face wet with a mixture of sea spray and tears." This from a woman whose parents had both been born in central Russia, far from any large body of water, though she herself was born in Paris and crossed both the English Channel and the Atlantic before she was four years old. How my father could say she was wasting her education when she was capable of hyperbole like that, I don't know.

It was during my father's absence that my mother and Moishe got word that their efforts had finally paid off.

The contest in which they had success was sponsored by a flour company and involved the writing of a jingle—the winning entry was to be professionally produced and become part of the company's radio advertising campaign. More importantly, first prize was five thousand dollars—an enormous sum in those days—and a cruise to the South Seas; though it's hard to imagine such pleasure cruises continued through those Depression years, apparently they did. The jingle my mother and Moishe wrote is lost, so I can't record it here; they didn't win first prize, and their contribution was never used by the flour company. They did win third prize, though, which was one thousand dollars, a set of stainless steel pots and pans and other kitchen paraphernalia, and a certificate redeemable at the grocer's for up to one hundred dollars worth of selected food products.

When my father came home from his trip, on Sunday evening, he was greeted by a nearly hysterical wife, two overexcited small children and a kitchen that looked, he used to say, like it had been hit by a tornado: the sink was filled with dirty dishes, the countertops were crowded with more dishes, open jars and boxes of food, the floor was filthy, particularly in one corner where a suspiciously fragrant stain still glistened. This was so unusual that he immediately assumed some calamity had befallen his family in his absence.

"Where were you?" my mother demanded. "I phoned and couldn't reach you."

"Bertie, what's happened?" my father gasped in reply, genuinely alarmed.

"I tried to ph-ph-ph-phone you," my mother stammered, tears streaming down her face. "No one knew where you were." First she hugged my father, then she stepped back and began to beat his chest with her hands. He allowed her to do this for a few seconds, then gathered her into his arms, where she nestled as still as a wounded bird taken into hand.

Through the shouting of his young daughters, who were grabbing at his trouser legs, my father could hear the soft shuddering of her sobs.

"I was sharing a room with Vogel, to save a few dollars," my father said when he understood why my mother had become so anxious, and this explanation stood unchallenged, then and down through the years of family lore.

"They said you checked out," my mother said weakly. "I was beside myself, I couldn't . . ."

"I did check out, of course," my father said. "I couldn't very well tell them at the front desk what I was doing. But I told them at the office. If you had phoned there, they could have told you."

"I didn't think."

"*I* didn't think, Bertie. I didn't think to let *you* know. It was Thursday, there were just a few days left, and it didn't occur to me that you'd call." He paused. "Why *did* you call?" He stood back, holding my mother at arm's length.

"Oh . . ." A smile broke across my mother's tear-stained face, the slightly crooked smile that had softened my father's heart the first time they met and still had as firm a grip on him, would continue to have for many years to come. "Oh, I completely forgot. We won, one of our jingles, Moishe's and mine. Third prize. A thousand dollars. I was so excited, I was calling to let you know."

"A thousand dollars!" Beyond that, my father was speechless, much to my mother's delight. He was a practical man, and whatever doubts or disapprovals he had harboured about her time-consuming hobby seemed to vanish at the mention of that sum—not a possible or projected or dreamed of amount, but a reality, more than ten times the amount of his weekly salary. "You have the money?"

"Not yet. I had to write back and confirm that I was who I am and live at this address. They'll send a certified cheque by registered letter."

"That you are who you are . . ." my father echoed, still trying to absorb the news.

"And half of it is for Moishe, for the Cahans, you know that, Harry."

"Of course."

"They can really use it. Moishe was beside himself when he found out, and Rachel was in tears. They were here for dinner Friday night. That was when I phoned you..." Her smile faded but didn't disappear. "Then we were *both* in tears."

Of all the arguments, fights and crises my parents had in their long marriage, none was as happily ended as this one; my mother would, years later, refer to it as "the time your father disappeared and I made three hundred dollars."

"It should have been five hundred," my father would grumble.

Then they would always laugh, both of them, as if the two events had been causally linked, as if it had taken my father's disappearance to allow my mother to win the money, although, in fact, she had won the money before she knew of his disappearance, and wouldn't have known of his disappearance at all—he would not, in fact, have "disappeared"—had she not won the money, and, as a result, tried to telephone him. The winning of the money, my father's safe return to her, to his family, to the tiny apartment in Coney Island, these were all remembered as a happy time, deliciously happy if all too brief.

⊗

Moishe Cahan was a short, heavy-set man whose thick mat of hair on chest and shoulders startled me, a boy of five or six, years later when the Cahans visited us once in the summer and he took off his shirt; so thick was the hair on his chest, he seemed more apelike than human. My mother used to swear that he was a kind, gentle, humorous man when she first knew him, that Rachel had plucked herself a peach, but the man I knew was bitter, irritable, stern. I went from feeling apprehensive about him to strong dislike during that visit, when I saw him slap the face of one of his sons, Manny, a few years older than me, for not immediately coming when he was called. This change in his personality was the result of the bad hand the

Depression had dealt him, my father said. It was because of that, I suppose, and my mother's deep affection for Rachel, that my parents didn't allow the disagreement over the division of the contest prize to ruin their friendship, although my father only barely concealed his distaste for the man. After Rachel's death, communication between them and Moishe—his children long grown—trickled to an annual greeting card, then to nothing.

"I should get seven hundred dollars," Moishe said.

My mother, startled, didn't respond, but my father, for all his earlier disapproval and ridicule, was now an active participant in the venture. "Why is that, Cahan?" he snapped. They were at Moishe and Rachel's apartment, which gave the other man a slight advantage. My father had brought a bottle of rye whiskey along and the two men had already enjoyed a celebratory glass, complete with *l'chayim, mazel tov,* and other toasts.

"Several reasons, Morgenstern. One, I discovered this particular contest. Berte, you'll bear me out?"

This was true, although my mother would surely have come across it too. The contest was advertised in both *Woman's Day* and *Family Circle,* magazines that both she and Rachel picked up for a nickel each where they did their shopping. That Moishe, who scoured the magazines the moment Rachel brought them home, had come across the ad first was only a testament to his idleness, not his greater zeal, but my mother didn't say that. She cast a glance at Rachel, who averted her own eyes.

"Two, I wrote the first line of the jingle."

"You wrote them together," my father protested. "All of them. I saw you with my own eyes."

"Yes, we did. I don't deny that. But every jingle, every poem, begins with a first line, and that is the most important line. Look at Shakespeare's sonnets—he didn't even title them, and we know them by their first lines. 'Shall I compare thee to a summer's day?' 'My mistress's eyes are nothing like the sun.'" Moishe's hands, which were hairy on the back but were unexpectedly small and well shaped, an architect's hands, flew excitedly about as he talked.

My father was an admirer of Shakespeare's sonnets, as Moishe well knew. "'When in disgrace with fortune and men's eyes,'" he shot back.

"Exactly," Moishe said, ignoring the sarcastic tone. "The first line sets the direction and tone of a poem, isn't that right, Rachel?"

All eyes turned to Rachel now. She was a better poet than my mother, though not necessarily better than my mother might have been, had she worked at it harder, but she possessed the enviable cachet of having published some of her poems, not only in the literary magazine at Hunter College but in several of the small, mimeographed journals produced in Greenwich Village, where she and my mother had shared an apartment before their marriages. But Rachel didn't answer. She stood up abruptly and turned her back on her husband and her friends, going to stand beside the open living room window and stare stolidly down at the streetscape below, where women sat gossiping on stoops and children played on the sidewalk, their voices lifting gaily in the heavy summer air. Though it was still early evening, her own children were already in their beds, a rule of their strict father's, and my sisters were at home with a sitter.

"Well, it *is* right," Moishe persisted. "Don't you agree, Berte?"

"In a poem, yes," my mother said slowly.

"And in a jingle too. The first line sets the direction, the tone... everything. It isn't the jingle entire, but without it, the jingle cannot be."

"But Berte wrote the jingle *with* you," my father began again, marshalling his forces. "You wrote it together, like Rodgers and Hart. You think Rodgers gets more money because people come out of the theatre humming his music even though they can't remember the silly words Hart writes?"

"That's entirely different, Morgenstern. Without the words, there's no song, without the *music,* there's no song; they're equal partners. Here, we both wrote the jingle, yes, I don't deny that I give full credit to Berte for her contribution; you know that, but *I* wrote the first line. Without that, the jingle couldn't have been what it became; we wouldn't have won."

"Third prize," my mother said quietly.

"If you'd used Bertie's first line, maybe you would have won *first* prize," my father said defiantly.

"Your darling wife didn't *write* a first line," Moishe said quickly. He thrust his chest out aggressively and clenched his fists. "*I* did, and we were away to the races. The jingle practically wrote itself. Isn't that right, Berte?" He didn't wait for an answer. "Listen, there were other times when Berte wrote the first line. If one of those had won, I'd be saying *she* should get a larger share."

My father threw up his hands and made a noise of exasperation. "Did you ever talk about these things? Bertie?"

But my mother wasn't listening to him. She'd gotten up and approached Rachel. She stood two or three feet behind her friend, gazing not *at* her, exactly, not over her shoulder, either, but at an indefinite point just above Rachel's shoulder. The two women stood motionless, two slender, dark-haired young women in similar light-coloured cotton skirts and sleeveless white blouses. My mother wore sandals; Rachel was barefooted. Rachel wore a tortoiseshell barrette in her hair, which was a coarse, crinkly black; my mother wore the blue velvet ribbon my father had given her in hers. Slanting evening sunlight streamed in through the window, illuminating their hair, their shoulders, their hands; my father couldn't see their faces. They stood so motionlessly that, when my father glanced at them, they appeared almost as if they were figures in a painting, perhaps by Monet, two women, sisters perhaps, perhaps lovers, certainly not rivals, caught in a moment of eternal time like flies enraptured by amber.

"Maybe you're right, Cahan," my father said after a long moment.

"I think he is," my mother said softly. She turned to gaze at her husband and there was on her face a look of such surprise and gratitude, an admixtured look such as he had never before seen, that it thrilled him to his bones. "Moishe wrote the first line."

"The first line *is* the most important," my father said thoughtfully. "And this one is a *good* first line. Not that I know anything about jingles. You two are the experts. But it's ... catchy. It ... catches ..." His voice drifted off. My mother had turned back to Rachel, who hadn't moved, and this time she had stepped closer, putting her hands lightly on her friend's arms, and my father found himself also engaged with hands—Moishe Cahan had come across the room with his extended, and the two men were shaking now, as if solemnizing an agreement.

"I knew you'd see it, Morgenstern," Moishe said.

When the cheque arrived, all four of them went to the Cahans' bank and it was cashed and the money divided according to the agreement reached that evening, seven hundred dollars to the Cahans, who, my mother would say, "needed it much more than we did," three hundred dollars to my mother, who set it aside for my sisters' college education. Afterwards, my father bought ice cream cones for them all. The shopping certificate, by agreement between my mother and Rachel, also went to the Cahans, but both households wound up with stainless steel pots and pans and other utensils, many of which were still in my mother's kitchen when she died.

Though they all remained friends and continued to see each other regularly—more so during the war, when Moishe was overseas with the signal corps and Rachel alone, less so after he returned and found a full-time job—there were no more contests; despite their great success, my mother and Moishe seemed to have lost their zeal for the competition. Rachel Cahan continued to write poetry, some of which was occasionally published. My mother continued to write poems too, but they were read only by my father, who had learned to read between their lines.

* * *

A Lake Named for Daddy

AFTER THE FUNERAL, they all go back to the house on Cameron Street, where sandwiches, chocolate squares, punch, and coffee prepared by two neighbour women are waiting for them. Toward the end of the afternoon, Gwen is standing in the front porch, her hand resting lightly on the withers of the rocking horse as she gazes blankly out at the poorly tended flower bed, the lawn, and the empty street beyond, when the man from next door, Dale Rolving his name is, touches her elbow gently. "She loved those flowers, Polly did," he says. Gwen thinks she can hear a sigh in his voice.

"Yes." She's all cried out, and finds she's able to manage a weak smile if she tries. "It's a shame she couldn't enjoy them much this spring."

"No," Dale says. He's looked after the lawn and shovelled the path for years now, with no payment beyond the occasional tray of slightly burned brownies Polly would force on him, but the flowers seem beyond him. Gwen put them in this year, on Victoria Day, as Polly always had, and Dale watered them, but they haven't thrived. A bachelor not much younger than Polly, retired from almost forty years in an office with the province, he's robust and enjoys being a help. Years ago, Gwen used to harbour hopes a romance might ignite between him and her mother, but nothing beyond a casual friendship ever developed, as far as she knows. In the last few years, they enjoyed trading stories about their porous memories, good-naturedly vying for the title of worst memory on the block. It was Dale who'd found Polly, in her web recliner in the backyard, looking as peaceful as if she were asleep, his call the one that alerted Gwen.

"I'm really going to miss the old girl," he says now. Gwen

puts a hand on his elbow, conscious of the way the current of consolation has smoothly reversed. A clatter of plates and a spike of unabashed laughter shake at them from the living room, where most of the mourners are still seated, reminiscing. Her brother Robbie and his wife Lorraine have things under control.

"She had a good life, though," Dale says. "Far as I could see. Eighty-three years is a good long span. Arthritis, yes, a little forgetful. So weak these last few months, but went without any pain; that's a blessing. And she sure was proud of you and Rob and those grandkids."

"Yes," Gwen says automatically. "She had a good life." It's clear to her that Dale doesn't know of Polly's stomach problems, doesn't know or chooses to pretend ignorance of the times she went out for nocturnal walks in her nightgown and bare feet, confused, then frightened when she couldn't find her way home. More than once Gwen was telephoned in the middle of the night by someone blocks away to come retrieve her mother.

"You going to sell the house?"

"I don't know. I just might move into it myself."

Dale grins. "That would be good, Gwen. I know Polly would have liked that. I know I will."

"It'll depend on whether your lawn-mowing comes with the deal."

"That'll depend on how good your brownies are."

He lets his long-limbed body fold into the wicker chair next to the rocking horse. He studies its wide-nostriled, slightly frantic expression pensively, his hand absently stroking the horse's flank, where once-bright colour has faded. "Polly told me a hundred times about this horse, but I forget . . ." he begins, his voice pitched in an almost apologetic tone.

"Oh, my dad made it," Gwen says lightly. She lowers herself carefully onto the wide arm of Dale's chair.

"I know *that*. The old database isn't that bad. But why all the . . . the sound and fury to it?"

"He does look wild, doesn't he. I don't know what my dad

was thinking." She shrugs. "Actually, I don't really know much about him at all."

"That one eye," Dale says, "it seems to follow you around the room."

Gwen allows herself a small laugh. "Kind of a saucy look, I'd say." She leans over and strokes the horse's smooth face. "He has personality, all right, my old horse. What the kids these days call attitude."

"He was . . . your father . . ."

Gwen's gaze cools slightly. "At Normandy. I was there a few years ago. There are thousands of crosses. It took a while to find his."

A silence falls on the porch. Gwen can hear the comforting murmur of voices in the living room and kitchen, the clink of glasses.

"I was there myself," Dale says quietly.

"Oh, I didn't know that."

"No reason why you should. Not something I talk about a lot."

"I'm sorry, I didn't mean to sound cross a moment ago"

"I didn't notice that you did." Dale stretches his legs, awkward in the sharply creased suit trousers. "It's a hard thing to lose your father in a war, a hard thing to lose your father when you're young, no matter what the reason."

"I barely had a father to lose," Gwen says. "I never saw him, he never saw me. He made that damn rocking horse just before he went overseas and he was dead before he had a chance to see any of his children ride on it. Robbie was barely a year old when he went overseas, and Mom was pregnant with me."

Dale shakes his head, as if to stir up the memories inside it. He still has a full head of hair, snowy white and neatly brushed, cut 1940s style. "Many's the time Polly described for me how he cut pieces of wood on an old table saw the fellow next door had in his garage—what's my garage now. Must have spent hours with rasps and sandpaper getting the shapes just right, then all that fuss with glue and clamps . . . way more than anything I'd ever tackle."

Gwen laughs again, a little stronger this time. "Your memory's not half as bad as you pretend."

"Oh, some things stick in it."

They sit in comfortable silence for a moment. Gwen gazes fondly at the rocking horse, admiring the craftsmanship anew.

"'*There's not a single nail or screw,'* Mom used to boast," she says, pitching her voice high, in a decent imitation of her mother. "'*Your father always said a nail is what they use to nail you with; a screw's what they use to screw you.'* She would always colour slightly when she said those words. *'A woodworker doesn't have any need for them.'* That's what Dad was, a cabinet maker, furniture maker, nothing as crude as a carpenter with a nail apron around his waist and his brains in the head of his hammer; that's what Mom always said."

Gwen puts her hand lightly on Dale's shoulder and laughs at that long-ago image. As always, when she thinks of her father, that deep hole in the centre of her life, Gwen's throat tightens and she feels again the bracing cold of the water of McDougald Lake, the lake named for her father, on her feet, her thighs, her belly and chest. It strikes her odd now that this should be happening today, when her thoughts should really be with her mother.

Then, surprising herself, she tells the neighbour the other part of the story, how when she was three two men in uniform came to the door of her grandmother's house, where she and Robbie and her mother were living. Polly was a nurse at the General then, in the emergency, and she worked long shifts. The rocking horse was upstairs in a room her grandmother and Polly had turned into a playroom, with bright wallpaper showing an endless succession of yellow ducks in blue ponds ringed with green and brown tufts of cattails. Gwen wasn't in the playroom, though; she was downstairs in the living room, playing with her dolls under the piano bench, her special place, and Robbie was outside in the backyard. Her grandmother was in the kitchen and when the doorbell rang and she went to answer it with a dishtowel in her hands, wiping away flour. She was, Gwen recalls, everything a grandmother was supposed to be, white-haired and plump, with pink cheeks and an apron. From her nest under the piano bench, Gwen saw the soldiers step through the door, but she was confused, thinking they were postmen. She knew the mail had already come, with no letter from Daddy again, but then she saw the tears rolling down her grandmother's pink cheeks and she knew it was something else.

"Does a three-year-old really know these things?" Dale interrupts.

"When the news comes that your father's been killed, you know," Gwen says.

After the funeral service, with its bugles and flags, her grandmother cut a gold star from a page in a magazine and pasted it on the glass of the front door. She picked Gwen up and showed it to her. "That's your daddy," she said.

"Robbie says he's in heaven, *with* the stars," Gwen protested.

"He is," her grandmother said. "But he's a star too. This one isn't really him, it's just a picture of what he's like. Don't you ever forget him, don't you ever stop loving him."

More than fifty years later, and another funeral, and she hadn't.

⊗

The last mourner doesn't leave until after eight o'clock. The few remaining sandwiches and pieces of cake are wrapped and refrigerated toward Gwen's lunch the next day, and all the dishes washed and put away. She means to spend the night, devote the next day to sorting through Polly's clothes and other things. Robbie and Lorraine promised to come over in the afternoon and lend a hand. Now she sits in gathering darkness on the porch, in the wicker chair the neighbour had filled earlier, just catching her breath. She's fixed a tall glass of iced coffee, a habit she picked up in New York, and is indulging herself in the cigarette she begged from her sister-in-law.

Funny how all that childhood stuff came pouring out,

stuff she hasn't thought about for years. Funny too, she thinks again, how, on the day of her mother's funeral, it's her father she's been thinking of, as if her grief has not yet found its proper form. *"Everything not tied down goes flying in a storm."* She smiles at the memory of one of her mother's favourite aphorisms. She puts the sweating glass of coffee on the chair arm and lets her hand rest on the smooth wood of the rocking horse's rump, and, eyes closed, she sees again the gold star on the front door, the five-pointed star that had been her father, feels again the chill waters of McDougald Lake that had embraced her.

That star and the rocking horse had been all Gwen had of him at first. Robbie had a first baseman's glove, way too big for him but he'd grow into it, their mother said, and a baseball he had to be careful playing with, it was so hard. When he was older, there was a gold watch promised for him as well, but there wasn't anything special left for Gwen. There were a few clothes in the closet of her mother's bedroom, shirts and the suit her father had been married in, and a tie, but they went to the Salvation Army and were gone. None of the cabinets he'd made, none of his furniture—he'd worked in another fellow's shop and hadn't been able to afford anything he'd made, Polly used to say. The only other thing of her father's that remained was a radio in a curved cherrywood mantelpiece cabinet he'd restored that would fill an honoured place in the house on Cameron Street until well into the sixties, when the radio stopped working. It went into the attic, probably is still there. Tomorrow, she'll take a look. It would be nice to polish the cabinet up, find some use for it.

They'd moved to Cameron Street after the war, to a small house, one of hundreds thrown up quickly and cheaply in the city for the families of returning servicemen. War widows got a special mortgage rate and even a nurse in the children's ward in Regina could afford one.

There was a playroom in the Cameron Street house too, and that's where Gwen remembers riding the rocking horse. She loved the horse, rode it until she was ten or eleven, older than when she should have stopped. The colours were still bright then, the brown and white of the horse's coat, the red of the saddle and bridle, the lustrous black eyes. Did it remind her of her father, she wonders; did riding it make her feel closer to him? But closer to whom?

On the day she was born, he was on a troop ship somewhere in the Atlantic. He was in Italy on her first birthday, England on her second, France on her third. There were letters home to Polly asking about the children, with special postscripts, "Tell Robbie and Gwen I love them" and a row of Xs her grandmother had explained were kisses, but no letters just to Gwen. There were photographs in grandmother's album, black and white snapshots of family groups, of a little boy, then a teenager, then a gangly young man. There was the formal wedding photo showing her father and mother; she was slender and radiant in a white fairy gown with tail and bouquet; he was stiff and tall in a black tuxedo, unsmiling. He looked more frightened by the prospects ahead in that photo than in the one of him in his uniform, baggy at the knees and cinched at the waist by a thick black belt, out of which he grins like a madman, hands raised in a what-the-hell gesture. Another photo remains; her brother has it, framed on the fireplace mantel: father, mother, and baby, looking like the holy family that day in the manger, the smile on Polly's face beatific as she gazes down at newborn Robbie in her arms, the father just behind her, his arms folded protectively around her, a look of solemn wonder on his handsome features.

But there's no photo of Gwen and her father.

Who *was* her father?

The years passed. Polly became head nurse, started to teach at the college. She never married again. Robbie played little league, with a glove bought for him till he was big enough, in high school, for his dad's old glove, but baseball wasn't really his best sport; he liked hockey better. He became a gangly teenager, a gangly young man resembling his father in the snapshots. He liked to work with his hands but had no special feel for wood. He went to work for Eisenbrenner Chrysler as a mechanic, later became a salesman, then a manager. He married Lorraine and they had three kids. Sometime during these years, what had been the playroom in the Cameron Street house was turned into a sewing room, where Polly's new Singer in its polished wooden cabinet held sway like a fine piece of medical equipment, and the rocking horse was moved to the porch. Robbie was welcome to take it home with him, but he preferred to let his kids ride it when they went to visit Granny, as a treat.

Gwen went off to the university, got her honours degree in English. Spent two years in Kenya, teaching bright-eyed children in dusty villages. She moved to New York and got a master's at NYU, then a Ph.D. at Dalhousie, wrote her dissertation on the new African poets, but she didn't teach right away. She wound up back in New York at a Catholic settlement house, working with street kids in Harlem, more sullen than their African cousins but just as bright. Polly visited her there, and it was clear how proud she was, her independent-minded daughter living on just a stipend, no salary really, sharing a three-room walk-up in the Lower East Side with another girl. Gwen had become a vegetarian, and Polly laughed at some of the meals the girls whipped up from beans, rice, and tofu. Gwen didn't marry.

Polly's hair went from black to white just like that, the year after she retired, and she began to shrink back into herself, never a large woman but now growing smaller, like a bird on a diet. She stayed active, with all sorts of volunteer work and her book club, but her bones became brittle. She broke her hip in a fall one winter, and a woman from home care came around every day. That's when Dale started shovelling the walk, mowing the lawn. Polly said she'd hire a man, but he wouldn't hear of it. Gwen moved home as soon as she could, to an apartment nearby. She got a sessional job at the university, and then, a stroke of luck really, a permanent spot came open and she won that.

That's where the story stands, she thinks. Anyone at the funeral, listening to the Presbyterian minister's service and the brief eulogy her uncle Robert had provided, would have had the sense of it: a family robbed of its husband and father had managed to muddle along. Polly did as good a job as she could, a fine job. She had a good life, raised two responsible, decent children. Robbie's a good man, a good husband and father, even though he didn't have one of his own to guide him along. As for Gwen herself, she knows she's thought of as a good woman, selfless, caring for her aged mother at her own expense. Anyone reading Polly's obituary in the paper would see as much. The story of a contented family, Gwen thinks, taking one last drag and putting out the cigarette. Beyond the screens of the porch, it's grown dark.

Oh, and there is something else. McDougald Lake.

In the late fifties, the government decided to name some previously unnamed topographical features after people killed in the wars. The postman brought a letter addressed to Polly saying a lake in northern Saskatchewan was to be named McDougald in honour of her husband—did she have any objection? There were hundreds of such letters—Gwen has no idea how the names were chosen, or how each particular name was assigned to this particular lake or peak or creek. That would have been all there was to it except for an idea a magazine writer in Toronto had. He read about the program and sold his idea to *Maclean's*. He asked the government to pick a few typical families for him and was given Polly's name, among others. He telephoned. The idea was that Polly and Robbie and Gwen would go up north with the writer and a photographer, the magazine would fly them up, pay the whole shot. They'd get to see McDougald Lake and the magazine would get a personalized story. Gwen was fourteen, and didn't want to go.

It was stupid, she thought. Way out there in the bush, no one else around for hundreds of miles, all those blackflies. Who needed that? And there were her friends she didn't want to leave, and a boy. But Polly insisted. "This is for your dad," she said, "you can do one thing for him," and Gwen went to her room sulking, stung by her mother's unfairness. She'd made it sound as if Gwen was always turning away from her father, when, in truth, it was *he* who had turned away from *her*.

The trip was set for the first week of July, right after school finished. They caught an early morning scheduled flight to Prince Albert, then transferred with all their gear—sleeping bags and a tent—to a bushplane barely big enough to hold them all. Gwen loved it, riding most of the way with her nose pressed to the cool window, but Robbie got sick, throwing up into the paper bag, and was embarrassed and grumpy for hours afterwards. The writer was named Ted, a short man with limp blond hair he was forever pushing back with his hand. He spoke quickly in a quiet voice. He was okay. The photographer had a German name like Hans or Helmut and hardly said a word the whole trip. He was a big man with thick, blunt fingers on hands that would have seemed more at home on a shovel or a sledgehammer than an expensive camera. Gwen didn't like him.

The plane bumped along on currents of air, a vast grey-green forest clawed by slashes of blue unfolding beneath them. The pilot, a small man with bright red hair, pointed out topographical features from time to time, in a noncommittal voice. McDougald Lake turned out to be about two hours northwest of PA, "a hundred miles past La Ronge by road, if there was a road," Ted said. He had a habit of saying something, then following it with a question. He did this so consistently, it didn't take long for Gwen to figure out the pattern. She didn't mind, but often, if the question was addressed to her, she didn't answer. Now he asked, speaking to Polly, who was in the seat in front of him, with poor Robbie, "Do you think they should build roads up here? How would you feel about people driving up to McDougald Lake?"

"I don't know," Polly said. She obviously hadn't thought about it one way or the other, though she'd certainly been thrilled when she heard about the naming, and excited about the trip. "I'd hate to see it turned into a tourist spot." She laughed. "You know, middle-aged men in Hawaiian shirts with cameras and pot bellies." She glanced at the photographer, blushing. His shirt was khaki, with epaulets and lots of pockets. Gwen, sitting in the back, smirked. Ted jotted something down on his pad.

"There she is," the pilot said, "hold on," and the plane began to bank. Polly held Robbie's shoulders, but there wasn't anything left to throw up and he was okay. Below them, Gwen could see an almost perfectly round bowl of cerulean water surrounded by spruce and birch trees. The lake seemed small at first, but it got bigger and bigger as the plane dropped toward it. Gwen peered out her window as the water rushed up toward them, and then they were down in a flash of spray. The plane bounced once, then bobbed gently on the surface of the water like a plastic duck in a bathtub. The pilot began to taxi toward the shore, a slight indentation in the lake's perfect circle where a natural sandy beach had formed between two stone outcroppings. A makeshift pier jutted out into the water from the beach, and the pilot tied up against it. McDougald Lake was separated from another, larger, lake by a thin band of forest, and there was a Cree community on the shore of the other lake, but planes supplying them often landed here, at this beach, the pilot explained, even though it meant a bit of a walk through the trees. "That lake can be rough," he said, turning to Polly. "This one's always smooth as a baby's backside."

Gwen didn't know if she liked that thought. She helped with the unloading and forgot about it. The water was smooth, completely calm and clear as glass. Kneeling down on the pier, she could see small fish in schools lazing around on the fuzzy bottom. She took off her sandals and jumped in. "Ayyy!" she shouted. *"It's cold!"* The water came up over her knees, almost to the cuffs of her shorts.

They made camp in a clearing up from the beach but just before the woods began in earnest. There was a birch with a thick trunk that divided into three equal limbs chest high, bark hanging in long curving loops from each limb. And there was a black spruce, taller than any tree Gwen had ever seen, with two chattering squirrels racing up and down its long body. They pitched the tent for Polly and the kids between the two trees, facing the beach and the lake. Ted and Hans or Helmut put their tent a little deeper into the woods. The pilot climbed back into his plane and took off with another roar of spray. Gwen felt frightened for the first time, but it lasted just a moment. She knew he'd be back the next day.

Polly had brought a picnic lunch of tuna salad sandwiches on white bread, potato salad, sweet pickles, and Thermoses of cherry Kool-Aid, which Gwen and Robby both loved. The lunch, along with food for that night's supper and breakfast for tomorrow, was wrapped in aluminum foil in a Styrofoam cooler packed with ice cubes. The day was already hot, but the ice cubes had retained their shape and the food was cool and fresh. Polly spread a blanket on the beach and they all sat on it and went at the sandwiches. Even Robbie had an appetite. Ted and the photographer had bottles of beer they'd brought in a small cooler of their own.

"The lake is deep," Ted said. "You can wade out for twenty, thirty feet, then, bam, it's over your head. In the middle, it's over a hundred feet." He turned to Gwen. "How did it feel, getting wet for the first time in a lake named after your dad?"

"I don't know," Gwen said, truthfully. She smiled, to show she wasn't being difficult. Polly had had a talk with the kids the night before. "We wouldn't be getting a chance for this trip if it weren't for them," she'd said. "So be nice to them, please. But remember that it's for us."

After lunch, the two men dug a firepit circled with stones and laid a fire to light in the evening. Then they all went for a hike, first along the edge of the lake, where Robbie, who had regained his normal good humour, demonstrated his skill at skipping stones, then through the dense woods to the other lake. In the distance, they could see the dwellings of the Cree village, shacks mostly, with a few tipis on the perimeter. They'd been told it would be fine to go over for a visit, but they decided against it. Maybe in the evening, when it would be cooler. Hans—that was his name after all—shot picture after picture, from behind them, on the sides, and from the front, walking backwards. He had three cameras strapped around his neck and he took turns with them. Gwen made sure she was looking away whenever he pointed one of them at her.

By late afternoon, it was really hot and the air was thick with blackflies. Polly and the kids had slathered themselves with musk oil and it seemed to keep them off. Ted and Hans declined and spent an hour swatting at their arms and faces, then laughingly begged Polly for the bottle.

Gwen went into the tent and changed into her swimsuit, a blue one-piece with ruffles around the leg openings. She felt self-conscious changing in the tent, imagining that Hans would be training his camera on the thin nylon. She looked good in the suit, though; she knew that.

Robbie had gone off with Ted for a talk somewhere. Hans was walking along far down the lakeshore, his hands stuffed in his pockets. Polly was lying on her back on the blanket with a book, wearing her big floppy straw hat and sunglasses, waving her hand at the flies.

Gwen walked across the hot gritty sand and into the cool water. Except for the tiny splashes it made as it gave way to her feet, the water was motionless. It felt cold at first but quickly adjusted to the temperature of her skin. She took a few more steps and the process repeated itself: first cold, just bearable against her shins, then finally comfortable. Another two steps and she was in up to her knees. Under her feet, the sand gave way to pebbles, slick with algae. She thought she could feel tiny fish nibbling at her toes.

The sun beat down like a torch focused on her head. She hadn't meant for this to happen, but here it was just the same, her stomach sinking and rising again, the skin on her back and chest and arms tingling, more than just the heat and flies, a sensation she can feel now, over forty years later, with astonishing vividness. *McDougald Lake.* Ted had brought along the plaque and fastened it to a tree, the birch by their tent, so Hans could photograph the family admiring it. Later, they'd been told, someone from the government would be up to erect something more permanent for it. On the plaque was her father's name, Donald James McDougald, the dates and places of his birth, March 17, 1917, Chopin, Saskatchewan, and his death, June 7, 1944, Juno Beach, Normandy, France. She'd run her fingers along the slightly raised letters of the cool brass plaque, and she was in her den under the piano bench again, the doorbell was ringing, two men in uniform could be seen through the front window. Grandma came to the door, a smudge of flour on her cheek.

Gwen took another step into the water, then another and another, the water washing around her thighs, then her hips. She made a little diving motion, as if she were flattening herself against the back of the rocking horse, and fell into the cold water, into the arms of her father at last. The sun beat down on her back and her face. She swam and swam and swam.

* * *

Promises

MY JESSE WAS AROUND FIVE, a precious little girl with wheat-coloured curls, the first time Andre Karl Walkingman saw her. She had a rosebud mouth just as small and perfectly formed as his own exotic mother's, he said. He was smitten, of course; you could tell that, though God only knows what Andre was thinking, because he was never much of a talker, still isn't.

Jesse, though, must have known, the way children can because their eyes are still not formed completely and can see things they wouldn't later on, what an angel he was, sent from above just for her. We didn't know then what Lefty was doing—I don't think even Jesse knew, really, didn't understand anyway—but Andre, whose child's vision has never left him, could tell something wasn't right, the way Jesse wound herself around his leg, and she must have sensed somehow he was the one who would set things right. I think I did too, with a mother's intuition. I didn't think, *This is a man who might bring my daughter harm;* no, I thought, *This is a man who might bring her good.*

Andre was just hired help in those days, a man with pride but humble at the same time. He was already the fastest tree-planter in the Kootenays then, and years later, when he and Jesse declared their love, he'd become the best, a man with reputation and respect. He took her into that log house he'd built with his own hands just as if she were a stray wolf pup needing nurturing. He was thirty-seven, she seventeen, just barely, and anyone could have had the law down on him if they'd thought of it, or if he'd been any man other than the one he was, everything right there in plain view.

He was not a Métis, as most people thought, at least not in the traditional way; rather, he was an *original* in an age of descendants. His mother was a Frenchwoman, the distinguished Simone Robinault, an anthropologist who had come over after the war to do her doctoral research and stayed; his father was a Saskatchewan Cree from the Piapot Reserve. They'd met when she came to the reserve to interview old ones and he—Will Walkingman was his name, still a bit bewildered from the shell shock he'd absorbed at Normandy but one of the few in those days who spoke both English and French well—hired on as interpreter. She was a striking young woman with raven hair and a mouth soft and round and red as a rosebud, from which emitted the most musical of sounds, sounds like those Will had heard floating above the farmhouses of southern France, where the mud had seemed to go on forever, an inland sea. Will, who was a passionate hockey player and worldly, fell crazy in love with Simone, the air between his ears crystallizing with a pure light for the first time in too many years for him to count. He pursued her, dropping everything to enroll in the fall at the university in Saskatoon, where she was teaching. It took him two years of education—not exactly wasted years, but hardly useful ones—to break down the wall of ice she had constructed around her, but when he did, the fire within came pouring out like lava from a revived volcano. All of this I learned from Andre himself, who is inordinately proud of his parents.

Their son was born the next year, not in a hospital, as worldly Will would have preferred, but in a sparsely furnished bedroom in his parents' clean government-issue house on the reserve, the same place where Buffy St. Marie, the singer, had been born a few years earlier. Andre Karl—they named him after Simone's father, who had died fighting for the Resistance—grew up in the best of both worlds, spending most of each year in Saskatoon, in a tree-shaded house on a crescent and in white men's schools, where he was spoon-fed the usual schedule of cultural armament, but summering on the sun-baked reserve, where he ran naked under the pale moon with his cousins and learned more elemental things.

He was seventeen in 1967, the year the flowers bloomed all over us down in the States, and he ran away, riding a cold and drafty CP boxcar to Vancouver, then hitching down the coast to San Francisco, where he spent the summer sleeping in Golden Gate Park and filling his heart with longings too ethereal to decipher. He did *everything,* polluting his body, but kept his soul chaste, the way his father, invoking the thread of the old ways, had taught him.

Hitching home in the fall, he passed through the Kootenays; something in the dark, fir-lined hills that press in like ribs upon the heart touched his, filled him with desire thick as the porridge his grandmother used to make on chilly mornings. He stopped, reached up and touched a tree, opened his eyes as if for the first time.

He didn't return for four years, but the place had never been out of his thoughts. By this time, he'd shaken most of the pollutants out of his system, absorbed two and a half years of university, been to Europe, and could play a passable blues guitar. He was a tall willowy man—six foot three or four, maybe more—whose spine seemed born to be bent into the perpetual hairpin required by the tree-planters' art, with shoulders heavy enough to keep his torso rooted to the ground and yellow, catlike eyes that couldn't possibly have seen as much as their glance implied. The first time I saw him, he came into Trudy's little place, where Lefty and I were drinking herb tea and sharing a sprout and peanut butter sandwich; he actually had to tuck in his head stooping through the door, there was that much of him, each piece piled on top of the other. He was the most beautiful man I'd ever seen, but I was so much in love with Lefty then, it wouldn't have mattered what he'd looked like, what he'd said, what he'd had in his hands. Still, I couldn't help noticing, and he did take the breath away, dressed in fringed buckskin pants and beaded mukluks, his lustrous black hair knotted into a braid thick as my arm that looped down his back and over his shoulder, like the strap of a gunnysack. Even Lefty noticed, looking over his shoulder to follow my stare. "Hmmp," he said through his nose. "Big Indian." But we all dressed like Indians in those days, and that didn't mean anything.

Jesse was just one year old then, still crawling, sucking her thumb and baby-talking, and who would have guessed what was to come. There's no way to predict the way love will go. That's trite, I know, but it's true.

⊗

It was a piece of equipment, something for his truck, I think, that brought him up our way that time and he stopped in to get some candles for his place, which was already beginning to take shape, up in the woods behind Kaslo. He'd bought some from me before, at the fairs where I used to set up shop, and claimed I made the best in the valley, which I appreciated because there were lots of other good candle-makers and one or two who did better, I believe.

He drove up our long driveway with no hesitancy, I remember, as if he'd been there before, and parked that thing under the crabapple, which happened to be in flower then, so it must have been late April, early May. I would have said that truck of his was a hundred years old, except it was a Henry J, and I know they only made them for a few years in the fifties. I was on the porch, just about the only part of the house that wasn't underground, melting wax, and Jesse was on the floor by my feet, playing with a half-starved kitten that had wandered in the day before and we were trying to fatten up with milk and soaked bread. "Indian," she said, her eyes going big as cornflowers as Andre swung out of the cab, his braids swinging. He was wearing two of them now, Willie Nelson style, though this was before anyone knew about Willie Nelson.

"It's just Andre Walkingman," I said, and Jesse looked up at me, as if I'd said something worth taking note of, I swear, as if that was a name she'd been waiting all her life to hear. Her eyes are grey, running the prism from gunmetal dark to cloud light, depending on what's going on around and inside her, and

I could see them changing, softening up like a roiling sky with weather blowing up.

"Hi, Kassoundra," he called to me, that was the name I used back then, that strong mouth of his wide as a book breaking open into a bashful smile, and I blushed bashful too, for reasons I couldn't say. "That your little girl?"

"My *big* little girl, this's Jesse. Rebeccah's having her nap, but Jesse doesn't need one anymore, do you, lamb chop?"

Andre came up the step and hairpinned over like he was going to scoop a little hole in the forest floor and gently spoon Jesse's roots into it, but all he did was tousle her head. The smile she gave him, throat arched up and head craned back as if her balloon was taking off to the sky, was like the aurora borealis; it was that bright and abrupt. "Hey, girl. You a candle-maker, too? Or you a candle?"

"I'm a candle burning in the night," Jesse said, and she hurled herself against his leg, pressing her cheek along the leather fringe, bringing a stream of tears, of happiness, I guess, to mine. Mother's intuition, like I say. I just *knew.*

A gust of wind battered against us then, chasing the kitten under the porch and splattering Andre's truck with apple blossoms big as snowflakes.

Jesse's my first-born and special to me, carrying with her all the reminders I have left of the "me" I used to be. Lefty always used to like calling himself a "draft dodger," then grinning and explaining he meant "draught," that it was the cold winds of Saskatchewan he was dodging. But I really was on the run from the war, or, I should say, my Robert was, and I was with him. We came to Montreal from Boston in 1968 and spent three bewildering months beating our heads against French, which he had flunked at Amherst, before we called it quits and split to Vancouver, where Robert found work as a deckhand on a salmon boat. That was great for him, and he would come back from his trips tan and slim, but he left me alone for long stretches, a little homesick and weepy in all that fog and rain and the brittle friendliness of the people there, even the other dodgers we got to know. I took some classes at Simon Fraser, which was still brand new then and had the smell of sawdust on its walls, but something wasn't right, with me, with Robert, with the two of us. We took off for the Kootenays with a couple from Michigan we met in the spring, a weaver named Danielle who everyone called Danny Girl and her man, Ted, who was a deserter. I loved it right away; it seemed so much like home, but Robert missed the action of the city, whatever that might have been, and the easy way he could lay his hands on speed, which he'd turned onto during those long nights on the boats. I was already pregnant but hadn't told him when he took off, just as well. Later, he took Carter's amnesty and now works for a TV station in Atlanta. We exchange Christmas cards, but he still doesn't know about Jesse. Once he was gone, it just didn't seem like it was his business.

Ted and Danny Girl and I moved onto a commune on a farm deep in the valley with the greatest people in the world, and, with Jesse growing inside me, it was the happiest time of my life, I believe now. Lefty was already there and by the time she was born, we were a couple, and then right away a family. "We might just as well say she's mine, even *believe* she is, Kassy, because she *would* have been, if you see what I mean," he said. I really believe that right then, when she was still so unformed and anonymous, he loved her just as if she were his own, what would come later the last thing on his mind.

He was already heavy into pottery, turning out bowls big as Indian baskets on a foot-powered wheel he'd built himself and rough plates thick as boards but with the grace of birds' wings from slabs he moulded just with his hands, which were always chapped. I took up the candles, and we struck out on our own. The piece of land we bought, up near New Denver, was a scrap, a triangular wedge carved off from the rest of a quarter section by a gravel road that cut an angle to avoid a wide spot in the creek, and we got it dirt cheap. There was already a shack there, an old prospector's dump, and we lived in that the first winter while Lefty built his studio in a cave the prospector had dug and began our dugout, which was just like a railroad flat laid sideways into the hill. When it was finished, with cedar strips on the inside walls and the stone fireplace, it was snug and dry as a sauna in there, no matter what it was doing outside, dark and furry everywhere but the front room with its multi-coloured glass. Going inside after sitting on the porch, I always felt like I was crawling back into the womb, back to where all the possibilities began.

Rebeccah was born there, and so was little Aaron, my darling boy, an accident the year before Lefty and I split up, and I was happy there, happy and blind. Despite everything, Lefty was a good man—I *think*—a good and loving man who was right for me then, though I guess that doesn't make any sense. He'd gone into Nelson that day I found out, taking some of his pieces to the shops. I was giving Jesse a bath in the big red ceramic tub he'd made for us by hand, her splashing around in the bubbles, still so much a baby at eleven, me sitting on a stool by her head, scrubbing her back. I reached around her with the slippery washcloth and rubbed up and down her chest, humming some tune to myself. I could feel the small swelling of where her breasts were just beginning and it made me so happy, thinking, *My Jesse's growing up, my little girl's becoming a woman,* and feeling a sense of oneness with her, as if she were *more* than just blood of my blood, child of my womb, but an actual part of me. She shivered, not from cold, I could tell, but a shudder of something like delight, and I pulled my hand back, my fingers tingling, as if I'd had an electric shock.

"Mom?" she said.

"Yes, honey bun?"

She hesitated and I took up the cloth again and began making soapy circles on her back. "What is it, honey?"

"If I ask you something, will you promise not to be mad?"

"Sure, honey, just don't ask me where the crown jewels of Russia are buried, 'cause I don't know."

"And not mad at Lefty? Promise?"

I swear, I didn't know what was coming—I was that blind, that stupid—just that it was something serious, and I quit kidding. "Sure, honey. You go ahead."

Beneath my hand, her skinny little shoulders rose. "I don't think it's right for him to put it in me, Momma. Is it? Lefty says it's okay, it's time now, it's no different than the other stuff we do, but, I . . ." Her voice dropped off, or maybe my ears had closed up. I tried not to show how frightened I was, to not frighten her. I've heard people say when you get a shock like that, it doesn't sink in right away, that you hear but don't *really* hear, but that isn't the way it was. I heard right away.

"What other stuff, honey?"

"You know, the stuff we do."

"I don't know, honey. Tell me."

Beneath my hand, her shoulders trembled, the way the sky does sometimes, just before rain. "I thought you knew, Momma. Lefty said . . ."

"Just *tell* me, Jesse. It's all right; I won't be mad. I *promised,* didn't I?"

But even before she could answer, I had her out of the tub, standing on the crumpled mat I'd thrown on the cool tile floor, and was wrapping her in a towel, folding her up in my arms, sanding at her skin with the towel as if to strip away whatever might have tarnished it, engulfing her with towel and my arms as if I could somehow force her back into my body or some semblance of it, back where it was safe and everything could begin again.

⊗

The part of the Anglican wedding ceremony I like best—and the part of ours I regret the most—is where the minister asks the guests to pledge they'll help the newlyweds make it through the hard times ahead. They do, of course, all of them meaning well, some of them maybe even thinking they'll be true to that promise, most knowing full well that they won't have the time, the patience, the interest. They're just guests, not part of the process.

At ours, Roger's and mine, there were over three dozen people, mostly my friends, people I'd met at school or through my church singing group, because Roger knew hardly anyone in the city, and after they made the promise, their eyes shining and hopeful, they greeted the people next to them and in the pews ahead and behind them, turning around to shake hands, hug each other, wish each other well, as if to cement the idea that we're all in this together, which we aren't, *can't* be, pretty thought though that is. Roger and I stood in front of the pulpit, facing each other, my neck a little stiff from gazing up, he was that tall, almost as tall as Andre Walkingman, our own eyes shining, but out of the corner of mine I could see the community behind us and I felt great peace, knowing their strength was there beneath and all around us, like a cushion of air thick enough we'd never be able to fall through. Then we turned back to the Reverend Tobin, who is a good if somewhat distant man, and followed him through the litany of our own promises, "for better or for worse, in sickness and in health, for richer or poorer ..."

I don't regret not keeping those, because they were really made just to myself—and, as it turned out, under false premises because Roger was not what he appeared to be—but I do feel I let those other people down. They made promises on my behalf they couldn't possibly keep, even if they'd truly wanted to.

It's funny, thinking about it now, that I would have done a thing like that, I mean marry a man like Roger for all those silly reasons—well, not silly, really, but so much unlike me—and I'm not even talking about the things about him I didn't know then, the debts and his urges, just the kind of man he was, a man like my own father but not like any man I ever thought I could love or would want to marry. But there he was, and I was frightened. I can laugh now, but it made sense then.

I'll always be proud of what I did after I found out about Jesse and Lefty. I didn't wait a minute, didn't try to find out his side; I just let the animal in me come out, fierce and sly. I had the kids dressed and packed within an hour and we were gone by the time Lefty came home, over to a neighbour's with a phone, where Danny Girl picked us up in their station wagon. I was in the lawyer's office in Nelson the next morning. I'd have been at the police right after if the lawyer hadn't talked me out of it, telling me about the questions Jesse would have to answer on the stand. That was too much for me; it wasn't revenge or punishment I was after, just to get her away from him, to get *all* of us away. We were in Vancouver the next week, living on welfare first, then student loans and the little bit the lawyer pried out of Lefty after he sold our place and headed back to Saskatchewan, where, for his sins, his hands must always be cold.

I'd been so long living with tallow and incense, the earth and sun all around me, it had been years since I'd read anything more complicated than Tolkien or *Watership Down*. I remembered I had a mind, that I'd done two years at Amherst before they'd kicked me out after a demonstration that got out of hand. I loved it at UBC and the kids loved living on campus in family housing, when we finally got in after a year in Kits sharing three rooms with all the cockroaches in the world. I hadn't thought I'd like Vancouver so much, after my first chilly time there, but things were different now, with the city or with me, and I did, but we were so poor, poor, poor. It broke my heart having to tell Aaron he couldn't have this toy or that he wanted so badly. Rebeccah had to wear Jesse's hand-me-downs all through Grade 10, when she started making her own money busing tables in a Greek restaurant. I had boyfriends, and we were happy anyway, a real family even without a dad, a little more normal than we were in the Koots, which suited the kids just fine, normal but off-the-wall like some of those fractured ones you see on TV sitcoms, self-contained, relying on each other, always something wacky going on. When I met Roger, he was just a nice man, a little older, friend of a woman in my art theory class in visiting from Calgary. There was no more menace in him than in a kitten, and he had a core of loneliness it flattered me to think I could fill. Our lives hadn't been alike in any ways, but we had some common interests—we both love Bateman prints and Beethoven played loud and board games—and he was homely as I am, sharp edged where I'm soft, a map of wrongly placed convexes and concaves. He was a widower, with two boys, one already in university but the other one still at home, a year older than Jesse and always in trouble. He thought a mother could straighten the boy out in time. I began to see things in Roger I was sure my own children would appreciate, though they said they didn't like him, sweet little Aaron, just seven, even calling him a "creep" right to his face, which hurt Roger but didn't daunt him. We didn't sleep together and it didn't seem important to him, but he was sweet and romantic, bringing me flowers and reading Shakespeare to me—not sonnets, but pieces from *Richard the Third* he liked that weren't really appropriate, though the gesture was wonderful.

"You really didn't know?" Andre Walkingman asks me.

"How could I have?" I say back. We are sitting on the log porch of his house, the Purcells grey-green and shouldery in the distance across the narrow strip of lake, Jesse making clinking sounds in the kitchen behind us as she fixes salmon salad sandwiches for lunch. Nothing in my life, not even Lefty, had prepared me, and despite everything I have been and done, I am just a normal person. I don't have vision beyond what my eyes bring me.

I say something to that effect and Andre laughs, not a mean-hearted laugh but a gentle one, filled with curves and corners, and looks at me with an incredulous smile. He is a man who sees the best and worst in people, often at the same time, without looking for either, and I believe he has a hard time accepting that this is a gift, that not all of us possess that sense. But he is willing to be generous.

It was Jesse who caught Roger and Aaron together, and she didn't waste any time afterwards taking off. Rebeccah was my strong girl, fifteen now; she's wiser than Jesse in some ways, steadier. Aaron was just bewildered, defiant and puzzled, trailing around the house in his pajamas with a teddy bear he hadn't played with in years, saying "Creep, creep, creep," over and over, like a magic oath you cast into darkness to keep spirits at bay. Roger went packing, but not before I called the cops. Didn't hesitate this time. Fool me once, shame on you; fool me twice, shame on *me*. But how I got fooled is something I'll never know. "Just too trusting," Andre says.

I got a call in the middle of the night the next week from Jesse.

"I'm home, Mom."

"No you're not. *I'm* home. You're calling."

"Real home, Mom, the Koots. I'm at Andre's."

"Uh huh," I said. I wasn't surprised, didn't have to ask her "Andre who?" and I started wondering why.

"I'm sorry if I worried you, Mom."

"I wasn't really worried, darling. Danny Girl called the other day. But I thank you for being sorry. Are you okay?"

"Sure, Mom. Mom, Andre isn't... I mean, this isn't what you're probably thinking."

I laughed at that, because, to tell the truth, I hadn't been thinking at all. "It's okay, honey; I wasn't thinking what *you* were thinking I was. Your old ma isn't that far gone, now, is she?"

We had a good laugh, and a bit of a cry, and a better talk than we've had since she turned sixteen, even if there was four hundred kilometres between us, all that space getting out of the way so we could put our arms around each other. I asked her to put Andre on the phone but he wasn't with her; she'd taken his truck and gone up to New Denver to look at our old place and used the pay phone at the gas station by the turnoff. "He's the one told me to call, Mom. I mean, I would have anyway, but maybe not tonight."

"I'll get up there as soon as I can, darling," I told her, but I didn't feel a real urgency. I hadn't done so well, and I didn't think she could do worse; no, I *knew* she had to do better.

I've been up there twice since then, though, staying with Danny Girl and Ted, who run a bookstore now in Nelson, and popping in on the lovebirds. I like the looks of them. The fellow I'm seeing now, Harvey, thinks I'm crazy. He's a teacher and has a degree in psychology and is a good judge of character, I think, but not infallible. I was always a bad judge, but I've learned some things, learned to trust my feelings even against all appearances. Harvey says a girl of seventeen living with a man of thirty-seven, an eccentric, a man who still wears his hair long as Andre Walkingman does, there's something wrong there, something *unhealthy.* Harvey is a city man—I don't mean that as a put-down—and a reasonable man, but I haven't taken him up to the Kootenays, so he hasn't seen them together.

First time I visited, I asked Andre, not in so many words, what his intentions were, and he told me this: "I love her, Kassy. I think I always have. I've always felt her waiting for me, ever since I came into this country, like some sort of a promise."

Andre has big hands, the skin on them hard as the scales on pine cones, but I've seen him pick up an injured bird with those hands and make them go soft as clouds, and I don't see any harm in them for my girl, short of what comes, come what may. I think about all the promises made to me in my life, the handful that were kept and all the rest that seem to have slipped away, like songs on the radio you get so used to hearing you *don't* hear anymore, and it seems to me you have to settle for what you can get when you can get it. The best is things spinning out almost the way you dreamed they would. Most things fall short, but maybe not too short. And what's the worst that could happen?

* * *

Scars

WHEN MY WIFE WAS FIVE, a tramp came to the back door of her home, asking for a handout. This was in the beginning of the fifties, several years after the war's end and long after the Depression, but there were still such men to be seen, riding the rails looking for work or running from it, cooking their scraped-together meals in hobo camps in the ditches near tracks, and no one thought to be frightened of them. Daphne's mother, who was still a young woman but already had a grandmother's heart, told him she would prepare him a lunch if he chopped some firewood.

This was here in Saskatoon, in the old stone Victorian on Saskatchewan Crescent Daphne's grandfather, who'd been a lawyer and councilman, had built for himself and his new young wife around the turn of the century, and there were two fireplaces. Daphne's father, who'd been wounded in the war and walked with a limp, was strong enough, but tended to fall behind in the chores. It was early autumn, shortly after the resumption of school, so her older brother and sister were away, the days still warm but the evenings crisp, and a fire was often lit after dinner.

Daphne skipped ahead of the hobo and showed him where the axe was kept in the garage, then sat on the grass, all golden curls, rosy mouth, and baby fat, watching as he took off his coat, hanging it on the picket fence, rolled the sleeves of his faded blue shirt, and began his work. Chips of wood smelling like medicine flew and one almost hit her.

"You're gonna get hurt, you sit that close, honey," the tramp said, offering a smile she remembered, years later, as curiously insincere. "Then yer mummy will be awful mad at me and I'll be out my dinner."

Daphne scrambled to her feet and backed off a few steps, but was reluctant to go farther.

"G'wan, now, Honey Miss. Here, play with this." The tramp reached into the pocket of his coat and took out a railroad spike, its sides rusted but shiny on the crown, and tossed it to her. She caught the spike awkwardly, the way she would have a rubber ball, pulling it to her chest, where it bounced off her breastbone, leaving a sore blue spot for days, and up to her forehead, the shiny crown opening a neat red pocket of skin as long as a thumbnail. Blood seeped from the cut and six stitches, expertly applied by Doctor Dempster, who practised from the front rooms of his house down the street, were required to close it. In time, a scar developed, a sliver of dead flesh smooth and hard and shiny as the head of the spike must have been. Even now, she's vain about it, brushing her hair to the side so that it's covered, and when we make love I brush my lips against it, that diamond of vulnerability drawing me closer to her, or so it seems to me.

⊗

In the third month of her medical practice, two things happened in one week that crystallized something in Daphne, like butter softening in the heat, then hardening again in the fridge in a different shape. One was expected, the other not. The expected thing was that she lost her first patient. It had been bound to happen, so she should have been prepared, and people had died on her before, when she was an intern, but it's different in hospital, where so much is oriented toward death and where people come and go, transient strangers who might as well as have died, because you never see them again. It's different to have a regular patient die, someone you've seen in the office, where getting better is what everybody works at.

The unexpected thing, which came first, was a letter from her first husband, Gary, whom she hadn't heard from in years. God only knows how he found out our name or address. The same way Daffy knew he was living in a commune in Arizona,

I suppose, through the old friend or two from those days she still saw now and then.

"Damn him all to hell," Daffy said.

⊗

My wife is in her forties but hasn't lost her looks. She's slim and tall, too tall for her own good, blonde as a field of straw, with eyes the colour and motion of bluebirds flashing through trees, Paul Newman eyes, and a girlish look. She's a doctor, as I've said, with as many male patients as female, and I believe many of them are in love with those eyes and her long, luxurious hair, those who aren't intimidated by her height. Her face has that same lean, almost bony quality that attracted me to her fifteen years ago, when she was paying her way through graduate school working as an occasional model, but her skin isn't as smooth. Harsh winters and dry summers do that. From across a room, her hair brushed to cover her scar and her makeup on, she seems perfect.

I don't understand change myself, but Daphne thrives on it. I'm a numbers cruncher at a bank, have been for twenty-seven years. I do it because I love numbers, love their motion and fluidity, the mystery behind them, the stability they represent—and that you can *trust* them—and always have, as much now as I did when I was a math whiz kid chewing up my teachers at Nutana Collegiate, in Saskatoon's leafy old neighbourhood. To me, the invention of the calculator represents the dawn of true civilization, not the steam engine or airplane or electric light. Daffy doesn't understand any of those things, certainly not my reluctance to try anything else. "How can you *not* be bored?" she asks me sometimes, and I grin in dumb amazement, all honest innocence, unable to comprehend why I should be. Bored is winter evenings with nothing to do but read, long summer weekends now that my children are grown and don't share their lives between their mother and me, keeping them for themselves.

But Daphne is always changing. When she was younger,

she was a chameleon, taking on whatever was forced her way. Now she makes her own. With her looks, naturally she wanted to be an actress, and she had small successes through high school, including Kate in *Taming of the Shrew* in Grade 12. She had plenty of talent, I suspect, but not the spark, the hunger; that became evident at the University of Saskatchewan, where she actually had to try out for roles, which forced her to quit. She holds no grudges about that. "Acting is make-believe," she's explained to me, "lying, essentially. You have to be a good liar to be an actress. I'm too honest." She blushes as she says this, explaining a fault with a virtue and seeking to transform it into a fault.

She met both her husbands, Gary the Jerk, as we both call him, and me, while she was at university, which was why I was nervous about her going to med school, though I'm really more secure in our marriage than that remark implies. Gary was all the excesses of the sixties rolled up into one neat package, except not so neat. His father was a postman, born here but with a Ukrainian accent he couldn't shake, his mother a Polish DP, a clerk at a library branch who worshipped books, and they'd slaved to get their children only the best: toys, clothing, food on the table, in a smallish house in a block where neighbours were a school principal, the assistant manager of a bank, the owner of a hardware store. Gary resisted all this, dropped out his first year at university, shortened his name from Lishnofski to Lish, let his hair grow halfway down his shoulders like a girl's and redolent with natural oils and dirt, hitchhiked, wrote poetry, protested against things he didn't understand, consumed whatever drugs were thrown at him, contracted a venereal disease. They have medicine to clear that up, but not his other ailments. He was back at school, his beard trying to catch up with his hair, when Daphne, who had a passion for literature then and wore her own hair tangled though clean, met him at a coffee shop where someone was strumming a guitar and singing in a sweet clear voice about an English lord who was unfaithful. They compared poems, went to her place, read e.e.

cummings to each other until dawn, became lovers when they were too exhausted to resist. Two months later, they married.

She dropped out then to support *him,* slinging hash. She with only a year to go, straight As, him with nothing clear. A year later, they were in Greece, hitching, sleeping on the beach, their blood turning to wine, and the year after that on a communal farm east of Prince Albert, both of them brown as shale, no drugs, no poetry, no politics, just sweat and aching muscles. Gary wanted to farm, really farm, but all organic, on his own, and they tried leasing a place but there's no money in that. Every cent you make goes into rent, machinery, seed, and you can't eat stubble and oily rags. Daphne had started painting by then, watercolours mostly, pastoral scenes, and some of them were good enough to sell. "You don't have to lie to paint," she says. "You paint what you see, what's really there." They went bust the second season and moved back to Saskatoon. Gary drove cab for a while, worked construction, drew pogey, went back to school. Daffy waitressed, painted; they got by. Gary got his teacher's certificate and they went upcountry, a little place north of PA. She loved the light there, the stark horizontals broken by pencil-thin spruce, slashes of dark across the light, and he said he loved working with native kids, unspoiled and fresh. She painted all the time, filling the walls of their rented house with canvases, selling the occasional one. He taught, coached basketball and the yearbook, and turned in on himself in a way Daphne could only barely sense, later couldn't explain. One day, she came home late with her easel and her oil-smeared smock and Gary's car was already in the driveway. "Sorry I'm late, hon," she called from the door, scraping mud from her boots. "I'll get dinner started in a jiffy." In the living room, she stopped short. The frames were there, each in its place, as if untouched, but the canvases had been sliced out with a razor blade, leaving blank windows of white scattered about the walls. Gary was in the den, the second bedroom they'd converted for him with a desk and shelves, marking papers. "The dump," he said when she asked where they were, but would give no explanation.

I met her two years later, when I was taking a weekend computer course in Regina. She'd left him that night, hitched into PA and found a job at one of the town's two or three galleries. That led to a better job, at a gallery down there. She did well, wound up managing the place, but she wanted her own. When she went to the bank for a loan, the man she talked to, who had a B.Comm., suggested she might consider sharpening her management skills. She was back in school that fall, in the commerce faculty, paying her rent by posing, both ways: for catalogue photographers, draped with clothes that are supposed to show while you melt into the background; and naked, at the art faculty, her chin high, eyes averted, as the eyes of the students filled with the form of her, not the detail, their fingers racing to capture that unyielding motion—invisible either way. During a break in my course, I went for a walk by myself, got lost, and wandered down a corridor I shouldn't have been on and past a door carelessly left open. I looked in, caught a glimpse of her, that was all it took.

After we got married, she quit the modelling but kept up with the classes and got her degree. Then she opened the gallery and seemed to be happy with it. My kids came to visit often, spending weekends, most of their summers. She and Gary had decided not to have children and now she would have liked one, but I'd had the vasectomy after my youngest was born. She didn't seem to mind, took to my kids. We all went to the Dominican Republic for Christmas one year. We bought a cottage up at Foam Lake. The gallery was doing well. I couldn't believe it when she told me she wanted to go to med school.

"I'll be thirty-five this year," she said. "It's time I did something with my life, don't you think?"

She quit smoking that year too, while she was cramming for the MCATs, as if she was thumbing her nose at whatever it was that had ever held her down.

⊗

Now here was this stupid letter from Gary.

"You wouldn't believe how together I am now," he wrote, "how *level* I am, in harmony with forces in the universe I never even suspected before. At one with the ripples."

I couldn't help but smile when I read that, looking up and catching Daf with her sleek, well-formed mouth in the wryest damn expression, as if she were sucking at something bitter at the root of her teeth. She wouldn't have shown me the letter, but I'd come home before her and noticed it with the other mail in the pewter tray on the foyer table, where the cleaning woman had left it. The name in the return address was Lishnofski and it took me a moment to place it. Then she couldn't very well say no when I asked her about it.

"Damn him," she'd said as she handed me the letter. "Still a jerk."

"I understand things are going good for you now," the letter went on. "You and I have always been tied together—even *before* we met, karma bringing us together because we were meant to be—so I can't help but think the peace I'm experiencing has something—maybe everything—to do with it. When I was going through hell, you went through bad times too. Thick and thin, richer or poorer, sickness and health, just like the vows say. I'm the stronger one of us, so I take the lead, I guess. I don't mean to; it's just the way things happen.

"What I'm getting around to is this: I'm glad you're good now, sorry for what came before."

Daphne was standing by the window, her back to me, when I looked up, my head shaking. "Jesus," I said. "What conceit."

"Damn him," she said again. "I'll never be able to wield a scalpel the way he can. Not if I practice till I'm eighty."

"From everything I've heard about the guy, I never would have described him as the stronger of the two of you," I said.

Daphne made a noise I took to be a laugh—an ironic laugh—but when I looked up I saw tears standing in those fierce blue eyes like whitecaps on the lake when the wind ripples the normally calm surface into brilliant Braille.

"Damn him all to hell," she said, but at that moment

I wasn't certain that the curse didn't spread widely enough to include me.

Two days after that, she called me in the middle of the day, asked me to come over to her office. That surprised me so much, I did right away. The waiting room was jammed but Lucy, the nurse Daffy shares with her partner Prentice, who's an older man, brought me right into her office. Lucy is a sweet kid and I swear, between her and Daf, it's the best looking clinic in the province. Waiting, I found myself reading the slanted, oblique letters on Daphne's framed diplomas. I could hear voices in the examining room next door, but not the words. After a couple of minutes, the door opened partway. "Sure," Daf said. "You can get dressed now." She closed the door behind her and I noticed there was a smudge on the lapel of her white smock, like a fingerprint left by a burglar.

"Oh, Robert," she said, and her face crumpled, the leftover smile fracturing into sharp lines like cracks in baked mud. "Mr. Brezak died. I was sure he was getting better and . . . damn it."

I had my arms around her and we stood folded up into each other in the middle of the office, with its dark oak and leather furniture I'd helped her pick out, the tray of gleaming instruments in the glass-doored cabinet, the diplomas hanging from the walls like open eyes, her small shoulders convulsing with sobs. I didn't say anything. I couldn't remember whether Brezak was the old gent with Alzheimer's and pneumonia or the middle-aged butcher with the bad heart. Brezak was one of them, Krulak the other. I thought about Gary and the way his name kaleidoscoped through his life, changing the way it suited him rather than constant like mine. "It's okay, baby," I said, but the words sounded so hollow, so useless, I didn't repeat them.

After awhile, the crying slowed, stopped. My arms were getting tired from holding her so tight, and my back was hurting from the way I had to lean into her; she's that tall. "This is stupid," she said. "I won't do this again."

"You *are* a doctor," I said, somewhat lamely, as if that really explained anything.

"I know." She sniffed and raised her head, gave me a weak little smile. "It won't happen again. Jesus, it better not or I'm in the wrong racket. Prentice will bust a gut when he hears about this. *If* I tell him." She took a tissue from the box on her desk and blew her nose. "Thanks for coming over. I just needed to cry a little and I couldn't bear to do it alone."

"Was there anything you could have done? About Blazak?"

"Brezak. No. Not a damn thing. It doesn't help much, though. I just need a thicker skin."

"It'll come," I said. "Just don't let it get *too* thick."

"A few more like this and I'll be covered with calluses."

I put my hand on her cheek, still hot and a little red. I could feel it all afternoon, back in my own office, where there never are tears, my fingers still tingling as they raced over the keys of my calculator.

The calculator is much like a crystal ball: you punch numbers into it—numbers like pieces of the past and the present—and it shows you the future. As many possible ones as different combinations of numbers you punch in. Mine has a light, sickly green face, with darker, fuzzy green numbers that grow more brilliant the darker it is in the room. I work with it so often, I keep the lights low in my office, which is nothing like Daffy's, furnished in functional, impersonal non-descript sticks of aluminum, polished wood, plastic, synthetic cloth. I sat at my desk, its top clear of everything but the papers I was working with, the neat in/out basket, an onyx and silver pen and pencil set Daf gave me for my birthday three years ago, and a framed photo of her in her hospital greens, taken the first day of her internship, my favourite photo of all the hundreds we have of her because her face is so open, taken unawares by the camera, overwhelmed. I looked from the face of the calculator to the photo—to *her* face—and I trembled.

* * *

Comfort

IN THE TOWN, TWO WOMEN lived together, not as lovers but as dear friends and constant companions, though of speculation among their neighbours and acquaintances there was no end. The one woman, the one we're interested in, was good-natured and good-hearted, but homely, and she'd been unlucky with men—one man dying on her, another abusing her and finally running off—and she had gradually resigned herself to living without their company. At the time of this tale, she had already endured the turn into her fifties and was reasonably content with the world and its doings, as much so, at least, as many of her neighbours who lived more conventional lives, with families and mortgages and all of their accepted deprivations and disappointments. As a child, she had been happy enough, and she'd been an optimistic young woman, with friends, lovers, and a career, but then had come a period of unhappiness, which she'd lived through, passed through, and more than merely survived but bested. She began the friendship with the other woman, whose story was something else entirely, and that had made all the difference.

Still, though she was not aware of it, the path of her life was not yet fully set.

This story concerns itself with sheets, pretty sheets with blue violets printed seemingly at random on a background of blush, 100 per cent cotton, 500 threads to the inch.

The woman's name was Violet, Violet Jakubowski; her first name, in this story, is reasonably important, but of the latter name there is no particular significance. Her parents had died—part of the unhappiness already mentioned. She was a schoolteacher, and if you have any stereotypes in mind for that profession, put them aside here. Violet was neither obsessively devoted to her pupils nor cold and manipulative—she was, as has already been said, good-hearted and good-natured; as well, she was efficient, imaginative, and conscientious, always prepared, usually punctual, memorizing the names of each student in a new class by the beginning of the second week, and never forgetting them afterwards, so her head was a huge repository of names and faces that she could connect together in a moment, as long as the face hadn't changed *too* much—meeting a former student ten or fifteen years later, beards could confuse her, but not much else.

Violet and her friend, Emily, had taken, several years since now, to sleeping in the same bed, though that activity was chaste, both in act and intent, rest assured. Their motivation was simply companionship and warmth.

"Oh, dear. I fear these sheets aren't much longer for this world, Emily," Violet said one Saturday, laundry day, in autumn as they remade the bed with linen fresh from the closet.

In their household, they had three sets of sheets for the queen-size bed they shared as well as an assortment of garage sale sheets for the double bed in the second bedroom, now reserved for guests, though they rarely had any, and the still-narrower sofabed in the living room. The sheets for their shared bed were of good quality but were old, too old for the women to remember precisely when they dated to, but easily ten years or more. Each set was laundered, in its turn, every three weeks, and, over the years, that had amounted to as many as two hundred washings and dryings, ironings and foldings. The sheets were thin, almost threadbare, diaphanous, translucent when held to the light streaming in through the bedroom window, which faced out onto a sunny backyard dominated by a spreading oak tree, but were soft as water, light as feathers fluttering to the polished hardwood floor from a tiny tear in the seam of the duvet they used in the winter. On Violet's skin, they felt comfortable, familiar, reassuring.

"Nor are we," remarked her friend, who could be described as no-nonsense for people who like that sort of phrase. She was also a teacher, a guidance counsellor, and Violet thought of her as someone wiser and both more precise and more eloquent than she.

"The others aren't much better."

"That's usually the way it is."

"I mean, Emily dear, that we're going to *have* to buy new ones one of these days."

"So, you don't think we can outlast them?"

Violet's comfortable face, always animated when she talked, settled into a blank-gazed repose for a moment. "Don't you mean . . ." she began, but, before she could continue, Emily hit her with a pillow and the two women erupted into simultaneous laughter, which sent them bouncing on the mattress, their hair flying.

Unusual behaviour for unmarried women in their fifties? Not really. The latest U2 was on the stereo as they worked. The evening before, they had dined on crab legs (frozen, and nuked, admittedly) and watched *Fargo* on video. The Saturday edition of *The Globe and Mail,* delivered to their door in predawn darkness and picked over at breakfast, awaited their evening edification and pleasure. Despite any and all appearances to the contrary, they were modern, sophisticated women. But they had sheets on their mind this afternoon, an old-fashioned preoccupation.

"I mean it," Violet said as they took tea in the living room afterwards, "about the sheets."

"I know, I know," her friend said. "But what do you propose to do about it?"

Ah, there was the rub, literally.

On a trip the two of them had taken to Mexico a few years earlier, Violet had developed a rash, painful and ugly red blotches that spread over her skin in shapes reminiscent of continents floating in the chilly curved seas of an atlas. Antibiotics had cleared up the condition, but in its place had come a skin sensitivity her physician was unable to treat, one that dictated huge changes in her wardrobe and household details. Wool, flannel, and other coarse material was unbearable, not just actually against her quick-to-ulcer skin but anywhere nearby, from where airborne fibres could easily find their way to her, setting off fits of twitching and squirming. All of both Violet's and Emily's old sweaters had long been given away, along with assorted skirts, jackets, coats, blankets, and wall-hanging weavings. Even silk, which seems so smooth, was implicated, along with most of the synthetics. Only cotton stood up to the stringent test of her skin's comfort—"and thank God for cotton," Emily liked to joke, "or you'd have to go to work naked." It was an old joke, told over and over again so that it had worn thin as the sheets the two women slept on, as comfortable. Violet would blush at that word, "naked," but Emily, bolder, would gaze at her frankly, her eyes filled with amusement and, Violet thought, perhaps something else.

Similarly, harsh household cleansers and any other kind of chemicals had been removed and banned from the house, along with most of Violet's small supply of cosmetics and all but the purest, most hypoallergenic of soaps and lotions. On her skin, dust could irritate almost as cunningly as sand or grit, but, curiously, she was not bothered by the usual allergies, pollen, mould, and dander. "Your nasal passages and lungs are healthy as those of a horse," her doctor had pronounced. He was an older man who reminded Violet of her father before his mind had begun to wrinkle like a prune. "It's just your skin that's hot."

All of which to say that buying something as seemingly innocuous as a new set of sheets was nowhere as easily done as said. The greater world to which Violet daily ventured was filled with hazards—should a student in wool brush against her, say, she cringed—but the house she and Emily shared had been made comfortable, secure against the irritations of the outside world that hammered at their door. But the balance was precarious, and both women knew it.

In fact, the conversation about the sheets was one they'd been having, off and on, for over a year now, since Violet had first noticed a small tear in the hem of the fitted sheet with the yellow roses, the once-bright blossoms faded now to a shade barely distinguishable from the once-blue background. The tear had been mended, but since then there'd been others, in all three sets, and an unfixable hole—unfixable except by a patch, which Violet was sure her skin wouldn't be able to tolerate—was beginning to take shape and spread like a colony of amoebas near the foot of the bottom sheet with the happy hexagonal shapes.

"It's always the bottoms that give the trouble," Violet said with a sigh, not the first time. Despite her frown, there was a mischievous gleam in her eye.

"What do you expect?" Emily replied to this observation, as she usually did, "They're the ones we lie on." This accompanied by a wink; other times, it might have as easily been a grin, or both.

But despite the conversations, nothing had been done. What could be done? Several years earlier, before it had become such a pressing issue, Emily had bought, on impulse, because they were on sale and the design appealed to her, a set of sheets they'd had every reason to think would be fine. But when they put them on the bed, after several washings, the slick cotton-poly blend of the pillowcase tore at the delicate skin of Violet's face like the menacing thorns of the wild roses she loved so much, and her calves and ankles, exposed beneath the tangled hem of her well-worn cotton nightgown, blossomed with patterns no designer of sheets or dresses would be likely to imagine. Several more washings, another attempt, the same result, and the new sheets were consigned to the closet in the second bedroom, where, with few guests to make use of them, and too big for the bed at any rate, they were as cast into limbo, a state not unlike that which Violet felt she herself occupied. What was to be done?

For some inexplicable reason—so ask for no explanation—this time Violet took action. On her way home from school on Monday, she stopped at the mall, wove her way through shoppers with more pressing matters on their minds than Christmas, still many weeks away, and hesitated for only a moment—frowning at her reflection in the polished store window and feeling her skin begin to tingle—before plunging through the gaily open doors of *La Boudoir Boutique.*

"Yes, ma'am, can I help you?" A nattily dressed young man with a ridiculously out-of-style moustache—"pencil thin" was the phrase that came to Violet's mind, though it wasn't really that slim—had materialized at her elbow.

"Yes, I was wanting..." She paused, and focused her attention on the young man's face, not just the moustache. "You're Johnny Summers, aren't you?"

"Yeah. I'm sorry, do I know you?"

Violet laughed. "You do, but I don't expect you to remember me. Though, actually, I've changed far less than *you* have."

The young man smiled, his cheeks dimpling. He was slim, the line of his jaw well defined, and a lock of his sandy brown hair lay with practiced casualness over his smooth forehead. "Don't tell me, then. Let me guess."

"All right, go ahead."

The young man gave her a quizzical look that made him look endearing and younger than she guessed him to be, in his late twenties. She couldn't remember what year she'd had him. His eyes, she noticed, were a shade of lavender that, on first glance, at least, didn't seem possible. "Are you a friend of my mother's?"

"No."

"You're not my long-lost Aunt Hennie, are you?"

"Hennie?"

"Henrietta. She—I guess you're not her—she moved to Australia in her twenties and hasn't been back since."

"No, I'm not her. Not Hennie."

"Well, let me see... No, I can't," he blurted out. "Just tell me."

"Miss Jakubowski. Davin School, grade seven."

"Oh, my god, you're right."

Violet laughed. "Well, of course, I'm right. I *do* know who I am."

"I mean, *I* know who you are. I mean, I recognize..."

"I know what you mean, Johnny." She put a hand lightly on his arm. "This happens to me all the time."

"Well, yes, I imagine it does. I only had one grade seven teacher, but you've had . . . hundreds of students, I bet."

"Yes, hundreds, not *thousands*. I'm not that old."

"I didn't mean . . ."

She laughed again. "Now I've flustered you."

"No, I only, I mean . . . how did you recognize *me*?"

"Oh, I never forget a student."

The young man smiled ruefully. "So it's nothing special, nothing memorable, about *me*."

"Now you're making *me* feel bad. It's just that *all* my students are special, to me. They're all memorable. But I'm just confounding the damage, aren't I?"

"Hardly damaged, Miss Jakubowski, no, not at all. Well, perhaps my ego's just a *tiny* bit pricked. Everyone likes to think they're . . . special." He smiled in such an endearing way that Violet, without giving it a thought, did something that surprised her, even more than it did him.

"Violet," she said.

"Violet?"

"That's my name. Call me Violet."

The young man hesitated. "I don't know if I could. I mean . . ."

"I'm not your teacher anymore, Johnny. It is all right to call *you* that, isn't it? Or do you prefer John?"

"John's what most people call me, but Johnny's fine, honestly."

"Good. So if you're Johnny, then it's only right and reasonable that I'm Violet. Miss Jakubowski's the teacher. *I'm* a customer. And, I don't know, perhaps an old friend?"

"Or a new one," the young man said, and there was something about the way he said it, and the way his lavender eyes caught the light—fluorescent though it was—that pierced her, like a fine wire, a wire carrying an electrical charge threaded through a vein to the source of trouble with an organ deep within the body, something she had read about on the science page of *The Globe and Mail* not long before. She had a strong impulse, which she resisted, to reach out and touch the fine hairs of that neatly crafted moustache.

They laughed, lightly, almost artificially, and after a

moment, the young man moved his eyes away from hers. "I'm forgetting my manners. Was there something you were interested in . . . Violet?"

"Yes," she said, almost primly, "I'm looking for sheets, the best quality. They have to be smooth as glass. But"—the skin around her eyes wrinkled—"softer, obviously."

"Obviously. I have just the thing." He began to move away, and Violet found herself following him through an aisle lined with plush displays of comforters, shams, and oversized pillows toward a counter where, she could see, an arrangement of packages containing folded sheets had been constructed in front of an oddly compressed bed, fully made but with the duvet and top sheet casually tossed aside, set at a vertical angle. "Top of the line, 100 per cent Egyptian pima sateen, 500 threads to the inch. None better, here or anywhere else."

"It's just that I have a skin condition," Violet began, as she fingered the satisfying material of the sheet on the display. It was heavy, crisp, its surface slick with a chemical coating she knew would have to be washed away.

"No need to explain," Johnny interrupted. "Skin condition or not, why shouldn't you have the best? And it isn't even all that much more."

The sheets *were* smooth, and one set she found, as she sorted through the pile on the counter, was very appealing, a warm pastelly pink scattered over with blue violets in a seemingly random pattern. Most of the others were plainer, in a rainbow of pastel shades but with no print. "Those are the ones for you, Violet," Johnny said, his voice suddenly soft, low, his chin lifting.

They were expensive, though, much more than she thought she should spend for sheets.

"Fully guaranteed," Johnny said.

"I don't take your meaning."

"You take them home, wash them a few times, try them out. If you're not satisfied, bring them back."

"Oh, Johnny, that's irresistible."

He didn't say anything, but his eyes rested on hers in a calm, steady gaze. After a moment, she looked back to the sheet in her hand.

"Surely they don't offer a guarantee like that. What would they do with sheets that were returned? You couldn't resell them."

"We don't expect any returns."

Flustered, she scanned the wording on the package. "Where does it say that?"

"It's a store guarantee, Violet."

"Store? You sure?"

"Don't worry, I'm not taking a risk. How do you want to pay?"

They concluded their business, and Violet, feeling both well satisfied and strangely unstrung, as if she'd drunk too many cups of coffee, gave Johnny a final smile and took her leave, the sheets in a bright yellow plastic bag with long straps swinging gaily from her hand. She could feel—*thought* she could feel—the weight of his vision on her back all the way down the long corridor to the escalator.

On Saturday, laundry day, the sheets would go through three washes, one with liquid detergent, two without, would ride the currents of caressing air in the tumble dryer, would sizzle under the hard, hot tongue of Emily's iron. The women would marvel at the feel of the material, its heft and weight—"almost more like actual linen, I think," Emily would say—and make the bed, standing back to admire the lovely pattern, that explosion of violets, before putting on the duvet, their throats tightening slightly with anticipation, their eyelids growing heavy with the presentiment of sleep. But that's on the weekend, five days away, and no explanation for the feeling Violet experienced *that* night as she lay staring into the darkness, Emily already softly snoring beside her, the air above their heads faintly redolent with the familiar smells that rise from the mouths of middle-aged women in their sleep, her skin so comfortable in its familiar bath of well-worn nightgown, well-worn sheet, yet somehow burning, *burning*.

* * *

The Gift

WHAT WITH THE TIME DIFFERENCE between Saskatchewan and BC, and the rental car being actually ready for him at the airport, Gerry found himself in his room at the Sylvia Hotel just past ten on an unnaturally bright Vancouver morning, with almost the whole day stretching ahead of him before his planned surprise visit to Lorna. As he stood at the window looking out at the metallic waters of English Bay, he felt, for the first time, a twinge of doubt. What if she wasn't pleased to see him? Lorna could be volatile, unpredictable, he knew that, but he shook the thought off, and it occurred to him that he should use the extra time searching for a gift.

He was still amazed by his audacity at even being here. But he didn't want to dwell on that—if he did, he was sure, he'd lose his nerve.

The previous day at lunch, he'd seen a woman who made his breath catch in his throat, and it had shaken him. He was standing in the lineup at the cashier in the city hall cafeteria when he caught a glimpse of her from behind, tight black tailored slacks over slim but rounded hips, and a mane of straight, luxuriant black hair, the backs of the heels of polished black pumps just disappearing from view. A minute later, as he was unloading his tray onto the table with the usual crowd, he saw her again entering the lunchroom, busty in a lavender sweater, full lipped, broad cheekbones—he couldn't tell whether she was native or Asian of some sort, Chinese perhaps, or Filipino; at any rate, beautiful. Breathtaking.

He kept finding reasons, without being so obvious that he'd embarrass himself, to look over his shoulder to catch glimpses of her, but the third time he twisted around, her place was empty and there was no sign of her, the group of women she'd been with continuing their conversation as if her absence was unremarkable. His heart sank. Then he caught sight of her coming back to her table, balancing a cup of coffee and saucer and a butter tart. Lunch finished, he lingered over a second cup of coffee, changing seats when his officemates went out for their usual smoke and stretch, so he could see her better.

When the woman started to gather her dishes, Gerry rose and made his way casually in her direction, coming abreast of her table just as she was getting up. He'd been right about her body—it seemed perfect—but up close it was clear she was neither as pretty as he'd thought, nor as young. Her cheeks were more flat than broad, her skin coarse, and her eyes, when she glanced at him, without interest, were dull, almost stupid. She was chewing gum.

Standing at the elevator on his way back to his office, he was struck by how he'd been so entranced, then let down, all within minutes. For the first time that day, he thought of Lorna, who was also capable of provoking extreme responses in him, soaring highs and plummeting lows. He was suddenly pierced by a desire to see her. He missed her, of course, but it was something more than that.

It was time to do something about Lorna, but he had no idea what.

⊗

That evening, Lorna was still on his mind—the girl in the cafeteria long forgotten—when Gerry got home to his neat two-storey house just a few blocks past the Broadway Bridge. He snapped on his computer, checked his e-mail, and was delighted to find a long message from her. The timing was perfect. Even better, she began the e-mail with an apology for her brusque manner the last time they'd talked. He'd phoned one evening, caught her by surprise and, apparently, in the midst of something. After a few minutes of what Gerry had thought was pleasant and affectionate small talk, she had made an exasperated sound and abruptly hung up, leaving him hurt and confused. Now she began her e-mail this way: "Gerry, I am *so* sorry for being rude the other day"—it was actually over a week ago—"but you caught me at a very bad time. Sorry, I can't explain, something with a parishioner. And—my cheeks are going red as I write this, so it's good you're not here to see me—it's a woman thing. Understand?"

Gerry shook his head and smiled with relief.

Aggravation and apology, tension and relief—it was the pattern of their relationship, and it couldn't go on.

He'd met Lorna while on a retreat at St. Peter's Abbey the previous February, shortly after his mother's death. They were drawn to each other, and, while nothing had happened that weekend except for a very clumsy kiss, he left the abbey feeling that something of significance had begun.

Back in Saskatoon, they'd not exactly dated but had seen each other a few times, going for coffee and springtime walks along the river, an occasional dinner. The kiss, familiar though it had been, was not repeated, not because Gerry hadn't wanted it to, certainly, but because an opportunity had not presented itself.

Then, at spring's end, Lorna, who had been studying for the ministry, was ordained and immediately found a church in Abbotsford, less than an hour's drive from Vancouver in the Fraser Valley. Since then, they'd become e-mail regulars—pen pals. The disastrous phone call had been his first attempt to go beyond the computer screen and clearly was a mistake. They kept saying they should have a visit, but neither had been able to get away. They were both busy people, Lorna especially, with her new ministry and her son, who was in law at UBC—one of the attractions of the west coast for her. Six months had passed and it was deep winter again, though mild, and Gerry was as uncertain about their relationship—was that what it was?—as he'd been on the afternoon of the kiss. If Lorna knew more than he did, she wasn't saying.

What was surprising to him about Lorna was that, while she wasn't particularly attractive—not anything like the girl in the cafeteria, at least not as he first saw her—he found her very appealing. She was a bit overweight—*plush* was the word that came to mind—with stringy hair and a gap between her upper front teeth he especially liked. She made him feel not aroused, especially, but unthreatened and satisfied, as if sex had already occurred. Not at all like his former wife, who'd been attractive enough to always make Gerry feel slightly uneasy, as if he had to explain himself.

After the apology, her e-mail was typical, full of pithy tales of her parishioners (Lorna had wound up mopping the floor herself after a mourner got sick at a funeral) and snappy observations (another parishioner had the obsequious manner of a hound dog). She'd been busy every evening this week, she wrote, and was looking forward to tomorrow, when she planned on relaxing and catching up on her reading in her apartment after work. As usual, the e-mail ended with the words "love, L.," but the electronically generated "love" seemed too dispassionate to be real. Gerry sat in his darkened study staring at the pulsing light of the computer screen, thinking again of his whirlwind romance with the girl in the cafeteria—that's how he'd come, self-mockingly, to think of it—and a plan gradually took shape in his mind, like letters appearing one after another on the screen.

Surprise was part of his strategy, so he neither e-mailed Lorna nor telephoned, but called his office to leave a voice-mail message and then, with ease over the Internet, booked a morning flight and arranged for a rental car. Everything fell neatly and quickly into place—he even, to his surprise, was able to get a room at his favourite Vancouver hotel, the usually all-booked-up Sylvia, calling just minutes after a vacancy came open. He had a bite to eat, packed a bag, and was ready to go before *The National* came on at 10 PM.

On the plane the next morning, Gerry had barely enough time to put his thoughts in order. Since the divorce—and he was amazed to realize it was over five years ago—he'd been at loose ends, dating a bit, throwing himself into his work, not feeling particularly satisfied at the office or home. Last winter's bout of stress or depression or whatever it was, he realized, had probably been a symptom of something larger. This thing with Lorna—even *thing* seemed almost too precise a word to apply to it, so nebulous was the reality it represented—was all that had captured his attention in the last year. But Gerry liked to be able to capture his ideas in a drawing, a map, a grid like those roads near the abbey they'd enjoyed walking on so much, and this was way too nebulous, too vague. Still, in every other way, Lorna was the most extraordinarily forthright woman he'd ever known. He intended to ask her a simple question—not to marry him, nothing as dramatic or romantic as that—but whether, in her view, what they were heading toward, if they were indeed heading toward something, was predictably disillusioning—a phrase she had used more than once—or enlightening.

Outside the Sylvia's window, two gulls battered each other noisily in midair. A lone sailboat struggled against gusts of wind on the shimmering bay below. Yes, a gift would definitely be in order, something to commemorate the event. Gerry headed for the elevator, turning his thoughts to this new problem. It had to be something perfect.

⊗

His mother's death had thrown Gerry into a slump. He wasn't in mourning so much as catching his breath—the funeral had taken place back in Alberta, where most of the family still lived, and he was there and then back in Saskatoon so quickly he didn't really have a chance to get accustomed to the idea of his mother being gone. They hadn't been particularly close—even when he was a child, she'd been cool and distant, or so it had seemed to Gerry—and she'd been sick and failing for several years, so her death was neither a surprise nor a blow. Nevertheless, two months later, he'd begun to have sleepless nights. Worn down and haggard after several weeks, he consulted his physician; it didn't take long before the loss came tumbling out.

"Whether you know it or not, you're grieving," the doctor

said, and prescribed mild sedatives and a good rest. One of the other city planners suggested a long weekend at the abbey, just an hour's or so drive east at a village called Muenster. He swore by the place for its restorative powers. The bucolic setting, even in winter when the acres of raspberry canes and towering firs rose out of a blanket of crusty snow, and the presence of all those centred-looking men in black robes, had a calming effect that was truly restful, Gerry was assured. His friend proved to be right.

Gerry had been raised disinterested United and was no longer religious in any way, but no one at the monastery seemed to mind that. Except for the cross in his small, narrow room in Severin Hall, which he took down from its nail and slid beneath the extra blanket on a shelf in the closet, none of the trappings or activities of the place were intrusive. The Benedictines—robed but otherwise seeming perfectly ordinary, especially the young, bearded Brother Randy, who beat Gerry three games in a row at pool and twice at Ping Pong—were more a visual oddity than a moral or spiritual presence, as far as Gerry was concerned. He found the Christian symbolism no more overwhelming than at the mall at Christmas time.

Gerry took walks in blustery wind through the woods to the farm, where he inspected the chickens and cattle but avoided the foul-smelling pig barn, and browsed in the library, where the forbidding collection of Christian books was leavened by a long-standing subscription to the National Geographic. After the first couple of restless nights, he slept soundly on the hard, narrow bed in his spartan room, even napped on it every afternoon. He stuffed himself on the meat-and-potatoes-and-cinnamon-bun meals and the oatmeal cookies from a constantly replenished jar in the guest wing lounge. Once, at the urging of the 5 PM bells, he even sat in the back of the chapel for vespers, where the prayers took the form of singing, slightly off-key but hypnotically pleasing, their content seemingly more Old Testament than New.

He ran into Lorna at breakfast on his second day, when, without hesitation, she joined him at the large dining hall table where he was sitting alone, contemplating a bowl of library-paste porridge and prunes.

"You look like you need some cheering up," she said brightly.

He raised his eyes to see a horsey-looking woman with a long face and slightly protruding upper teeth transformed by a wide, completely guileless smile. She was about his age, early forties, with a nondescript haircut and dressed in baggy sweats. Not at all the sort of woman he would normally be attracted to, but almost exactly the sort who fit with his own appearance, his own place in the world.

He laughed. "I didn't use to think I did. Then I didn't think it showed."

"Oh, it shows," the woman said. "It shows."

They immediately fell into conversation so deep that he barely noticed the porridge going down—she'd had a not-altogether-different experience with her father's death—and they were on their second cups of coffee when it came out that she was a divinity student at the Lutheran seminary in Saskatoon. She suffered from a learning block with languages and was spending a few days at the abbey preparing for a Greek exam she'd already flunked once.

"I need to build up my strength," she said.

"Moral strength or intellectual strength?" Gerry inquired mildly.

"My *physical* strength. My moral strength already does arm-wrestling with my intellectual strength, thank you very kindly."

Like Gerry, she was divorced, but her divorce had cost her dearly—she'd been in her second year at the *Anglican* seminary, on full scholarship, but the bishop had disapproved and support was withdrawn.

"My being married to a Jewish man didn't bother him," she laughed, "nor did he care about his being a bastard, but divorcing him did. The Lutherans heard about it. They might not have liked the idea of a Jewish husband, but he was gone, so what the hell. They welcomed me with open arms—well, as open as Lutheran arms ever get."

This brought gales of laughter from two of the plumpish women among the group that had gradually filled their table, one of them, as it turned out, of Swedish background, the other, a luminous woman in round spectacles, a Finn.

"The Lutherans have too many restrictions," Lorna said with a mock sigh, "but I'm learning to live with them."

"Ya, so?" singsonged the Finn, who was part of a group of writers spending two weeks together in the former convent on the abbey grounds. "Not restrictions, *etiquette,* don'tcha know."

"And *you're* studying to be a Lutheran minister?" Gerry inquired.

"And your point?" Lorna shot back.

"Anglicans are easier going," said one of the other writers. "All they really care about is dressing nicely on Sunday."

"Oh?" said Lorna, arching one eyebrow. "You've obviously never witnessed an argument over which type of sherry to serve with lunch."

Again laughter, but, after a pause, she added: "Still, the world would be a better place if everyone in it was Anglican. Certainly no wars. The Lutherans *like* to fight." She pronounced this in an almost angry tone that struck Gerry ...as curious.

"I don't know," piped in a thin, dark woman, another of the writers who'd been listening to the flow of conversation without saying anything, "Jews don't really care about anything but dressing nicely for synagogue on the Sabbath, but they still manage to have plenty of wars."

"Tell me about it," Lorna said, winking. Then, adopting a broad aping of a Yiddish accent: "Of Jews, I know plendy."

Over the next few days, Gerry and Lorna took all their meals together and several times went for walks through the snow after lunch. At the abbey, the noon meal was called dinner and was the heaviest of the day, homegrown pork chops or chicken swimming in cream gravy, heaps of lumpy mashed potatoes, apple pies fragrant with cinnamon and nutmeg. If Gerry didn't get some exercise after eating, he would sink into sleep back in his room. On these walks, along a straight-as-an-arrow grid road system and through long lines of planted spruce windbreak alive with chattering birds, Gerry told her how, growing up on the farm, he'd always wanted to be an artist, but, getting lost in the city on his first day of university and registering late, he'd been channelled off into architecture, which he'd immediately fallen in love with. And then how, again because a course he wanted was full, he'd stumbled into city planning, which, again, transfixed him—it was the public nature of the field rather than the private satisfactions of the artist's life, even the architect's, that appealed to him, he said.

Lorna, for her part, told him about her life as a graduate student in sciences, then marriage, motherhood, the "predictable disillusionment" that seemed to feed on itself. She mentioned her husband only occasionally, and when she did she referred to him—not with bitterness but certainly not with affection—as "the asshole."

"If disillusionment is so predictable, it's a wonder people don't do something to avoid it," Gerry said, without really having thought it through.

Lorna's long, elastic face—almost rubbery, Gerry thought—stretched this way and that with smiles and frowns as she talked, and her hands fluttered about her body in wild gestures like the begging chickadees. Now, she shot him an almost glaring look and he was taken by the complete frankness of her expression and the way that, when her face was entirely in repose, the features took on a very pleasing aspect, almost pretty—no, she *was* pretty.

"Right, like you and your mother," she said. For a moment, he thought he'd offended her, but then those features reassembled themselves into a smile, the smile he was coming to appreciate more and more. "Anyway," she added, "without disillusionment, there couldn't be enlightenment, right?"

On the third day, the day before Lorna was to return to

Saskatoon and take her exam, their walk took them to the abbey's small cemetery, where they counted forty small stones for brothers, many of the inscriptions in German, and another four larger ones for abbots. The graveyard, which was surrounded by a double hedge of evergreens—cedar on the inside, spruce on the outer row, with a muffled corridor between them safe from the constant wind—was dominated by one stone larger still, standing over the grave of the abbey's founder, Father Bruno. Lorna's Latin was good enough to be able to translate most of the mysterious bits on the stones: "Natus" for born, "Mortuus" for died, and so on. Then they stood in silent meditation for a few minutes while Gerry said—finally—a proper goodbye to his mother.

On the way back, chilled a bit by the cold wind that was reddening the tip of Lorna's nose, they stopped to feed a trio of unusually fearless chickadees, which fluttered close to their outstretched hands, darting down to snatch a broken peanut, then hot-winging it to a low-lying branch in triumph. Suddenly, without warning, they found themselves in an embrace, locked in a nose-bumping kiss that was not passionate, particularly, but far more than what mere friends would share. It was as if they had known each other for a long time, had shared many kisses.

"I'm really sorry," Gerry said, disengaging himself and stepping back, embarrassed. "I shouldn't have done that."

"Oh?" Lorna's rubbery face made itself into a mask of mock disappointment. She didn't appear embarrassed at all. As she had in the dining hall that first morning, she adopted a parody of Yiddish accent: "Und vy not?"

⊗

Lorna was not easy to buy for, he knew—he'd agonized over her birthday, which fell in May, when they'd known each other barely three months, and his choice, a pass to the jazz festival, was both inspired and welcome, but the ticket wound up going unused, since she'd left for the coast already when the festival came around. Her interest in clothes seemed to be nonexistent—she habitually wore sensible, almost shapeless suits with straight skirts a size too large, leaving Gerry still uncertain what her body was like. She wore next to no jewelry, no perfume at all. A book, which would have been easy, since he knew her interests, or thought he did, was far too impersonal for what he wanted to convey with this gift. Art, though bulky, seemed promising; he had in mind something like a raku vase or a delicately worked metal box, but he left his mind open and set out in the rented car to Granville Island, where, a friendly woman at the Sylvia's front desk assured him, there were a number of shops selling high-quality crafts.

He browsed through two such shops, one a co-op filled with lovely pottery, the other the studio shop of a glass-blower, without finding anything that seemed right. He took a break for a lunch of steamed mussels, thick bread, and a beer at Bridges, a good restaurant overlooking the water, sitting outside in the cool sunshine and breathing in the salt air. He allowed himself to consider the possibility of living here and wondered what the job prospects would be like at Vancouver city hall. He'd managed to acquire a good track record in his half a dozen years in Saskatoon and his years in Prince Albert before that. Vancouver, with its recent influx of well-to-do Asian immigrants retrofitting narrow lots with enormous houses, was crying out for his talents and vision, he decided.

After lunch, he took in two more shops, again without success, then drove to Kitsilano, where the desk clerk had told him he might also try. As he browsed through one shop after another on West Fourth Street and Broadway, he rehearsed possible speeches he might make that evening to Lorna. Twice, passing pay phones, he weakened and almost called her, fearing she might have made an unexpected date, but he fought off the impulse, determined that he'd fare better if he didn't give her an opportunity to think too long about possible replies. The memory of how she'd hung up on him still stung.

In each shop, he found several items that seemed almost right but not quite. Gerry had never been an enthusiastic shopper of any sort or particularly adept at selecting gifts—he remembered one Mother's Day when a kitchen appliance, a toaster oven he thought his mother would like, had provoked a cold, sarcastic response—and he sensed that, with Lorna, he might do more harm than good with a poor choice. He grew increasingly frustrated as the afternoon progressed. Perhaps flowers would be better. Lorna, he knew, was partial to yellow roses.

Finally, in a shop around the corner from Broadway on Eighth Avenue, he found a glass and copper box that struck him as perfect. There was something Biblical about the box, the hammered copper, the pastel shades of the stained glass, that reminded him of St. Peter's and would, he hoped, have the same effect on Lorna. He remembered sitting with her in a sunny lounge area near the chapel filled with ferns of various types, a priceless fragile harp adorned with a "please do not touch" sign standing nearby, the sound of canary song drifting toward them from a large cage the monks kept further down the hall.

"I could sit here forever, it's so peaceful," Lorna had said. Gerry had been pleasantly surprised, because he'd been thinking the exact same thing.

The box cost $150, but Gerry thought it well worth it. Still, for a reason he couldn't later explain to himself, he hesitated, placing the box on the counter while he took another sweep around the shop, which was empty except for him and an officious sales clerk wearing sand-coloured suede slacks and matching loafers.

"This box is exceptional," the man had said when he took it out of the display case for Gerry to examine.

Noticing the time—it was past three, and he should be getting a move on, he knew—he suddenly remembered the rented car halfway down the street. "I'll be right back," he told the clerk and went out to feed another quarter into the meter. He couldn't have been gone more than a couple of minutes, but when he returned, his mind made up to buy it, there was a man and a woman in the shop, and the man was holding the stained-glass box in his hands.

The man, who looked vaguely familiar, was holding the box up to the light streaming in through the shop's windows and smiling in what struck Gerry as an enigmatic way. He was dark-haired, handsome, no taller or heavier than Gerry, dressed in rumpled black slacks and what looked to be a cashmere sweater, cream coloured. The woman, who was obviously with him though she was a few metres away, twirling a display of earrings, was stunning, a tawny blonde wearing a tight leather miniskirt and black stockings. Her lipstick was a pale pink, and Gerry could see her lips moving as she blew the man a kiss across the shop. A number of items were already stacked up by the cash register, and a shopping bag full of parcels, some of them gift-wrapped, sat on the floor near the man's feet. The unmistakable smell of money seemed to waft off the couple.

Gerry went right up to the man. "I'm sorry, but that box is mine," he said. "I mean, I already decided to buy it. I set it down there for a minute while I went out to feed the meter."

The man gave Gerry a curious glance, as if he'd just been asked for change by a panhandler. In that glance, Gerry recognized him, or thought he did: it was David Duchovny, the actor who had played the youthful FBI agent in *The X-Files,* a television series that Gerry knew had been produced in the city. He was less than a rabid fan, but had sometimes watched the show, and was certain that's who the man was.

"I'm buying this," the man said. There was no apology or explanation, just the simple statement of fact. Even the man's voice sounded familiar.

"You don't understand," Gerry said. "That's my purchase. I just set it down there while I went out for a minute. It's mine."

Again, Duchovny, if that's who it was, gave Gerry an odd look. "Right," he said, and started to move away, around him.

Without really thinking, Gerry reached out and took the box from the man's hand, plucking it from his grip the way he might take a memo someone in the office was handing him, except that this man wasn't handing him the box.

"Yes, right," Gerry echoed. "I'm sorry."

"The fuck you are," the man said, and before Gerry could brace himself, he grabbed the box back, using both hands.

"Listen," Gerry said. "You don't understand..."

"I understand that you're an asshole," the man said. Could he really be David Duchovny? The show wasn't being made anymore; surely he didn't still live in Vancouver. He squared his shoulders, as if to ward off a blow, a gesture that, later, struck Gerry as ridiculous, laughable. "I'm buying this box," he added.

"Listen," Gerry repeated, frustration rising in his throat, a wash of pale red sweeping across his vision as if tiny veins had ruptured in his eyes. "That box is mine."

"You're a liar," the man said. No, it couldn't be Duchovny. "You're crazy. Get out of my way or..."

He hesitated and Gerry, moving strictly on adrenaline, stepped forward and to the side, blocking his way. "Or what?"

The blonde woman was suddenly beside them. She placed a slim manicured hand on the man's arm and levelled a cool, long-lashed gaze at Gerry. "Why don't we ask Robert?"

At the sound of his name, the sales clerk, who'd been staying conspicuously out of the argument, stepped forward from beside the cash register. Gerry's heart sank.

"You remember, I was looking at that box," he said nevertheless. "I went out for a minute to feed the meter. It must have been clear to you that I was coming right back to buy the box. I said I'd be right back."

"Well, yes..." the clerk began.

"Didn't I ask you how much the box was?" Duchovny, if that's who it was, interrupted. "I said I wanted it." Gerry saw the two men exchange glances.

"You did," Robert agreed.

The man turned to the woman. "You heard me say it was just the thing for Priss. It was there on the counter, I picked it up."

"I put it there, for god's sake," Gerry said. He was as angry as he ever recalled being, but he knew it was hopeless. "Just for you, obviously. You must think the world is your oyster.

I hope you really want that fucking box, because it's yours." He turned on his heel, but not quite fast enough to avoid the smug look that blossomed on the man's face, not even a good enough actor to mask it. Then he was out the door, the tinkling of the bell following him down the street like the bells that rang at St. Peter's for vespers or vigils.

There was a bitter taste in Gerry's mouth as he started the car and edged into the Broadway traffic. It was almost 3:30 now and he knew it would take him over an hour in rush-hour traffic to get to Abbotsford, where, he was certain, Lorna would be finishing her day around five. At a stoplight, he noticed a shop proclaiming imports from Israel, and, though he'd given up on the idea of a gift, he pulled over on the next block and walked back. As soon as he was through the door, its bell gaily tinkling, he saw something that caught his attention: it was gold Hebrew letters strung on a soft black string around the neck of a paper cutout model. "What do they say?" he asked the friendly woman who came out of back room to assist him.

"Oh, it's names. It's individual letters, see, so we can make up any name."

"It doesn't have to be a Hebrew name?"

"No, we translate the name into Hebrew phonetically. It works for any name, really."

"Could you do Lorna?"

"I'm sure we have before. I'll just ask my partner. She does the phonetics."

While he waited, Gerry admired the necklace again. Greek would be even better, he supposed, but Hebrew was inarguably Biblical, and the necklace was lovely. He was certain that Lorna would like it, even if she didn't necessarily wear it often. He didn't imagine she'd want to wear it to church or church functions, or while visiting parishioners.

Within minutes, the gold necklace, in a tasteful box and gift-wrapped, was in his jacket pocket and he was heading back downtown, toward the highway east, and, as he'd estimated, he approached the Abbotsford exit just past 4:30.

Abbotsford was a conservative community, he knew, a place where the school board banned books, homosexuals were frowned on, and women ministers met resistance, although Lorna, by her own accounts, seemed to be thriving. He wondered how someone like Robert, that sales clerk, with his soft pants and soft eyes, would fare in this town, then shook his head, laughing at himself.

For the next hour or so, things went exactly as he'd planned. He'd looked up the address of the church in a phone book at the Sylvia, and found it with no difficulty, arriving at ten minutes to five. He parked across the street from the modern-looking building, with a sloping roof in the shape of a wing. The highest, narrow tip of the wing enclosed a stained-glass window that made Gerry recall the glass and copper box for a moment, and he patted the small package in his pocket to reassure himself it was there. Had that horrible man really been David Duchovny? It seemed inconceivable now—surely he'd been wrong. But things had worked out for the best. Lorna would love the necklace, he was sure. Maybe he should see if *The X Files* had a website, send Dochovny an e-mail thanking him. He could just picture the puzzled expression on the face of the actor when he read it. He got out of the car feeling lighter-spirited than he had in months.

He paused to admire Lorna's name, Reverend Lorna Williams, on the board outside the church announcing the topic for Sunday's sermon: "The role of the gospels in the new millennium." The heavy front door was unlocked, the church apparently empty, but when he called "Hello," a female voice answered and a moment later Lorna, wearing a navy blue suit and flat shoes, came through a door to the left of the pulpit, her eyes widening with surprise, her rubbery face going quickly through a number of compositions before settling on apparent pleasure.

"What on earth are you doing here, Gerry?"

"Aren't you glad to see me?" He took her in an awkward embrace, their cheeks touching.

"Of course, but... You really should have called. I've got a million things to do tomorrow."

"I want to talk to you. Don't worry, I won't get in the way. I've got a hotel in town. You have to eat. I want to ask you a question." All of this came out in a rush, and Gerry realized adrenaline was still coursing through his veins. Calm down, he told himself.

They went to an Italian restaurant Lorna said she liked, just a block from her apartment building. It was an unpretentious neighbourhood place, Tony's, with a view of the snow-capped mountains further to the east. They ordered spaghetti—Lorna's with meat sauce, Gerry's with clams—and small tomato and onion salads, a basket of Italian bread, and a bottle of good Chianti. When the salads came, Gerry was careful to avoid the onions in his. He was uncertain whether to tell her about his encounter with the Famous Actor, so he let her carry the conversation. She was telling him a funny story about a wedding she conducted the previous Sunday, and that ran into a convoluted tale revolving around the youth drop-in centre she was struggling to establish. "Honestly, some of my parishioners seem to think teenagers belong to a different denomination—why should we be doing anything for them?"

"The spirit of ecumenicalism?"

"Yeah, right." She put down her wine glass and looked at him fondly. "Gerry," she said, putting a hand over one of his. "I'm talking too much. Tell me why you're here."

"I want to ask you a question. But wait, first I've got something for you."

He took the small package from his pocket and presented it to her gravely. "This took some doing," he said with a wry smile. "I'll tell you about it later."

Lorna looked at the box with apprehension for a moment, then carefully, using a neatly filed but unpainted fingernail, loosened the tape and removed the gift-wrap. She opened the box and took the necklace out. For a moment, they were both silent.

"It's your name," Gerry said. "Lorna."

She looked up at him, and something about her expression made his heart lurch. "It's Hebrew letters," he said lamely. "Phonetic letters. It says Lorna, honest." He laughed nervously. After a moment, he added: "I thought it would remind you of St. Pete's."

Lorna put down the necklace and carefully folded her napkin, laying it across her soiled plate. Her face darkened, and, to Gerry's surprise, she began to cry. Very slowly—as if in slow motion, he thought later—she stood up, an ordinary looking woman, slightly overweight, in a wrinkled suit that seemed to have been designed for an even larger woman.

"You asshole," she said. Despite the sting of the word, her tone was not rancorous or bitter; rather, she sounded almost amiable, much the way she had at the abbey when she'd used that term to describe her husband.

Without a further word, she took her coat and purse and walked away from the table, out the door, down the street. Gerry sat stunned, staring at the necklace, Lorna's napkin, his plate, the smudged glass containing the dregs of his wine. After a suitable length of time, he paid the bill and began the long drive back to his hotel.

* * *

Careless

AT THE BANFF SPRINGS HOTEL, Peter ran into a man he knew who was sharing a room with a slim, youthful looking woman who protested, when someone remarked how much like a kid she seemed, “Oh, but I’m old, I’m old.”

The man’s name was also Peter, and whenever the two met they referred to each other as Peter M and Peter F, the F standing for Frankenheimer. The last time Peter M had seen or talked to Frankenheimer, who was just an acquaintance, really, not a friend, was two years earlier. Frankenheimer had just broken up with his wife, had left her and his three children, and was living in a mother-in-law suite in the basement of a friend. He had no job, no car, no money. “Just my self-respect,” Frankenheimer had said, smiling sourly, when Peter inquired, “and that won’t get me far.”

It had, though, or so it seemed. Banff Springs was far from cheap, and Frankenheimer and his young woman friend had just emerged from a new Lexus when Peter spotted them. They were well decked out in Hugo Boss sports clothes and carrying matching sets of soft-sided Samsonite, and then there was the woman herself, youthful looking and alluring, really quite splendid, despite whatever she may have thought of herself or felt compelled to protest.

Peter and Barbara had checked in only minutes earlier and were standing in the lobby, about to go out for a walk, when Frankenheimer and his friend arrived, and, after introductions, they agreed to meet on the tennis court an hour later.

As they strolled through the gardens, not yet in full bloom, Peter told Barbara about Frankenheimer’s breakup, two years earlier, and how, when he’d commiserated, the other man’s one regret seemed to be the separation not from his two natural children, a young boy and girl, but from the eldest, who was adopted, a Cree boy who had given him and his wife nothing but heartache since puberty. The boy had run away, gotten into drugs and other trouble, and had wound up in hospital, almost dying, from a beating. Peter recalled wondering if worry and strain over this boy hadn't hastened the end of Frankenheimer's marriage. At any rate, he appeared now to be over any remorse, any reversals of fortune, and was prospering.

"Peter M," he'd exclaimed when he entered the ornate hotel lobby and saw Peter, "how's it hanging?" He thrust his hand forward and Peter, though he disliked shaking hands, always had, saw no alternative but to grasp it in return. Frankenheimer's grip was firm and dry, the shake sincere but brief, like the goodbye kiss of a former lover. Peter had had only a fleeting look at the woman Frankenheimer was with, but, the handshake over, the two men stood back from each other, and as the conversation circled around them, he allowed himself a good look, and he fell immediately in love with her.

⊗

Peter had always considered himself a fortunate man. His wife was still beautiful, and, after twenty years, they still loved each other—or, that is to say, he believed Barbara still loved him, and, up until that moment at the Banff Springs, he still loved her. His children were healthy and brilliant, their teeth straightened and bright. His job—he was a petroleum geologist, finding places where other people could drill holes and find things of value—continued to be interesting and rewarding. He was forty-three, a conventional man but capable of charm and insight, and his life was about to change utterly.

Frankenheimer was a petroleum engineer—one of the people who drilled the holes where Peter told them to—who had fared badly in the fortunes of the oil patch, losing his job when prices went south the last time, though clearly he had recovered. That had never happened to Peter, who, working for a succession of juniors, had always ridden out the storms, always landed on his feet. This did not confer any superiority, moral or otherwise, on Peter; he knew that, but he could not escape the feeling that Frankenheimer had somehow been careless.

"I'm in real estate now," Frankenheimer told him. He also introduced him to the woman he was with, whose name was Ingrid, which, Peter thought, was just right. She had a long neck, making her appear somewhat like a gazelle, graceful and fleet, with dark, alert eyes and short, swept-back dark hair. It seemed to Peter that Frankenheimer was careful not to use the word "wife" while still making it clear that their relationship was proprietary.

Later, on the tennis court, Peter was able to admire her long shapely legs and the firm slender sweep of her arms, the delicacy of her wrists, although her backhand was strong. Even her feet were small and precisely shaped, as if they, and not the expensive athletic shoes she wore, had been shaped on a cobbler's last. She moved like a ballet dancer, and Peter wasn't surprised to learn that she'd gone through ten years of lessons, had even tried out, unsuccessfully, for the Royal Winnipeg school.

"Was that a disappointment?" he asked.

"Oh, of course. God, I was sixteen; I thought my life had come to a shattering end. It hadn't."

They were having drinks on the patio beside the court, the four of them—Frankenheimer and Ingrid, Peter and Barbara, who had no way of knowing, of course, that Peter was in love with another woman. He liked the way Ingrid said "shattering," liked the matter-of-fact way she said, "It hadn't," without elaboration, liked the way she held her gin and tonic, the pinkie of her right hand extended just so, delicately but without affectation, liked that the fingers of that graceful hand were unencumbered with rings, liked the bright red shade of her nail polish, though ordinarily he didn't care for nail polish at all and Barbara never wore any, liked the cool way she gazed at him, liked, he realized with a start, everything about her. He felt, simultaneously, uncomfortable and exhilarated.

The four had already agreed to have dinner together, and, back in their room for showers and to change, Peter eyed his wife as surreptitiously as possible as she laid out her clothes, and, wearing a pink slip, sat at a dressing table, drying her hair with an electric blower. She had not become fat, had not lost the muscle tone in her legs or arms, had not let herself come apart. Her conversation was as intelligent and witty as ever, her hair as lustrous, but Peter was struck now by how plain and uninteresting she was. He found himself gazing at the woman he'd lived with for almost half his life with the same dispassionate disinterest he'd bring to bear on a check-out clerk at the supermarket.

"They seem like pleasant people," Barbara said suddenly, enthusiastically. She always enjoyed meeting new people.

"Yes," Peter said, but he turned away, afraid that his eyes would betray him.

⊗

It was at dinner that Barbara made the comment about Ingrid's youthfulness. Ingrid had laughed at something Frankenheimer said, and Barbara, completely ingenuously, Peter was sure, said, "Ingrid, you're such a kid." Then she'd blushed, and quickly added: "Oh, I didn't mean that the way it came out. I just mean you're so youthful. It was a compliment, honestly."

Ingrid touched Barbara's arm lightly. "Not to worry. I didn't take it the wrong way. Oh, but I'm old, I'm old. I'm probably the oldest person at this table." She crinkled her face to accentuate the lines around her eyes and mouth, but that only succeeded in making her look adorable, Peter thought.

Barbara's gaffe, unintentional though it may have been, struck Peter as clumsy, Ingrid's reply deft and modest. It turned out then, though, that Ingrid *was* older than she appeared. Like Frankenheimer, she'd survived a failed marriage, and had a daughter, eighteen and in her first year at the University of Calgary. Looking closer, Peter could see the faint lines around her eyes that the funny face she'd made a moment earlier had called to his attention, lines that even the skillfully applied makeup hadn't been able to completely hide, lines produced by the irresistible wrinkles that leapt like excited puppies to the tops of her cheeks when she smiled or laughed, both of which she did often. None of this new information did anything to cool Peter's ardour.

Both couples had come to the hotel for the long weekend, a chance to get away, as Barbara put it, "from the grind"—her omission of the word "daily" in the familiar phrase rang in Peter's mind as emblematic of the something that had suddenly gone missing from their marriage, though he had no way of knowing if she felt the same way he did, and he doubted that. Since the two Peters no longer worked in the same industry, it was not surprising that their paths hadn't crossed for two years, and there was no reason why Barbara and Ingrid should have met—Barbara was a high-school math teacher, Ingrid a physical therapist. It turned out, though, that the two couples lived not all that far from each other, since Frankenheimer and Ingrid had moved to Roxboro the preceding year, and Ingrid's daughter had graduated last spring from Western, where Peter and Barbara's son was in Grade 12 this year. And, as it developed, the two women had a mutual friend.

They laughed at how small a world it was, while still so large, and Frankenheimer regaled them with tales of the real-estate world, which, huffing and puffing, was continuously pressing outward at the city's borders. "Don't let them kid you, Peter M," he advised, "the world is getting larger, not smaller. Soon we'll be laying out subdivisions in outer space." He winked. "Gated communities."

The two women excused themselves after the entrée

and went to the ladies' room. "What do you think of her?" Frankenheimer asked, beaming, his tone conspiratorial. "Isn't she something?"

Peter nodded, smiling wanly, but he couldn't speak, his heart was so full. Later that evening, he and Barbara would make desultory love and Peter would lie awake long into the night, his eyes closed but his mind bright, revisiting a vision that had come to him at that moment. It was a vision of the future that both disturbed and solaced him, a future in which he and Barbara were separated but in which Ingrid and Frankenheimer—Peter F—persisted; still, it was clear to him, the sheen of their relationship was all surface, and shallow, that it would only be a matter of time before Ingrid saw that—it was clear from the diamond-like brilliance of her cerulean eyes that she could see very well indeed—and that he would have his chance. It would only be a matter of time.

After he composed himself, he inquired as to Frankenheimer's adopted son. "Oh, that turned out all right," Frankenheimer said, almost casually, almost as if he didn't care. "Actually, much better than we expected."

* * *

A Love Story

THIS IS A LOVE STORY. That is to say, it is a story about love. But also, perhaps, something else.

Here are the characters: Arthur, Joanna, Emily. A man and two women—already, you can see the possibilities, may even think you see the way the story might go. Maybe you do. Maybe not.

Arthur and Joanna were happily married, well, reasonably so. They'd met in university and were married the year Arthur graduated. Joanna, two years younger, never finished. She was skeptical that her fine arts degree would do her any good anyway. She knew her limitations, and she was no painter, not really. Arthur's computer degree was as good as money in the bank, and he went to work for a big firm, rose quickly through the ranks, and was the manager of his department by the time their first daughter, Linda, solemn-faced and owl-eyed like her mother, started school. There were two other daughters as well, Lani, the unexpected blonde, and little dark-haired Laurel, who was always called LaLa the Laugher.

"I am a man surrounded by women," Arthur used to proclaim, making this sound like a comical complaint, because it's widely known that a father craves sons. In fact, his daughters were his delight, and later, what he would miss the most were his dear daughters. But we're getting ahead of ourselves.

Time passed; Arthur prospered; Joanna became restless and returned her attention to painting, joining a small co-operative studio nearby; their daughters grew, fine, strong-willed girls who took after their mother physically, fine-boned and large-eyed, but resembled their father in the way they saw the world, as a problem to be solved, an obstacle to be bested. They did well at school, except for Lani, who was a slow reader; excelled at sports; sold summer lemonade from a front-lawn stand. The family's first house became cramped and they bought a larger one, in a better neighbourhood, closer to a better high school. A woman came to clean every Tuesday afternoon. They bought a cottage at the lake, a sailboat. They were healthy, happy, lucky.

In October, Arthur was a featured speaker at a conference in Calgary. By this time, he had his own consulting company, Webwise Associates, and a national reputation as a good hand at helping small businesses get the most out of the Internet. At the panel on networking where he spoke, he met a woman almost half his age, or that's what he told himself, shaking his head in disbelief. He was now almost forty, and she was barely out of her teens, the same age Joanna had been when they'd gotten married and just a few years older than his daughter Linda, just started at university, following her mother's footsteps in fine arts. But Joanna had never seemed as young as this girl was, this Emily, so slim, so lithe, so fresh, so frankly admiring—and, eventually, adoring—when she looked at him. He knew it wasn't right, thinking of her as a girl, but he stumbled over the shape and sound of the word "woman"—no, this Emily hadn't yet grown into that word, even though here she was, a briefcase and a laptop beside her, and, he discovered, a responsible job at a hot West Coast software designer shop. A whiz kid.

Emily's face was a match struck in a darkened room, a brief, small flash of brilliant illumination. Looking at that unblemished face made Arthur think of his own, of how it must look like a weary sigh, stale and faintly unpleasant.

"I'm old enough to be your father, you know," he admonished her, and she replied, coquettishly and inexplicably, "I *love* my father."

He didn't think of Joanna, still attractive, faithful in her application of cleansing and firming creams and other beauty aids—no, he didn't think of Joanna at all. And he directed all his energy to *not* think of Emily—"I am not going to embarrass myself over this girl," he told himself, "not make a fool of myself." He had never been unfaithful to Joanna, to his "women at home," and there was no reason to start now, no matter how alluring Emily was. Nor would that be fair to Emily, he knew, a young girl—woman—who could have her pick of men. Arthur watched with a combination of amusement and envy as the young men at the conference clamoured at her heels like excited dogs.

Still, she was enticing, and, despite the attentions of all those young men, seemed genuinely interested in him. After Arthur's morning talk, where he first noticed her, she was part of the group that went to lunch, and he found himself sitting next to her in the noisy restaurant, where people had to put their heads close together to be heard. Her conversation, at first, seemed naive, girlish, giddy, but when talk turned technical, he was impressed by what she had to say; she was clearly no fool.

"That's very good," he said, in response to a comment she made about his talk. "You were listening."

"Oh, you," she replied, blushing, her almond eyes slightly expanding, and placed her hand lightly on his arm, and it was as if that word, that "*you*," was a knife slicing through his flesh and bone to the quick deep within him, as if her small, delicate hand was not on his sleeve but sliding between his shirt buttons and caressing the feverish skin of his chest.

Over the three days of the conference, he noticed, she wore the same pair—or could she have owned several identical ones?—of mauve leggings and two different oversized tunics, one olive green, the other a musky brown, making her look like one of Robin Hood's merry crew, and he wondered if she washed the leggings nightly in her hotel sink or if the fragrant odour emanating from her was not a leafy perfume, as he'd first imagined, but the natural smell of her body. Indeed, Arthur found himself imagining various intimate details relating to Emily: the colours of her underwear, or if, other than the leggings, she even wore any; the shaving of her legs and underarms; the many minutes of brushing it must take each night and morning to keep her shoulder-length honey-brown hair so shiny and sleek. He thought of his daughters, envisioning them at their vanity mirrors as he'd seen them so many times, hairbrush in hand, Linda's and LaLa's long dark tresses, so much like their mother's, Lani's tight blonde curls that resisted brushing, and he smiled fondly before willing the images away.

But despite this infatuation—that's the word he used himself to describe it—Arthur resisted temptation. On the last evening, he sat beside Emily at the banquet and allowed himself thoughts of what the night might bring, but thoughts only. In the hotel lobby, he gave her a quick hug but declined her invitation for a nightcap. He felt old but virtuous as he stood at the elevator, watching as she and a few of the younger men disappeared into the lounge. Old, yes; virtuous, yes. He thought of the confession Jimmy Carter had made in that famous interview, that he had been unfaithful in his heart. That was one way to look at it, but not the only way. He was certain of that.

Two nights later, he was making love with Joanna. As he kissed her, the image of the younger woman flickered through his mind just for a moment, like an electrical surge, and the next morning, in the shower, recalling that surge with a pang of guilt, he thought that if he had had sex with Emily it would have been just that, having sex, while making love with his wife was still that, making love. And that night, as he and Joanna lay panting, sated, beside each other in the damp sheets, he'd been as certain of his love for his wife as ever. He wished she would roll over on her elbow, brushing a lock of her dark hair, just beginning to grey, from her eyes, and ask him, perhaps in only a mock serious tone, "Do you still love me?" That would give him the opportunity to say, after a moment's hesitation, for effect, "Yes, but not the same way I once did. Slower, deeper, longer." It was eighteen years past their first roll in the hay, after all, almost twenty years, and a fire can burn at a certain pitch only so long. It banks, but is just as hot. And it can flare.

⊗

A couple of months later, Emily phoned Arthur at work.

"Hi, it's me."

"Excuse me?"

She laughed. "You don't remember me? I'm deeply hurt."

"It's a bad connection," Arthur said.

"It's Emily." Just that, no last name, no "from Vancouver," no "We met at that conference in Calgary, remember?" But his blood quickened; he could feel it.

"Of course. What are you doing here?"

"How do you know I'm here?"

"You sound close."

"Oh, I'm close. I *am* close."

They agreed to meet for lunch.

⊗

It was a Wednesday. Wednesdays were studio days for Joanna. Here's how her day went, all routine.

7 AM The alarm goes off.

7:15. Out of the shower.

7:25. First cup of coffee. She starts breakfast for Lani, who is fifteen now and in that awkward stage, and LaLa, who's twelve: orange juice, oatmeal with brown sugar, cinnamon, and sliced bananas. Linda is eighteen, dieting, and already gone to make an early class; Joanna considers herself lucky if Daughter One has half a glass of juice in the morning. Arthur looks after himself: juice, coffee, a muffin, jam.

7:55. The last of them out the door. "Don't forget my dentist appointment," Lani calls. Her braces are coming off today. "I'll be at school at 12:30," Joanna calls back. "You be ready."

8:15. Her own breakfast, a poached egg, slice of whole wheat toast, second cup of coffee. The paper, and a frown over the wrinkles and jam stains Arthur has left in it.

By nine she's on her way, comfortable in jeans, a T-shirt and cardigan, the old navy blue wool cable. There's been a lull in the weather and the snow has turned to slush, so she's wearing boots with rubber soles. At the studio, she changes to sandals, a paint-stained smock. Donna and Patsy, the two women she shares space with, are both already there, already hard at work. Donna is a sculptor working in clay, Patsy a painter, like Joanna, though her taste is far more abstract. At 10:30, the three of them will duck next door to the café for coffee and cigarettes, a little gossip. Then back to work. The canvas Joanna is working on is bigger than she usually tackles, forty-five centimetres by seventy-five, a forest scene, one towering tree, a smaller one, a carpet of moss and unexpected wildflowers, and, in the upper right corner, a totally surprising bright red parrot, its yellow beak wry and ironic, the punctuation point on a mouth filled, if one could hear it, with witty, colourful oaths.

So intent was she at her work, Donna had to call twice. "Lunch? Joanna? Earth to Joanna. You going to melt right into that canvas?"

"Oh, God, look at the time," Joanna cried. "I've got to pick up Lani." She flew out the door, the seat of the Subaru wagon warm under her from the electric doohickey Arthur bought for her, down Halifax Street to Seventh Avenue, then to Broad. Ordinarily, she would have cut across to Albert on Dewdney, but today there was an obstacle of some sort; it looked like a little red Honda and a forest green minivan had been in a fender-kiss in the right turning lane, the two drivers engrossed in an arm-waving pantomime beside them, so she zoomed through the underpass and turned right instead on Saskatchewan Drive, and, on impulse, took a left on Smith. She was so late, she needed to call, and she was sure she remembered seeing a phone booth on the corner of Smith and Twelfth. And sure enough, there it was, and there, a parking space, not half a block past it, just past a restaurant she and Arthur had often said they should try someday. She slid the Subaru in over a ridge of icy snow, a little crooked but good enough for just a minute, and darted out, not even zipping up her jacket, just clutching the two sides together at her breast.

And thus it was that, at precisely twenty-two minutes after noon, on Wednesday, February 15, the day after St. Valentine's

Day, as it happened, she passed by Stella's Bistro, the rubber soles of her boots squeaking on the slick snow, turning her head to the left against a gust of wind so that she saw, as clear as day, through the plate glass window, her husband lean across a table toward a plain young woman with long brown hair and kiss her on the cheek.

⊗

Emily had been very frank, if anything. She made it clear that she was in the city on business, but that the deciding factor had been personal.

"I was a very silly girl in Calgary," she said. "I played the flirt and let an opportunity pass by."

"We do that," Arthur said obliquely.

"I don't want to anymore," she said. Her meaning was crystal clear.

Arthur took the deepest breath of his life. The girl—woman—was as lovely as anything he'd ever seen, her eyes enormous, warm and deep, her lips moist and full, her face luminous, lit from beneath the transparent skin by what appeared to be nothing less than unabashed adoration. She was, in one five-foot-five-inch package of 110 pounds, exactly what the word "temptation" was coined to convey.

"That's very sweet of you," he said. "No, more than sweet. Flattering. Generous. *Exhilarating.* Well . . ."—he looked away for a moment, to compose himself—". . . shattering. Really." He moved his water glass to one side so he could reach across and take her hand without risk of upsetting it. He cleared his throat. "You know, I think, that I'm married."

"I know."

"I have daughters."

"You said."

"I love them very much. My daughters."

Emily's smile was heartbreaking. "I'm a daughter myself," she said sweetly.

"I love my wife."

"Oh."

"That's the sticky point."

"Yes. I see."

They sat in silence for a moment, Arthur's hand warm on Emily's cool fingers.

He cleared his throat. This was, he realized, the hardest thing he had ever done. "We can be friends," he said. "I'd like us to be. But not lovers. No."

Emily's smile was even more heartbreaking now. "That's so sweet. I mean it. Thank you."

And it was at this moment that Arthur lifted himself from his chair and leaned over the table, careful with the wine and water glasses, and kissed Emily on the cheek, a kiss as chaste as any a father might bring to his own daughter.

⊗

These are the facts, what we might call the bones of the story. The story may be true; you may have heard it from Arthur or Joanna, perhaps even from Emily, who believes herself blameless in everything that flowed from that kiss.

These are the bones. So too are the argument that night, the dark well of hurt unexpectedly opened, the separation that ensued, the divorce, Arthur's ensuing love affair with Emily—a real love affair this time, not an imagined one—and its inevitable demise, his eventual marriage to someone else, someone older, far more suitable, Joanna's marriage, even the suicide years later of one of their children, outgoing, exuberant Lani, who'd seemed at first to take it all the easiest but secretly blamed herself, the dentist, those damned braces. Was Emily to blame for that? She wouldn't believe so, if she knew. Certainly Arthur blames himself, but this is not a story about blame.

But what *is* the story about? Is this a love story, as we were told at the beginning? Every love story, as we know, is a coin, with its heads and its tails. Or is this, rather, a story of infidelity? Or of renewal? Or is it, perhaps, a story about chance, about the *cruelty* of chance?

What was it exactly that Joanna saw in that window? Was it Arthur who kissed Emily—or Emily who kissed Arthur? Would it have made a difference? Is this a story about perception? What *was* it about?

We'll have to ask Arthur or Joanna themselves, ask Emily. All are married now, happily married. Well, reasonably.

* * *

Party Girls

WHEN PAUL AND CHUCKY'S father was in his eighties, he developed what Paul thought of as a compulsive interest in an old boyfriend of their mother's, a man he referred to as "your mother's lover, the man who went back to New York." Their mother had been dead for over ten years, and after a lengthy period of intense grief, she had gradually been receding from their father's thoughts. Now she returned with what might be called a vengeance, as if she were haunting him, tormenting him from the grave.

"She never really loved me," their father complained once. "She was so gay and I was so serious, not her type at all. I got her on the rebound, you know. She was broken-hearted; she needed distraction and there I was, serious and solid. I served a purpose, then I became habit."

"Father, that is absolute bullshit," Chucky said, unable to control herself. Paul's sister was the kind of person who suffered fools only badly and had no favourites.

"I'm sure it's not true Mama didn't love you," Paul, always ready to mollify, said, even though he had his own doubts. It had never been lost on him that he used the affectionate terms, like Mama and Papa, while Chucky preferred the more formal. This wasn't the only area, he felt, where he and his sister had their gender traits slightly mixed up: he had always been the conciliator and mediator in the family, even as a child, preferring compromise to confrontation, unlike Chucky, who had blow-ups and had run away countless times. It was he who had taken piano lessons, and as an adult loved the opera and the symphony, while Chucky had been into gymnastics and now cheered her sons at little league and hockey. Paul had mentioned this any number of times to Kate, his wife, who always laughed good-naturedly or smiled knowingly.

"Oh, she was fond of me, affectionate," their father went on. "I don't mean I was a *bad* habit. She was used to me; I was a good husband and provider." He paused to glare, first at Chucky, then at Paul. *"And* father. Fond, yes, but love, no, I don't think so."

"I say again, Father, bullshit. B-U-L-L-S . . ."

"But if she had married that man, that . . . Bronstein!" he went on, ignoring Chucky, and pronouncing the name of his rival as if it were a non-fatal but unpleasant disease, "you two wouldn't be here, don't forget that. There might have been two children, they might even have been called Paul and Charlene, but they wouldn't have been *you* two. Different genes. Different role models."

Paul and Chucky exchanged glances. Their father's value as a role model was something they'd discussed—argued about—many times, without resolution. Chucky, for all her breezy self-confidence, considered him a failure, and blamed his failures for having wounded her; she wouldn't—couldn't—forgive him. In her view, he'd never made enough money, never gave the family the kind of home or comforts she, at least, thought they deserved, never was anyone she could take pride in. Even when one of his plays went to New York, it was only *off*-Broadway.

Paul had been closer to his mother, but held his father in high regard—he was the kind of decent, solid man Paul aspired to be himself, and, Kate assured him, he was. Nevertheless, he would sometimes watch his own children at play, or creep into their rooms late at night to observe them in their sleep, and the weight of parenthood felt heavy on his shoulders—not just its daily obligations, which he was more than prepared to cope with, but its siren song, its husky insinuation of liability.

⊗

It happened that sometime late in spring, Paul had to go to New York on business for a week. One evening, he found himself in his hotel room, dinner finished and an hour or so to kill. He'd been unable to get tickets to the show he was interested in, and just as well, because his legs were killing him from so much walking. The Manhattan telephone book, a big fat thing, was sitting on the desk next to the phone; on an impulse, he picked it up and turned to the Bs, looking for Bronsteins. By this time, he had heard the name often enough to remember it. Bronstein, of course, was Trotsky's true name, and it had permanently lodged, with distaste, in a crevice of memory of his father, still an unrepentant Stalinist.

There were dozens of them. Paul didn't know the first name, and, since the man was probably about his father's age, there was a good chance he was dead. But his father's compulsion must have been contagious. He dialed the first listing, A. Bronstein on West Seventy-sixth Street. There was no answer, so he went on to the next, Abraham Bronstein, on Bleeker Street, in the Village, more appropriate, he thought. Here, there was an answer, a youngish-sounding man.

"Mr. Bronstein? I'm sorry to bother you; I'm looking for a man named Bronstein who would be in his eighties, probably—perhaps your father? The man I'm looking for spent a year or two in Toronto in the forties. I believe he was involved in the theatre, an actor, perhaps."

"I'm sorry, I don't know anybody like that," the man said. He sounded sympathetic, but offered no suggestions.

Paul dialed the next number, no answer, then a disconnected number, then spoke to a woman who, again, was sympathetic but of no help, then a man who was suspicious and a woman who hung up before he could fully explain. But then, as he was beginning to feel he was wasting his time, his call was answered by a young woman who interrupted him: "That's my grandfather. I'm pretty sure. He was a stage designer, Murray Bronstein; he won a couple of Obies. He worked on Broadway for years, but he used to talk about an experimental theatre he was part of in Toronto when he was just starting out."

"Used to?"

"Oh, he's alive. I just mean he doesn't talk about that stuff anymore. My grandmom is really sick and he focuses on her pretty much all the time. But he's probably the man you're looking for. What's this all about?"

Embarrassed, Paul explained as best he could without revealing the actual situation. "Well, the man I'm looking for—and I think you're right, it is your grandfather—was a friend of my parents, back in the forties, right after the war, I think, in Toronto. My mother was an actress and my father was a playwright; that's the theatre connection."

"There were some people he used to mention," the young woman said, "but I don't remember their names. And, as I said, he hasn't spoken about that time recently."

"My parents *never* spoke of *him,"* Paul said with an apologetic laugh. "My mother died ten years ago, and my father's doing okay but he's getting a little cranky."

She laughed. "That's a good word. My granddad's like that."

"Anyway, one day, right out of the blue, he says, 'I wonder whatever happened to Bronstein?' He couldn't remember his first name or much about him, just that they were friends. He thought he was from New York and that he'd gone back there."

"Granddad's a New Yorker all right," the woman said, laughing again. "Through and through. That time in Toronto was the only time he ever left the city, and when he did talk about it, it was usually to say what a bore Toronto was. Sorry, no offence."

"None taken," Paul said, and he took the opportunity to press for the old man's address and phone number.

"He's always home," the young woman said. "He just looks after Grandmom, never goes out. I should warn you, he's a little hard of hearing."

And so, two days later, on a splendid shirtsleeves afternoon filled with sun, Paul found himself alighting from a taxi on a street in the Bronx two blocks off the Grand Concourse, a tree-lined boulevard that splits the borough in two like the stem of a leaf. From watching too many Hollywood movies, doubtlessly, he had been fearful of the borough's reputation for crime and racial tension, but the big thoroughfare seemed prosperous and peaceful, bustling with people of all types darting to and fro like skaters in bright Christmas sweaters on a pond. As the cab had slowly edged down the side street and he allowed his eyes to take in the scene around the apartment building, he was reminded of the east Toronto neighbourhoods of his youth. Women in twos and threes, some young, their hair in curlers, some old, with kerchiefs on their heads, Mediterranean and Slavic features prominent on their cheerful faces, chatted on the stoops of tenements; the pair of young women across the street from Bronsteins' building sat with their knees spread under their drab flowery dresses, cigarettes in their hands. Nearby, two little girls skipped rope, the singsong of their chant just audible above the sounds of traffic from the busier street two blocks away. Paul checked the address on the piece of paper in his hand again, comparing it with the raised numbers on the arched glass above the building's wide front door.

He entered a lobby, found the name Bronstein on a long list of tenants, and rang the bell beside the name. He glanced at his watch, and, after a minute, rang again. In a moment, a voice crackled on the intercom. "Nu?"

"It's Paul Olefsky from Toronto. I phoned..."

"Come up, come up," the voice interrupted. "Take the elevator, maybe. It's 11B, not 2B."

Paul smiled at the sly joke as he waited for the creaking elevator, which began its descent on the sixth floor but paused interminably on the third, mysteriously so, since it was empty when it finally arrived. On the phone, he had been as circumspect as possible, mentioning only his parents' names, Toronto, and the fact that he was in town. Would a brief visit be possible? "There's something my father wanted me to ask you." The voice on the other end of the phone, first feeble, then booming, then weak again, was agreeable but vague. "I don't remember your parents," the voice said.

Now, as Paul stepped out of the elevator on the eleventh floor, his nostrils wrinkling with the smell of cabbage and garlic, and something else, slightly sweetish, which he couldn't identify, he saw a bald oval head with large ears and a toothy grin appear in the open doorway just a few steps to his right. "So you found it?" the bald head inquired.

"I did."

"So come in then. You're here, you might as well."

Bronstein was a small man cloaked in an inescapable implication of having once been larger. It was clear from the roundness of his stooped shoulders under a frayed black cardigan flapping at his hips, the gauntness of his cheeks, and the bagginess of the pleated corduroy trousers held together at the waist by a knotted terry cloth bathrobe tie and up by faded red suspenders, their elastic sprung. The raggedly trimmed moustache above his moist upper lip was too large for his caved-in face; even his bedroom slippers seemed to have been fashioned for a larger foot, flapping noisily as he led Paul down a dim corridor made narrow by stacks of ceiling-high newspapers lining one wall. They emerged into a brighter kitchen, beyond which Paul could see glimpses of a cluttered living room. All of these signs were familiar to Paul, whose father had undergone a similar process of shrinkage, and, with so much in his life gone, unwillingness to throw things away.

"That's some city you live in," Bronstein said. He was at the sink, running water into a kettle. Above the hiss of the tap, Paul could hear the gurgling and sighing of the refrigerator. "Sit, sit." He gestured to a tarnished chrome chair pulled out at an angle from a table cluttered with dirty dishes, a crumpled copy of *Variety,* and pieces of scattered paper scribbled on in blue ink in a broad, loose hand. "Too hot in the summer, too cold in the winter kind of thing—or is it the other way around? And windy all the time. All the time chapped lips in Toronto." He peered at Paul through small, rheumy eyes that appeared to be lustrelessly black, as if they absorbed light rather than reflecting it. "And if that ain't enough of an insult for you, I don't remember you. What did you say your name was?"

"Paul Olefsky. It's not me, though, it's my parents." Paul had sat down at the table and now found himself in the uncomfortable position of having to look up at his host, whose stale breath rattled as it wheezed out of his lungs past irregular, yellowed teeth. "My mother, really. Her name was O'Brien before she married my dad." Mindful of the granddaughter's warning, he spoke louder than normal, without shouting, and was careful to enunciate each word.

Bronstein stopped fussing with the teapot and cups and gave Paul a long, lopsided look. "O'Brien? You're talking Louise O'Brien?"

"That's my mother."

"The actress?"

"I think we're talking about the same person." Paul smiled.

"Blonde? Blue eyes? A body like ... well, a beautiful figure."

"I don't remember her ever being blonde, but I've seen pictures of her that way. And I'm afraid she'd grown a little plump in her later years."

"She married someone named Olefsky? No offence, I'm just surprised. She wouldn't marry me because she wouldn't marry outside her faith; that's what she said."

"Olefsky's Polish," Paul said. "We're Catholic." Then, after a long moment during which, as his neck began to ache, he and Bronstein gazed at each other as if trying to fathom the other's meaning: "You wanted to marry my mother?"

Bronstein made a bellowing noise that Paul realized was a laugh, though it seemed particularly mirthless, more a noise of pain or surprise. "Wanted to marry her? I was mad for her, insane for her, crazy for her, nuts for her. Disconsolate when she turned me down. Don't tell any of this to my Sophie; she sees red when she thinks of her rivals, so many of them there were, she thinks. But don't worry; she's deaf as this teapot." He clinked a teaspoon against the side of a creamy white china pot with a single rose design. "She's in the next room, sleeping maybe, but there's no need to whisper."

With that, he turned his back on Paul and set about spooning loose tea leaves from a canister into the teapot, pouring water from the steaming kettle over them. Sighing heavily, he cleared some of the litter from the table and set out two matching china cups, their rims chipped, and saucers, and a coverless sugarbowl, its contents crusted. He opened the door of the noisy refrigerator, bent inside, and retrieved a perfectly round, glistening lemon, which he then set about slicing on the counter.

"Disconsolate," he repeated. "You think I wanted to go back to New York? Toronto was boring, but there was work there. New York was nothing to me in those days. Still, things worked out, kind of thing. But did I want to come back? Is that what you asked me? No! But what could I do? Stay and ...?" His voice trailed off and he turned back to Paul with the lemon slices artfully arranged on a small china plate, its chipped rim looking like the battered mouth of a grinning hockey player. He slumped into the seat across from Paul. "She asks about me, your mother?"

"I'm sorry, Mr. Bronstein, I thought I made it clear; my mother's dead. She died ten years ago."

"Dead? Louise dead?" Bronstein looked first aghast, then crestfallen, then bemused. "Well, what do you expect? She's an old woman. Old people die." He gave Paul a meaningful glance and a small note of hopefulness slipped into his voice. "Still, ten years ago ... she wasn't so old then."

"She had cancer," Paul said. "She was only sixty-seven—you're right, too young to die, really."

"She was robbed," Bronstein said, his voice going suddenly bitter. "*You* were robbed."

Although he had never really cried for his mother—he had tried to on the day of her funeral, but the tears refused to come—Paul felt a stinging behind his eyes now. "We *were* robbed," he said softly. "You're right."

"*I* was robbed," Bronstein said. "I mean, back then ..."—he waved his hand vaguely.

"I'm sorry, I don't understand," Paul said.

"She wouldn't marry me. What, you're as deaf as my Sophie?"

Paul took the crooked opening of Bronstein's generous mouth to be a grin. "Oh, I see."

"So, if she's dead, to what do I owe this honour? Tea?"

"Please. No, it's my father, Mr. Bronstein. This is . . ."

"Sugar?"

"Yes, please." He helped himself, hesitantly stirring half a teaspoon of the clumped sugar into the cloudy tea. "This is a little embarrassing."

"Embarrassing? Lemon? Fresh from the A&P today." Bronstein cleared newspapers off the other chair and sat down, extending the little plate. Paul noticed that his fingernails were dirty and ragged.

"Sure."

"How can your mother's death be embarrassing?"

"No, not that. Certainly not that." Paul frowned as he squeezed the lemon slice into his tea. The faint smell that had been nagging at him, he realized now as the sharp scent of the lemon cut through it, was vomit. "You'll laugh, maybe, Mr. Bronstein."

"I could use a good laugh."

"My father says my mother . . . never loved him. That she married him on the rebound . . . after you."

"Rebound?"

"You know . . . bouncing back."

"I don't know that expression."

"It's a basketball term. The first shot misses the hoop and bounces back. Then someone scores on the rebound."

"Ha. I like that. Very sexual kind of thing. Your father, he's a basketball player, maybe?"

"No . . . it's just an expression; everybody uses it. He was a playwright. Joseph Olefsky, Joe Olefsky. You don't remember him?"

"Playwrights, no offence, are a dime a dozen." Bronstein gave Paul a shrewd, assessing look. "You a playwright too?"

"No, nothing like that. I'm a computer analyst."

"So even computers get neurotic? I was right not to get one."

Paul smiled weakly.

"Your father, he ever had a play on Broadway?"

"Off-Broadway, years ago. Most of his plays were produced in Toronto and that's all, little theatres. He hasn't written in years. After we kids came along, he got a job in advertising... you know how it goes."

"I know, I know. It goes, it goes. Usually, it leaves you behind."

The two men sipped their tea. Paul let his gaze wander around the kitchen, from the cracked and worn reddish-brown linoleum to the dusty baseboards to the stained, paint-chipped cupboards.

"So...?" Bronstein finally inquired.

"This is stupid. I'm sorry." Paul put his cup and saucer firmly on the table. "I'll just go."

"Stupid as it might be, stupider still is going without doing what you came to do. All the way from Toronto? That's a long way."

"I'm in the city on business, Mr. Bronstein. But you're right. May I ask you a question?"

"What else have you been doing?"

"You were in love with my mother?"

"Who did you say she was again?"

Paul got up. "I'm going. Thanks for letting me come."

"Don't be so fussy. So maybe my memory's not so good, you ever think about that?"

A wave of dizziness lapped at Paul, but he pushed it aside and sat down. "You're right. I'm sorry."

"Don't be so sorry, either. Drink your tea. More? There's plenty."

"No, thank you." He took a deep breath. "Listen, Mr. Bronstein... my mother was Louise O'Brien. An actress. You knew her in Toronto fifty years ago, or more. You were in love with her?"

Bronstein peered at Paul. He put down his teacup and took a pair of glasses from the pocket of his cardigan. He laboured the wire arms over his ears and adjusted the nosepiece. He looked at Paul again, thoroughly, as if reading an important note, then removed the glasses, carefully folding them and returning them to his pocket. "Louise O'Brien, you look a little like her, maybe. Was I in love with her? Sure, didn't I tell you already? I was crazy about her, nuts about her, insane..."

"And was she in love with you?" Paul interrupted.

"Ah." Bronstein massaged the upper bridge of his nose with

the thumb and forefinger of his right hand. "That's the question. Isn't it?"

"That's the hammer on the nail," Paul said, using an expression of his father's. He smiled slightly.

"Just because sometimes my memory ain't so good, don't mean I'm senile." Bronstein lowered his hand and squinted at Paul. "So don't tell that's the question when we ain't come to the question yet. *Here's* the question: Because if she loved me, then maybe . . . maybe what?"

"I don't know," Paul said.

"I'm your father, maybe?

Paul reddened. "No, it's not that. The math doesn't work."

"Okay, then, didn't love your father, didn't love you, didn't love . . . you have sisters, brothers?"

"A sister."

"Okay, didn't love your sister. Is that what you're worrying about? That the whole thing was a lie? The whole ball of wax?"

"I don't know. I don't know what I'm worrying about."

"You don't know? Why worry about something you don't know what it is?"

"I don't even know that I *am* worried." Paul laughed. "Was I worried when I came here? I don't remember. I think maybe you're *making* me worried."

"Me? If you're not worried, what the hell are you doing here? You'll pardon the expression."

"I don't know why the hell I'm here, pardon the expression yourself." Paul got up. "Thank you for the tea, Mr. Bronstein."

They went into the hallway, but Bronstein, holding a finger to his nose and gesturing with his other hand, turned right instead of left, leading Paul through the living room, its walls lined with framed playbills and signed photos of smiling men and women. They picked their way carefully around islands of books and magazines scattered about on what must have once been an expensive Persian rug, faded but still beautiful, and past a baroque sofa spread with old copies of *Variety* and *Billboard* and *National Geographic,* to a doorway through which he could see a large bed piled high with what appeared to be quilts and pillows. Bronstein gestured with his hand and Paul stepped gingerly into the room, from which the smell of stale vomit and bleach emanated. The window was closed, the air heavy, hot, dense with dust.

"What colour hair does your mother have?"

Paul sighed. "She's dead, Mr. Bronstein."

"Does ... did. What colour *did* she have? Was she still a blonde?"

Paul had to think for a moment. "She'd been grey for a while, but, no, her hair was brown. As far as I can remember, it always was."

"See? You think I'd be so crazy about a brunette? The Louise O'Brien I knew was a blonde." He gestured with his thumb into the bedroom. "So was she ... *was,* she still is. Party girls, both of them."

"My mother was a party girl?"

"What? You're smiling. You don't even know what I mean. And don't ask, my young friend. About your mother, there's some things no man wants to know."

A small noise arose from the bed, from beneath the heap of bedclothes; the noise grew to a moan and the quilts began to stir as Paul watched, fascinated. A hand threw itself out, followed by an arm, its shape obscured by the baggy sleeve of a bright red nightgown, then by the head of a woman, wrinkled and waxy, her distinctively blonde hair so thin and sparse Paul could see the dull white of her scalp. The moan grew in pitch, wavered, dipped and rose again, gradually shaping itself into a distinct word: "Mmmmmmmmmmm ... Murray?"

"I'm right here, Pumpkin," Bronstein said, his voice rising. He moved around Paul and sat on the edge of the bed, taking the woman's hand gently in his own. "Look, we've got company."

The woman's head rotated slowly in Paul's direction and her eyes narrowed, widened, narrowed again. Then, as if exhausted by this effort, she slumped backwards again, expelling air like a punctured balloon.

"Okay, pretty girl, that's right, you rest now," Bronstein said, stroking her hand. "I'll tell you all about it later." He looked up, smiling sheepishly at Paul. "She's not at her best, poor thing. The spirit's willing; the flesh, forget it. Don't be fooled, though, her mind's all there, she's sharper than I am, ain't you, old girl?" He rose, chuckling, and made an abortive effort at straightening the bedclothes. "Okay, okay, so we'll see you later, sweet thing. You rest."

He was rewarded with a gentle snore, to which he smiled broadly. Placing his finger by his nose, as he had when he'd led Paul into the room, he now led him out, through the minefield of the living room, down the narrow hallway and to the door, where he paused and gave his visitor a meaningful look.

"So you see how it goes, party's over."

"I see," Paul said lamely.

"So you'll give my best regards to your mother?"

"I will."

"And to your father, too, what the hell. No hard feelings after all these years. Let bygones be gone kind of thing." He shook Paul's hand, his grip surprisingly strong, and gestured to the elevator. "Live and let live, and why not? We won't live forever. Soon enough . . ."—here he rolled his eyes up and made a slashing gesture across his neck—". . . curtains."

Out in the street, the afternoon still bright and warm, Paul was struck again by the peacefulness of the scene, the gatherings of women and children, the tricycles on the sidewalk, the flowerpots on windowsills. He looked at his watch and was startled to see only half an hour had passed since his arrival. He lit one of his infrequent cigarettes and stood watching the two girls jumping rope—were they the same pair he'd seen before? They were too old to be home on a school day, but there they were just the same, bare legs flashing under their skirts as the girls jumped, landed softly on the rubbery pavement, and lofted effortlessly into the air yet again, the process repeating itself seemingly endlessly, their chanting voices rising and falling with the same rhythm.

"You are a clown," that's what Chucky would say if he told her of his visit, dismissing both the question and the answer, if there was one. He wondered what his father would say, if anything: *"That man? You went to visit your mother's lover?"* He wasn't sure. Kate, Paul knew, would think it all a grand adventure, would want to know all the details, what things looked like, who said what, what happened next. What *had* happened? He gave the jumping girls another look and began to walk toward the Grand Concourse, the plangent voices of the girls still ringing in his ears.

* * *

Spiders Across the Stars

"The only people for me are the mad ones, the ones who are mad to live, mad to talk, mad to be saved, desirous of everything at the same time, the ones who never yawn or say a commonplace thing, but burn, burn, burn like fabulous yellow roman candles, exploding like spiders across the stars."

—Jack Kerouac, *On the Road*

WHEN CLASSES ENDED in late April, Ben and Gail loaded the back of his 1955 Pontiac convertible and made the long drive to San Francisco, west via Winnipeg and Regina, south through Montana to Oregon, then through the moonscapes of the bitterly dry Columbia Valley to the coast. It was 1965, a year after the free speech movement had jolted Berkeley, but two years before the Summer of Love, when thousands like them poured into the city to live on the streets, smoking grass, painting their faces, and driving themselves wild on the plaintive strains of the Dead and the Airplane. Driving south, they sang along to the Beach Boys on the car's scratchy radio.

They knew no one in California; their plans were shapeless and elastic. It was just where they knew they wanted to be.

On the south Oregon coast, they stopped at the sea lion caves in early evening to soak in the sunset over scenery that mesmerized them, the spray from the waves breaking on the jagged rocks below leaving a fine mist of salt on their faces. It was almost closing time, and the girl operating the elevator said this would be the last trip down. They watched the raucous lions and seals with the others in their group, tourists in loud shirts. On impulse, Ben grabbed Gail's hand and the two of them pressed themselves into the damp shadows.

After the elevator's rise, they made love on rocks slick and salty from spray. When the elevator girl came back looking for them, they were already straightening their clothes, flush-faced and exhilarated.

"Everything starts now," Ben said.

He was twenty-one, just through with his third year at University of Toronto and not at all sure that he wanted a fourth. He was from the Lakehead, a tall, angular boy with a sharp nose, unkempt dusty brown hair, and piercing black eyes that settled on people with naked interest. Both his parents were teachers and devout Baptists; his eldest brother, Thomas, had gone to divinity school and was now serving his first congregation; and a sister had married a missionary and disappeared into Africa. Ben had no clear idea of what he believed or wanted for himself. He'd always been good at writing and had been working on *The Varsity* and covering U of T games for the Canadian Press, which opened up possibilities for him, but he was starting to think he was more attracted to poetry than journalism, though he had yet to actually write a poem.

"I'd say it already has," Gail said, smiling. She had to shout to be heard over the crashing of the surf on the rocks below.

She was nineteen, the youngest in a brood of seven girls and three brothers, but she had been cheated of the kind of doting affection many babies of the family receive. When she was five, the very day before starting school, her mother had been stricken with a never-diagnosed ailment that left her weak and unsteady on her feet. The burden of looking after the youngest children had fallen on the two eldest sisters, who were rivals for the eye of their father, a conductor with the CN who often was away from their home in the Sault. Gail had grown up feeling apart and unloved, like the planet farthest from a cold distant sun in some science fiction galaxy. She was coltish and pretty in a dark, unconventional way, her hair chopped short as a boy's. That had attracted Ben the first time he saw her, at the student union, where she had a job flipping burgers.

They held hands as they walked back to the car from the sea

lion cave. Ben whistled a sprightly tune for the next few miles, the dramatic coast unwinding to their right like a spool of film. They'd been sleeping together for less than a month but fit together so well it felt as if it had been going on for ages. They were still surprising each other, but there was a comfort between them neither had experienced before, as if each of them had deciphered part of the code that explained the other.

Gail was most conscious of that comfort during the long stretches on the drive down when they were silent. She squeezed Ben's arm and thought she'd remember all her life those moments in the mountain night when the stars pressed down on them like a lover's breath and the radio crackled with unearthly static.

⊗

They found an apartment on Fell Street, just a few blocks south of the intersection of Haight and Ashbury, though that conjunction had no special meaning then. The windows in the living room had been painted shut, but Ben managed to pry them open; they overlooked the entrance to the freeway and the hissing of tires disturbed their sleep. There was no furniture, but the landlady allowed them the use of an old foam rubber mattress a previous tenant had left behind. They laid it right on the floor until Ben, who had learned a bit of carpentry from his grandfather, built a frame out of two-by-fours and plywood.

They sold the Pontiac, and, with the small stake that Ben had saved from his CP work, had enough money to get them started. They paid their first month's rent, begging their way out of the damage deposit, and bought a few pieces of furniture and kitchen stuff at a second-hand store. They'd told the suspicious guard at the border they were visiting friends and would be in the country for a couple of weeks, so working was strictly illegal. Just the same, Gail got a job waiting tables at the Foster's on Divisadero, where the tips were decent. After a few shifts, she was able to treat herself to a doctor's visit and a long-overdue birth control pill prescription. Ben, meanwhile, was looking around, answering a few ads in the miscella neous help wanted column in the *Chronicle* every morning. He wound up spending much of his time hanging out at the City Lights bookstore, Ferlinghetti's place, and prowling North Beach, where the topless craze was barely a year old. Carol Doda was the big name on the strip, drawing in huge crowds to the Condor. There were lots of other dancers, though, and an endless stream of joints up and down Broadway, each with a fast-talking man at the door coaxing passersby in, carnival barkers in gaudy sport shirts with cigarettes dangling from their lips.

"What about you, sport? Wanna see something you ain't seen down on the farm?"

"Not me," Ben protested, laughing.

"Sure, 'less you'd rather get your jollies thinking about it and playing pocket pool. They ain't gonna bite cha."

He hadn't been in one of the bars, but a fascination with the colour and popcorn-and-tobacco smell of the strip kept him walking it, watching the tourists. Now he shrugged and backed away, suddenly shy. He took refuge at the Cafe Del Sporte, on the corner of Columbus and Broadway. Despite its name, it was dark and sedate as a church, filled with old men sipping espresso and playing checkers. He was sitting at a table by the window one afternoon, reading a paperback copy of *On the Road,* when a man about his own age with an unruly beard and a twisted mouth approached him.

"You stole that, didn'tcha?"

Ben looked him over—he was dressed in patched jeans, a red-checked cowboy shirt, and faded denim jacket—but his expression was hard to read. "So? What's it to you?"

The young man's face hardened beneath the sandy beard, making Ben think of a slide he'd seen in his geography course last term of glaciers grinding over mountain granite. He leaned over, his face hovering close enough for Ben to see that the twisted mouth was the result of a scar on his upper lip, perhaps from an automobile accident, and abruptly sat down in a vacant chair across from him. The stone face cracked into a grin. "Just admiring your style."

He flipped his jacket open so Ben could see a book in his waistband. He took it out and laid it on the table between them: *Under Milkwood,* Dylan Thomas's eyes and cigarette smouldering from the paperback cover.

"Blaze," the young man said, extending a surprisingly delicate hand. He pressed his palm against Ben's and quickly withdrew it, so that the two hands merely slid together. "Where ya from, cowpoke?"

"Canada," Ben said with a self-conscious laugh. "Toronto the Good."

Blaze hesitated just a moment. "Oh, yeah. Morley Callaghan. *That Summer in Paris.* Leonard Cohen." His eyes glanced at the book in front of Ben. "What brings you down here? Aiming to join up with the beat generation?"

Ben smiled, embarrassed but engaged by his companion's directness. "Maybe not join. Take a look."

"Huh! Cautious man." He reached into a shirt pocket for a battered old Luckies pack, tipped a hand-rolled cigarette from it, and lit it with a match from a packet so worn the printing on its cover was unreadable. "You're just a trifle late. Year or two, I'd say. Ginsy's doing Europe, Jack's drunk back east, Corso's in the desert looking for truth, and God only knows where all the rest of them are." He squinted up through his smoke to see if Ben was registering all this. "I'm about all that's left. You'll have to make do with me."

⊗

The scruffy guy Ben brought home said he was a poet, but, except for the beard, he didn't fit Gail's idea of what a poet should be, though she found him oddly appealing, with a broken-toothed grin that reminded her of one of her brothers. At the U of T, she'd taken a course in Romantic poetry from a gaunt man with a manicured moustache bobbing above the stem of his pipe and leather patches on the elbows of his beige tweed jacket. He would recite often from Keats and Shelley, his eyes closing and his voice resonating as he spoke the words by heart; his class attracted a clutch of young men who seemed to have patterned themselves after him, the same patches on their tweed elbows, their cheeks even gaunter than his. His retinue included a handful of serious young women in black leotards and peasant skirts. Gail admired them but felt distanced from these lithe women whose long dark hair hung gracefully below their shoulders. She would see them around the campus, these young men and women, in small groups arguing over coffee in the commissary, or alone, moving as if in a dream, their burning eyes focused on some distant point.

Blaze was nothing like the young Toronto poets.

For one thing, he had nothing but contempt for the Romantics, calling Keats "laughable," Shelley "corny, old, mouldy." For another, he didn't seem to actually write anything himself—in this way he was much like Ben—although he carried a dirty, spine-broken notebook folded in his back pocket and would occasionally whip it out and scribble brief notes. He did this with the stub of a pencil he kept in the Luckies pack beside the half a dozen homemades he rolled every morning.

Meeting him for the first time, Gail immediately was wary of the attention he lavished on her; when she came home from the restaurant, Blaze insisted she sit down at the kitchen table and brought her a cup of the strong black tea he'd brewed in their chipped brown teapot.

"Ben tells me you're his mornin' and evenin'," he drawled, although she was sure Ben hadn't said anything remotely like that. "I can see that, can see why."

Gail blushed despite herself. "I'm the breadwinner," she remarked dryly, although she knew that was a sore point with Ben.

"Man doesn't live by bread alone," Blaze said, winking.

He was wide-shouldered and muscular, with no hips or ass to speak of, wedge-shaped as a football player. Blaze was lanky, but there was nothing gaunt about him: the skin of his cheeks above his beard was tanned and glowing with health, and the cornflower-blue eyes that reflected light above the high bones were filled with humour and electricity. His hair was a birds' nest of russet brown that irresistibly attracted his hands, his long, usually dirty fingers raking through the tangled strands when he talked, which was almost always. He came from somewhere in Wyoming and spoke with a lemonade twang that Gail found, depending on her mood, either charming or maddening.

His worn-at-the-knee button-fly Levi's seemed as dark indigo and stiff as the day they'd been bought, suggesting to Gail that they'd never been washed; his gaudy cowboy shirt with imitation pearl snaps, Gail would soon learn, was one of several he owned, in different colours. He claimed the scar on his lip was a keepsake from a barroom fight with a Marine in Saigon, "from talkin' through the wrong end of a broken beer bottle." That brawl was as close as he'd come to seeing action overseas, he said, and as close as he wanted to come. The war was heating up now, and Blaze, who'd been a draftee, was grateful to have been there before things got too bad.

"That shit is going to fly like hornets in a hailstorm, mark my fuckin' words," he said, shaking his head. He launched into a rant about the war that was filled with New Lefty language Gail had heard around campus that spring. She gave him a second appraising look.

Blaze and Ben hit it off so well that he almost immediately became a fixture in their lives. Blaze had a room in North Beach, on one of those tiny crooked side streets, illuminated by a bare blue light bulb and furnished with a foam rubber mat, sleeping bag, and a table made of a packing crate. But he spent more and more time at Ben and Gail's place, crashing in their living room, curled up in the oversize beanbag chair. Gail didn't blame him for not wanting to go home—the one time she was with Ben when they dropped in on him, she was repulsed by the urine stench in the hallway and his sinkful of unwashed dishes. "Welcome to my Parisian garret," he said, winking at her. He insisted on lighting a candle and pouring glasses of acidy wine from an opened bottle he produced from a tiny pantry. Gail got the one wine glass, while Blaze and Ben drank from dusty water tumblers.

He and Ben would almost always be out when she got home from the evening shift at ten and would come dragging in at any hour, frequently after she was already in bed, and sit up till dawn, drinking cheap red wine. They'd sleep till early afternoon, just about the time she was putting on her uniform and getting ready to go.

They spent hour after hour at City Lights, sometimes boosting a book but mostly browsing, and at the Del Sporte, where they nursed espressos, watched the old men at their checkerboards, and argued over the merits of this writer or that one. They also prowled the city, the black Fillmore and Hunter's Point districts, where Blaze introduced Ben to the wonders of sweet potato pie and after-hours clubs where you could listen to jazz all night for the price of a coffee; jangly Chinatown and Japantown; gaudy Fisherman's Wharf; serene Golden Gate Park; and always the North Beach strip, where Blaze would tease Ben for his refusal to enter any of the girlie clubs.

"I don't need that," Ben said, although it was days and days since he and Gail had made love—their schedules so disparate and Blaze's presence so constant. "It's the *guys* I'm interested in, the guys who go in those places. I can see them just as well outside as in." The men he meant were shy middle-aged tourists, glancing about before going in, unself-conscious bumpkins from the country in boots, and loud-mouthed sailors, always in groups of three or more. He was constructing a tragic theory about such men that he imagined might form the basis for an epic poem, although the few notes for it he jotted down on napkins from the Del Sporte usually went missing.

"Yeah, those cats are strange, man, but they could be me and you," Blaze said with a grin.

Wherever they went—wherever Blaze took Ben and, occasionally, on her evenings off, Gail—they avoided the tourist spots and wound up in dives Blaze knew, cheap Chinese restaurants where theirs were the only white faces, black bars on Fillmore Avenue bristling with hostility and the exotic smell of marijuana, fag joints in the Tenderloin where a crowd of muscular young men in leather jackets gathered around Ben, eyeing him like horse traders at an auction.

Once, the three of them went to an anti-war rally in a park downtown, a ragtag crowd of college students, old women with net bags, and steel-eyed men in workshirts handing out Trostskyite newspapers. They stood on the sidelines to watch and listen to the speeches and chants but declined to take up signs. "I had my war, man," Blaze said, and again Gail felt intrigued by him, despite her better judgment.

On one of Gail's paydays, Blaze led them down a winding North Beach street to the Green Mountain Cafe, where, for $2.25 each, they got a full Italian meal, including a glass of wine so harsh it would etch glass. A bargain, she agreed, but after tip and trolley fare, still almost ten dollars out of her purse. She'd balked at paying for Blaze, but the pressure of Ben's knee against hers under the table and his sharp glance changed her mind. One weekend, they hitchhiked down the coast all the way to Big Sur and had hamburgers and endless cups of spice-scented coffee—Gail paying again—at Nepenthe, a cafe chiselled into the rock above a spectacular sweep of ocean, where Henry Miller was supposed to be a regular, though they didn't see him that day. Nor did they ever see any of the other luminaries—writers and musicians—Blaze claimed to know, there or at any of the other places he and Ben went.

"Whyn't you be nicer to Blaze?" Ben asked Gail after one of those threesomes.

That surprised Gail, since they'd had a pleasant afternoon at Fisherman's Wharf watching the boats, and, to her mind, she was always as nice to Blaze as the situation required. Perhaps she didn't initiate conversations with him, didn't go out of her way to include him in things she said to Ben, but she always answered his questions, was always polite, always laughed at his jokes. "I'm not in love with him," she said.

"What the hell's that supposed to mean?" Ben snapped.

"Nothing. Just what I said."

They glared at each other and in the moment of silence, Gail imagined Ben's face softening. "I guess I have been spending a lot of time with him," he would say. "I'm sorry, honey, I've been ignoring you, haven't I? Taking you for granted? I won't be so dumb again, honest." Then he'd take her in his arms.

But all Ben did was shrug. "Well," he said, letting whatever he meant trail off.

One night, her sleep was lurid with kaleidoscopic dreams of threatening sky, angry surf, mythical creatures, and falling. When she awoke, she found Ben out like a light beside her, Blaze in a coma in the beanbag, and the whole apartment stinking with an unfamiliar, heavy smell.

"Tea," Ben explained later when he came yawning into the kitchen in his underwear. "Boo."

"Grass," Blaze chimed in from the chair, stretching.

"Marijuana. Blaze copped it."

"Heavy shit," Blaze said. "You gotta try some, Gail Momma."

The thought appalled her, but Ben's dark look if she refused seemed even worse. "Okay."

"We're tapped out now," Blaze said. "Have to score later."

"Oh yeah," Ben said. "You got any bread, honey?"

Money was becoming more of an issue. There was a pitiful pittance left in their reserve fund, and they could just barely live on Gail's pay and tips. Blaze always seemed to have a dollar or two on him, though he had no visible means of support. Ben had more or less given up looking for a job, with no explanation, but hadn't stopped spending a few bucks a day on trolley fare, coffees, and Red Mountain wine, which came in two-gallon jugs. And now there was the grass; despite her reservations, Gail soon developed a taste for the stuff. She could take it or leave it, she told herself, but taking it was just fine. The more she smoked it in his company, the better company Blaze got to be. She found herself looking forward to watching his long, graceful fingers rationing a thin stream of ground leaf into Zig-Zags, the darting lick of his tongue along the edge of the papers, the skin around his blue eyes wrinkling in a grin above it.

⊗

One afternoon, Ben and Blaze came out of City Lights with books in their belts—the man at the cash register behind the high counter never gave them a glance—and sauntered over to the Del Sporte. "Do get me an espresso, won't you, there's a good fellow," Blaze said, handing his book, a volume of essays by Artaud, to Ben. "I'll join you in a nonce."

Ben watched him continue down Columbus to the Chinese grocer on the corner. A couple of minutes later, he joined Ben at their favourite window table, from which they could watch the street go by. "Sorry, man, they were out of goat's cheese." He produced a fist-sized round of gouda from his shirt, followed by a loaf of sourdough in a paper bag. He tore off the end of the bread, spraying crumbs, and, with his pocketknife, began to peel the reddish-brown rind from the cheese.

"Shit," Ben said.

"Hey, who you with?" Blaze asked. "Robin Hood and his merry men or the sheriff of Nottingham?"

"We're giving to the poor?" Ben asked skeptically.

"Who's poorer than us? Do pass me the sugar, my good man."

Before Ben knew it, they were boosting almost every day. They eased up on the books to make more room in their jackets for fancy cheeses and packages of cold cuts from groceries, never going back to the same place. The food was joined by a wild shirt for Ben, a beret for Blaze that he took to wearing to keep his wild locks in place, and a card of silver earrings that Ben gave to Gail.

"Where did these come from?" she asked suspiciously. They were the drop style she liked, and the small reddish stones appealed to her. She had chosen to ignore the food that mysteriously appeared in the fridge, since it was a welcome addition to the macaroni and cheese that had become their staple.

"They just seemed to call out to me to take them home to you," Ben said, with what he hoped passed as a romantic smile.

"So they're stolen?"

"I wouldn't put it that way. They've been liberated. Gone to a better home." He put his arm around her and gave her an inexact kiss.

"I don't want stolen goods, whatever you call it," Gail said, sending Ben into a funk that, as it progressed through the day, made her feel as if she were the criminal.

When she came home from the restaurant that night, there was no sign of B & B, as she'd started calling Ben and Blaze, nor the earrings, which had been on the orange-crate coffee table when she last saw them. One of her older sisters had a pair just like them, and now she was feeling a little sorry she hadn't been more gracious. She stayed up later than usual, with hopes of making up, but Ben and Blaze were still out when she went to bed. She woke in the middle of the night to the unceasing traffic sound from Fell Street, and was surprised at the absence of Ben's warm body beside her. Nor was he in bed in the morning, or anywhere in the apartment. She had a cry, wondering if she'd ever see him again, then had a shower, unsure whether to be anxious or angry. When he did come home shortly before she left for work, on his own and looking none the worse for wear, he acted as if nothing out of the ordinary had happened.

And what, she wondered, had?

The next time Ben brought her a gift of shoplifted booty, a slim fountain pen that allowed her to write letters to her siblings in graceful pale blue loops, she accepted it with grace.

⊗

Ben had started writing poems. He'd gone beyond the napkin stage and was now jotting down thoughts, observations, and descriptions of people he saw in a boosted black-covered notebook like Blaze's. He had no more knowledge of metaphor and prosody than any other high-school graduate but did have a natural facility for language. He set about teaching himself, setting a quota of first five, then ten similes and metaphors a day. Soon, his notebook was filled with images like "the moon deep as a well . . . the moon a well" and "my heart hammering like a tattoo . . . her heart a tattoo on her lily chest." Eventually, these random lines began forming themselves into poems.

He showed a few to Gail, but was suspicious of her quick approval. "You're just saying that because . . ." he said.

"Because of what?" she grinned.

"You know . . ."

"I don't. Because I love you? Because I'm standing by my man? Because I wouldn't know any better?"

"Jesus," Ben said. "Keep your shirt on."

"Oh, it's on," Gail said.

Blaze's approval was harder to win but easier to believe. "Bullshit," he said of the first few things Ben showed him. "Abstract bullshit. Detail, man, detail. Don't give us this 'oh, woe is me, the world is just so cruel' shit; give us a punch to the nose so we taste the world's cruelty in our own blood."

It took a while for Ben to make any sense of what Blaze was trying to tell him, but gradually the poems began to become harder, more shapely. "Not half bad," Blaze said grudgingly, and Ben was more pleased than he'd expected to be. "Now just stop with the 'me-me-me' shit and tell us something we don't already know about the world."

Blaze never seemed to write any poems himself—he was going through a dry spell, he shrugged—but he was always reading a volume fresh from City Lights: Ferlinghetti, Snyder, Corso, and Ginsberg, of course, plus some of what he called "the older cats." He turned Ben onto them too, "the wise old sages of the poetry racket," like Williams, cummings, Pound, and Thomas. And he seemed to know what he was talking about. "I don't gotta always be *writing* poems, man," he explained. "I talk poetry, I dream poetry, my *life* is poetry."

And it was true, Ben thought, that Blaze's everyday speech was often infused with a flavour that was just this side of poetry. When he was stoned, he could cast a spell with words that would have Ben's also-stoned head spinning, although the next day he could rarely remember more than a phrase or a word or two.

Coming out of City Lights one afternoon in early July, Ben's head was buzzing with images from a new poet, Frank O'Hara. Out of respect for the poet, he hadn't lifted the book, but he was eager to get over to the Del Sporte and write a few things down, ideas of his own. "You go on; I'm just going to grab us a bite," Blaze said, heading down Columbus.

"You've already been to that one," Ben called after him.

"That was weeks ago, man, be cool," Blaze said over his shoulder and continued down the street to the grocery.

For some reason, Ben didn't go on to the cafe but lingered on the street, waiting for Blaze. Good thing he did, too. Blaze was back in a minute, moving fast. "Holy shit, let's make tracks," he hissed, taking Ben by the arm. As he spun around, he caught a glimpse of a Chinese man in an apron charging out of the store.

They boogied down Broadway as fast as they could without actually breaking into a run, trying to look cool and casual. As they passed the Condor, Blaze took a sharp left turn, hauling Ben behind him and surprising the doorman, who, weeks earlier, had given up trying to entice them.

"Jesus, that was close," Blaze said. He stuffed his beret in his jacket pocket and ran his fingers through his snarled hair. "I'm getting careless in my old age." They found a table in the dark lounge and ordered beers from the waitress who was there in an instant. "You got enough to cover this? Two fuckin' bucks for a beer, Christ!"

"Let's hope I do, or we'll be running from the sheriff again in a minute," Ben said, digging in his jeans.

The celebrated Doda didn't work afternoons, but the blonde dancing onstage now was impressive; after they'd paid and settled down, they turned their attention to her.

"Jesus," Ben said.

"The wonders of modern science," Blaze said.

They were able to nurse their beers through two more girls, who drove the last vestiges of poetry out of Ben's mind for the day. Back out on the street, he declared he was heading home, which suited Blaze. "I haven't been at my pad for days, man. The goldfish must be beside themselves."

Later, in bed, Gail was suspicious. "Where've *you* been today?" She snuggled into the hollow between his chest and shoulder.

"Whaddya mean?"

"You know."

"No, I don't. Nowhere. Can't a guy come home early? Can't a guy make love to his girl?" He started laughing.

"Sure, sure," Gail said. "Say, whatever became of that guy, what was his name? Blame?"

Ben fell asleep feeling happier than he had for quite a while. Coming to San Francisco seemed to make sense now. And he felt as if something was about to change for him, most likely for the better. He thought maybe he'd start looking for a job again, this time more seriously.

But three days later, on his own down on Market Street, where he'd gone to register with an employment agency, he ducked into a strip bar. There was no one pursuing him, no pal pulling his elbow, just the impulse. His minister brother, who often seemed to be watching over his shoulder, clucking his tongue when Ben boosted books, was nowhere to be seen.

He ordered a beer, feeling a twinge of guilt at spending Gail's money this way, and let his gaze settle on the girl gyrating on the stage, but his mind quickly wandered. Since the incident with the Chinese grocer and the hideout at the Condor, he hadn't seen much of Blaze. He wondered why. Gail was also on his mind. That terrific night they'd had—shit, that was the same night as the close call with Blaze—hadn't brought them closer together, as he'd thought it might. Instead, it seemed to have pried them further apart. When he'd told her of his resolve to find a job, she had snorted. "Better ease into it so you don't sprain something." She'd seen the hurt in his eyes and given him a quick kiss. Then she'd gone off to her own job.

When Ben got back to the Fell Street apartment, it was

empty of all traces of Gail, except for a note. She wasn't mad, just didn't think there was much of a future for them, she wrote in a careful, slanted hand, obviously using the pen he'd given her. The other night was lovely, but just a shooting star. She and Blaze were heading down to LA to see what was happening there. She hadn't meant things to happen the way they did—they just did. She hoped he wouldn't hate her.

"Hate you?" Ben said aloud, shaking his head. Then: "Just a shooting star. Where did *she* come up with a line like that?"

He went right over to Blaze's place, thinking he'd bloody his fucking nose for him, but was relieved to find the door hanging open and the room empty, the foam mat and sleeping bag gone, the packing-crate table lopsided and derelict. He shook his head at the filth of the place, a burnt crust on the hot plate, a carpet of discarded girlie magazines, and a broken-backed poetry book or two on the floor. His heart was still rattling in his chest, but by the time he got off the streetcar at Fell Street, he was breathing normally.

There wasn't much to sort out. He made a deal with the landlady, leaving her the little bit of furniture they'd accumulated and a pile of books—surely they were worth something. He headed back for Toronto, via the thumb, thinking he'd get a job, earn as much as he could in the rest of the summer, and go back to school in the fall. He might take that poetry class Gail had talked about.

Months later, he got a letter from her, addressed to him at his parents' and sent on. As soon as he saw the Wyoming postmark, he tossed it away, unread. Later, he was sorry, and went looking for it, but the trash had been taken out; it was too late.

* * *

The Unattempted Kiss

THE NAME IN THE HEADLINE was Rowman, a senator from Ontario who'd been caught with his hand in the till. Some forty years had passed, but the unusual spelling, the unnecessary "w" in the middle, made Zelaro think of Taffy Rowman, a girl he'd taken on a date one night when they both were freshmen at Michigan, in 1964. He'd been half in love with someone else, and she hadn't seemed all that interested in him, either, so he hadn't even attempted to kiss her goodnight, just took her gloved hand awkwardly in his and thanked her for the pleasant evening—well, he was sure he hadn't exactly said *that,* not *pleasant.* It was only later, halfway back to his own dorm, that the image of her perfect face—translucent skin, crackerjack eyes, and Crayola'd mouth—shining in the ice crystal halo light outside Forrest Hall, the girls' dormitory, sprang into his mind and he began to kick himself for letting opportunity deke him that way. The name of the other girl, the one he'd thought he'd been in love with, was long since lost, but he had never forgotten Taffy Rowman, whose father had been a Hollywood director twice nominated for an Oscar. His films occasionally popped up on television, and they never failed to remind Zelaro of her.

He could see her face now, as clear as if it had been captured in one of her father's films and he'd just seen it on the TV that so often filled his nights, nights that doggedly resisted sleep. Since his wife's death, eight years earlier, Zelaro's life had been rudderless—he seemed to merely cruise through his days, on autopilot, but the nights were bottomless, filled with Joyce's ghost, the ghosts of his parents, other nameless and faceless ghosts.

Like him, Taffy had wound up in Canada, and, like him, she had become a writer, though not a journalist. She had written several books, social histories with, so he gathered, a slightly leftist leaning. He hadn't read any of them, though he'd always meant to, but had seen reviews, all of them favourable. There'd been no contact between them—not since that one inconsequential date all those years earlier—and he had no idea if she remembered him or if, for that matter, she'd ever given him a second thought.

All of this went through Zelaro's mind now, and this time, for no particular reason, he resolved to look for one of her books on his next visit to the library—no, he would go that very evening. Supper finished, the house empty and silent, there were no other demands on his time. He folded the newspaper and tossed it aside. Senator Rowman and his problems didn't interest him in the slightest, nor did anything else on the front page, and those, he thought with a sniff, were the top stories, the best the paper could provide. These days, he often despaired over his former profession.

"That was the news?" he would always say at the close-off of the radio or TV report, smiling at the self-mockery his sarcasm implied. *"That* was the *nooze?* It was more like the snooze."

What *did* interest Zelaro these days was all inside him, in his head, where he could reach for it any time, more like a favourite book studded with turned-down page corners than a radio, where you had to flip the dial and take your chances on what you'd hear. The surprises were not what was there but what would surface at any given time, in what order. Zelaro would never have said that the past had any great hold on him, any greater on him than on anyone else. But, the truth was, that was where, for the past eight years, since Joyce's death, he lived, gathering dust, just like any other relic.

On this particular day, for no particular reason he could name, he shook off some of that dust.

⊗

The day John Kennedy was killed, November 22, 1963, Zelaro was working in the wire room of *The Detroit News*, eighteen years old and in the third week of his first newspaper job, as a copyboy, a job he had gotten only through the good turn of a friendly neighbour who worked in the paper's advertising department. It was the events of this day that, more than anything else, made up his mind for him about his future and sent him off, the following autumn, to journalism school. At a little after eleven o'clock, the bells rang on the United Press machine and a bulletin from Dallas came clattering across, saying simply "JFK shot." Zelaro was the first person in that large city to know.

He dined out on that story for years after, especially relishing the part where he rushed into the newsroom to spread the word and the city editor, Bill Holdon, an intimidating Second World War veteran in a wheelchair, had growled at him, "Come on, kid, don't fool around about things like that."

Zelaro was not really a storyteller by nature, though he'd made his living writing stories for newspapers and magazines for over twenty years. He had spent countless hours with mayors, MPs, premiers and prime ministers, cops, robbers, murderers, generals, movie actors, and famous people of all stripes, his mind littered with enough characters and anecdotes to fill half a dozen volumes of memoirs. But at parties or in gatherings at the bar, when others would fill the air above their heads with delicious stories of their own and others' adventures, Zelaro would usually be a listener, too forgetful or uncertain of the value of his own recollections to want to trot them out for other people's inspection.

He always listened to other people's stories with interest and appreciation, his head cocked to one side, as if to make certain the avenues of reception were prepared and clear, his cold blue eyes focused on the face of the speaker. At story's end, he would laugh, a strong, honest laugh signifying genuine amusement. Sometimes he would shake his head gently from side to side, as if saying to himself, "That is too much, really too much."

But Zelaro rarely offered a story of his own. Occasionally, with his journalism days long behind him, and now safe and secure within the warm bosom of government, he still told the JFK story, though, as that distant day receded further into the past, and was not even part of many people's personal memories, it held less currency. He liked also to tell another story from his early newspaper days, how, as a young reporter in Detroit, he was dispatched to the scene of a horrific murder and interviewed several neighbours and passersby, including, as it turned out, the murderer himself, who, having disposed of his weapon, was drawn back to the scene, where he stood like any other gawker. "This guy was so cool," Zelaro would say, meaning calm and collected, not hip, "telling me about the suspicious vehicle he'd seen in the area, a black van with a tiger stripe on the back. That even got into my story."

Other than the few stories like that, in which Zelaro was a character but the focus was on others, he rarely talked about himself, a characteristic he had learned from his parents. Zelaro was a good guy, his colleagues would often comment among themselves, but hard to know.

Zelaro found two of Taffy Rowman's books at the library after checking the catalogue to remind himself of her right name, Daphne. One was a history of agitprop theatre in Canada, the other a biography of Merlin Bouchard, the Quebec-born photographer who had documented the lives of migrant workers on the Prairies in the years just before and during the Great Depression. Both books had numerous photographs and struck Zelaro as being a bit skimpy on text. He had no real interest in the photographer's life, but he skimmed through the book to get its flavour. The theatre book he read with relish over the next few evenings. It was engrossing, meticulously researched, well written.

The library owned one other book by Daphne Rowman, which turned out to be a somewhat iconoclastic biography of Stephen Leacock. Zelaro put a hold on it and by the time he was through with the theatre book, it was waiting for him.

In the meantime, he'd placed an order at Buzzwords, his favourite bookshop, for a fourth book, which he'd found in Books in Print but not in the library's catalogue. The Leacock biography punctured several holes in the humourist's mythology and went so far as to declare him not all that funny. Zelaro found it delightful. The book he'd ordered, when it came, turned out to be a sharp-eyed look at advertising that he found fascinating.

From the dust jackets of these books, Zelaro developed a brief glimpse of the author: She had degrees, in sociology and art history, from Michigan and Toronto; she'd followed her husband, like Zelaro a draft dodger, to Canada in the late sixties; she lived in Toronto with her two children and a dog. In fact, the dog, an amiable-looking golden retriever, was featured prominently in the author's photo on the back cover of the advertising book. There was no further mention of the husband. Of more interest to Zelaro in the jacket photo was the author herself: a still-striking woman (this book, when he checked the copyright, turned out to be a decade old) with a clear, intelligent gaze and dark girlish bangs, carefully arranged to look careless. If he passed her on the street, he was sure, he would recognize her as the girl he had failed to kiss all those years ago.

The evening he finished the advertising book, he sat down at his home computer, called up the web, and did a search of her name. He found several sites, including one that included her e-mail address. He sent her this note:

"Hi, Taffy,

"You won't remember me, Guy Zelaro. We had one date, first year at Ann Arbor. I've always regretted there wasn't a second. I've read a couple of your books, and just recently the advertising one. Just wanted to say how much I enjoyed it. You nailed the bastards."

The next day, there was this reply:

"Hi, Guy,

"On the contrary, I remember you very well. I share the regret. I used to see your byline in the *Globe* and always thought you were probably the same boy I knew—Zelaro isn't that common a name. Seems like it's been quite a while since I've seen it, though—what's become of you? The 'Sask' and the 'gov' in your e-address suggest the where and the what—am I right?"

She closed the e-mail "Fondly, Taf."

⊗

Zelaro's parents were Holocaust survivors, Hungarian Gypsies who had managed to emerge from the other end of the dark tunnel of Treblinka by pretending to be Jews. This greatest of ironies was at the heart of the combined resentment and gratitude that nagged at Zelaro's father, though neither parent really ever discussed the camp experience itself. All his father ever said was that, bad as it had been for the Jews, it had been worse for the Gypsies. As a child, Zelaro knew very few Jews, but as an adult, he came to know many, including two who became close friends. He watched with interest as they and their families coped with the banal but mostly harmless discrimination still levelled against them, and wondered how he would stand up under something more stringent.

As for Gypsies, there were few of them in his childhood life, and gradually they disappeared. His parents always identified themselves as Hungarians, and Zelaro did too. Other than Joyce, he couldn't think of a single person he'd ever told the truth. It was not a big deal, after all. Being a Gypsy was more a state of mind or a way of life than anything as definitive as nationality or religion. That's what Zelaro told himself, at any rate.

Guy was an only child, and was doted on. He was close to his parents, and probably would not have left the country—would have taken his chances with the draft board, courts, even prison—had they still been alive when the time came. But their health had never been good and they both died relatively young, his father when Guy was at university, his mother a few years later. At least she had the satisfaction of seeing her son on a successful path, working on his first reporting job after graduation, back in Detroit at the *News*.

As he pondered a response to Taffy's e-mail, Zelaro considered certain confluences of events: his father's death, from a heart attack, had come not long after that one memorable date with the luminescent-skinned girl; his mother had been diagnosed with cancer earlier, within a month or two of the Kennedy assassination, seemed to have it beat, but then succumbed to a relapse a few years later, just weeks before Zelaro's draft notice arrived. When it did, he'd already thought it through and left for Canada without hesitation.

He resisted the notion that there was any discernible pattern in these events, or that there was anything pushing him and Taffy Rowman together, but, like a schoolboy enmeshed in a romantic daydream, he felt a definite magnetic force pulling him toward her.

As it happened, he had had lunch earlier that week with a colleague, a married woman he was friendly with, who told him the following story:

As a young woman at university, she had been stalked by a quirky man who turned out to be the brother of a recent acquaintance. She learned of this connection by accident during a conversation with the other woman. She also learned that the brother—the stalker—was long dead; he had killed himself years ago. This left Zelaro's friend wondering if she had played any part in the man's death.

"What do you mean by stalk, exactly?" Zelaro asked.

"I'm probably exaggerating," the woman said. "We went on one date and then he wouldn't take no for an answer. He kept hanging around, phoning, sending me gifts. After a while it got creepy. Wherever I'd go, there he'd be. There wasn't ever any violence, though, or even the threat of it."

"How did you get rid of him?"

"No court order or anything dramatic like that. I just finally got through to him that I wasn't interested. I had to be a lot blunter than I was comfortable being."

"Doesn't really sound like stalking to me," Zelaro said, but in a reasonable tone so the woman wouldn't get defensive. "More like persistence. Men used to be like that." He laughed. "Maybe still are."

"Oh, you're probably right," his friend said agreeably. "I was really sorry I used that word in describing it to his sister. But she didn't object. Apparently he'd done it to other women."

Zelaro replayed this conversation several times as he composed his reply to Taffy. The last thing he wanted was to seem invasive.

⊗

Zelaro's wife, who had been a special needs teacher, died in the most pointless of ways. At a four-way stop in suburban Regina, just after dark, she looked both ways, then edged her little yellow Toyota into the intersection, only to be broadsided by a couple of teenagers in a pickup truck. Joyce was killed on impact; the second teenager was thrown through the windshield and was taken to hospital, covered in blood, where he died. The driver received not a scratch, but was sent to jail for eighteen months and would have two deaths on his conscience for the rest of his own life. Zelaro, who was numb for months after the accident, remembers vividly the look of sullen resentment the boy's mother shot him as they left the courthouse, as if the whole thing had somehow been his fault.

⊗

"You're a regular Sherlock Holmes," he e-mailed Taffy. "Saskatchewan and government, but not necessarily in that order. Like so many others of my tribe, I succumbed to the romantic notion—myth?—that I could maybe make a difference. Believe me, as director of communications for the education department, even with the NDP, differences I might make are rarely ones to be proud of."

He wondered if that sounded too cynical, but thought it perhaps caught an echo of her own tone in the advertising book, which he was now rereading. Before hitting the Send button, though, he did go back and change "tribe" to "trade," concerned she might think he was referring to Gypsies. That was ridiculous, of course, since no one knew that about him, probably could not know, but, having made the change, he left it.

⊗

Zelaro's father had been a violinist, his mother a dancer. That is to say, he taught the violin to a succession of sweaty-palmed young less-than-virtuosos at a private academy in Detroit, while she instructed classes in ballet and folk dancing at a similar school in the suburb of Deerfield Park. His father wore a suit and tie every working day; only the flowered peasant skirts and black tights his mother favoured gave any hint of his parents' backgrounds, but then peasant skirts and tights were common among the dancers his mother taught. Just as they were closed-mouthed about their experiences during the war, his parents rarely spoke about their families or their own childhoods and lives as young adults in Europe. But young Guy was able to piece together a few things: they were both raised among large extended families in travelling caravans that worked the countryside and towns of Hungary and Romania, a lifestyle the boy found all but impossible to imagine. His parents met while working in a musical troupe and didn't care for each other at first; they were thrown together during the tumult of the war. After his mother's death, Guy found himself wondering if, though they'd been affectionate enough, his parents had ever really loved each other, or if theirs had been a marriage of convenience, as if they had turned to each other for comfort.

⊗

Their initial e-mail exchange was in the fall. By April, when an education ministers' meeting brought him to Toronto for three days, Zelaro and Taffy had become regular e-mail correspondents. It was only natural that they would want to meet. He'd let her know—as casually as he was able to muster in a carefully crafted note—that he'd be in town, and she'd quickly written back to invite him to dinner. He countered that, since he'd be on expenses, he should take her out to a restaurant, but she insisted.

He knew more about her and more about her current thinking on a variety of topics than he did about many of his friends: she was divorced, her children grown and away from home; she was against globalization, for the demonstrators, sympathetic to the Israelis but to the Palestinians as well, horrified by the September 11 attacks but equally horrified by the attack on civil liberties and the invasion of Iraq. She, in turn, knew more about him, at least at a slant, than almost anyone before or since Joyce. Sitting at his computer in the darkened den, the only light radiating from the screen upon which the motion of his fingers produced words, he found it possible to lift some of the restraints he normally felt on himself—up to a point.

Since his wife's death, Zelaro had gone on dates with a number of women and "been involved," as the saying goes, with one or two, but nothing had stuck—he hadn't really wanted anything to stick. He sometimes thought, in an admittedly perverse way, that he was lucky: he and Joyce had been married only eighteen years; he had no reason to think they would have fallen out of love with each other, but the fact was they still had been *in* love, and that was a comfort to him. He regretted they didn't have children, of course—there was no living reminder of her—but he had his memories, and they were untainted. He had no great desire to replace her.

But—and this was so curious—he had this memory of Taffy too, the flawlessness of her face shining in the frigid air, the not-attempted kiss. He knew he was not in love with this woman he didn't really know, but—he admitted this—he was in love, well, half in love, with the idea of her.

⊗

He called from the hotel at noon of his second day in Toronto to ask if he could bring anything.

"No, just yourself. I've already got a nice bottle of white wine in the fridge. And I've got some slivovitz, if you're so inclined. I'm making something I'm sure you'll like." Slivovitz—that was the famous Hungarian plum brandy. Was the "something" goulash? What did this woman expect? What had he said?

"Slivovitz," he said aloud. "Should I be bringing videos of your father's movies?"

As impulsively as that came out, he knew it was a risk, but she responded with an immediate, full-throated laugh. "Oh, I've got them all, don't worry about that. And no, I won't show even a one of them to you, don't worry about that either. Not even a minute's worth."

Zelaro had struggled to be forthcoming with her. He'd mentioned that his parents were Hungarian, but no more. "When I was eight or nine, I noticed a tattoo on my mother's arm for the first time," he wrote in one of his e-mails, composed late at night. But he deleted that sentence before sending.

The row of digits forming a blue smudge on the upper wrist of his mother's left arm was still as vivid to him now as when he'd first seen it. Usually she wore blouses or dresses with long sleeves, but on this day, as he remembered it, she was in the bathroom in her slip, standing in front of a mirror. He wouldn't ordinarily have been in there with her, but she'd called him to get her something.

"What's that, Mommy?" he asked, touching her wrist gingerly.

"Oh, that?" The compact she held in her other hand clattered into the sink, and the hand darted to grip her wrist, covering the smudge. Young Guy was amazed by the look of consternation, confusion, and tenderness she gave him—at least, those were the emotions that the unexpected look that swept over his mother's features appeared to convey to the boy.

Almost fifty years later, he could still remember that look and the one of utter helplessness that succeeded it, and how the boy he then was had pondered their meaning. Joyce, who had come into his life long after his mother's death, always, inexplicably, made him feel as if he were somehow close to her again. Now, thoughts of Taffy Rowman were bringing his mother back into his life one more time. It was odd, but thinking about Taffy didn't bring Joyce to mind, as he would have expected, but his mother. Sitting at his computer late at night, rereading an e-mail from Taffy, he could almost smell the rich spice of his mother's perfume.

In the taxi from his hotel to Taffy's home in the Beaches that evening, the thought crossed his mind that, with parents and wife dead, no other known relatives and no siblings, there was not a soul in the world who knew he was not just Hungarian but a Gypsy. Did that matter? No, of course it didn't. Yet he looked forward to the moment when he'd be able to tell this woman. He didn't know why it was important, but it was.

* * *

A Man of Distinction

My own grandfather was a man of modest means and ambition. Nevertheless, his impact on the family, if not the greater world, was considerable. While his gesture may have seemed small and merely personal to him, he changed the course of the family's future, radically and permanently, by immigrating to the New World. He made other changes to his life, his outlook and behaviour which further modified the fortunes of the Bell family, setting the feet of his children and theirs in directions which would have been unimaginable to my grandfather's own father, my great-grandfather, who, it would appear, had no ambition whatsoever.

—from *My Life, In and Out of Medicine,*
a memoir by George Alexander Bell, MD
Montreal: Medical Press, 1957

MY GRANDFATHER WAS A MAN of distinction, but also of distinctions. He was a generous supporter of his church, and his name, George Alexander Bell, anchors the central panel of the magnificent triptych of stained glass that stands behind the altar of the First Presbyterian on Albert Street, where, even to this day, my family enjoys a privileged place. He also gave his name, along with that of a colleague, to Bell-Timmins Syndrome, a rare malady of the nerves they discovered while working with patients suffering from multiple sclerosis, and to the Bell Clinic at the General Hospital. And, last but certainly not least, he was one of the four dozen souls who perished, through no fault of their own, in the celebrated sinking of the Andrea Doria, the luxury Italian liner that went down off the coast of Nantucket in 1956 after a collision with another ship.

Even one of these distinctions would be enough to cast anyone's grandfather into larger-than-life proportions, but four is truly heroic, transforming the shadow George Bell cast on our family into something akin to that of a giant oak in an orchard of cherry trees. Forgive my hyperbole, but that's the effect my grandfather's storied memory has on me.

I never had any idea there was a secret hidden in that shadow, that there was yet another distinction that I, and perhaps no one else, was aware of, a distinction I myself may have inherited.

Children daydream of glories, but since I've been an adult I've always thought of myself as a person bereft of distinction. I'm a violinist, but not a particularly good one. I play in the symphony orchestra, one of many anonymous faces in the string section, sustained and made secure by reliable competence, but I am no soloist or disciplined enough even for a quartet. I play in the occasional theatrical production, and other musical odds and ends. I find this satisfying enough.

And I teach, of course, as one must, and manage to make a decent enough living. In fact, I'm a pretty good teacher, a better teacher than a violinist, which is to say I'm good at communicating my thoughts to students, good at getting them to respond, good at motivating, and I'm patient to a fault. I have a good eye and ear for talent, and I've had several students over the years who, I readily recognized, had more of it than I do.

I will never have fame or fortune, will never bestow my name on anything, and I know it.

None of this particularly distresses me. Of course, I would prefer to be better at what I do—who doesn't? As a youth, I daydreamed of a soloist's life, as do all promising music students, even though I knew that to be unlikely. But despite my shortcomings and disappointments, I cannot say that my life has been one of disappointment. I have a lovely wife, two wonderful children, a fine home—what sounds like a litany of expected clichés, except that my life has been happy. I never had great expectations for myself as a musician—that was my parents' dream, really, particularly my father's. His own life had been stunted by the shadow of *his* father, my eminent grandfather, and he had allowed himself to recede as a personality, like a recessive gene that produces certain characteristics or disorders in alternating generations. He was a lacklustre student, bringing that part of his life to a sudden end with the outbreak of war in 1939; he joined the army, but flat feet kept him out of action. Later, he had an undistinguished career as a civil servant. I doubt if he knew his father's secret; if he did, he kept it to himself.

As his father was his burdensome pride, his children were his liberating hope, what he chose to live for. My sister showed an inclination toward science early on, as my father had not, and, through the dint of his will and her own, she overcame a mild learning disability and has become a physician of note. She hasn't yet identified a syndrome, but she's still young. I showed some small promise at music. It was actually my *mother's* idea that I take up the violin, after an initial venture at piano, with an inept teacher, proved frustrating. At any rate, I showed sufficient promise with this instrument for my father to seize on, enough promise and competence to get me through the long series of classes, trials, recitals, graduate schools, the long series of teachers, some terrible, some inspired, none as good as I am, I'm afraid, but one memorable one, at least, with the gift of patience that informs and inspires me even today. I often think of him, long-legged Mr. Greenshields, with his shiny elbows and smelly pipe, as I instruct a clumsy student, whereas, up until recently, I rarely thought of my grandfather, all his distinctions rolled up together. He's been dead for many years, and, at any rate, I never knew him.

And yet my grandfather haunts me, as he does my sister. She has given in to his ghost; a large, ornately framed photograph of him, all whiskers, scowl, and starched collar, adorns one wall of her private office in Toronto, next to the degrees from Harvard and Johns Hopkins. On particularly difficult cases, she tells me, she occasionally confers with him.

"How would you proceed, Grandfather?" she asks aloud, the "Grandfather" she addresses him as no more formal than it should be, considering that neither of us really knew the man, his final ship having gone down while we were both small children. I have no actual memory of him; she, two years my senior, claims a fuzzy recollection. He is, she says, a presence in her life nonetheless.

Not so in mine, not that way. Until now.

He was an author, of course—men of distinction usually are. He'd written a number of articles for the medical press and one surprisingly readable popular essay on nerves that appeared in *The Reader's Digest*. And, just a year before his premature death in 1956, as if prophesying his own quick end, he'd written a modest enough memoir, which lay in a desk drawer until its discovery after the memorial service—his body, of course, was never recovered—by his wife, my grandmother (she was one of the lucky ones who got into a lifeboat and was spared), who quickly arranged for it to be published. I have all these publications and other writings, in manuscript form, as well as his letters to my grandmother and a few to his children, and some of his favourite books, but they had all lain uninspected and unread, in a trunk in the attic, for years. My own son, Alex, made the discovery.

"What are these books, Dad, do you know?" he asked me. "What language is it?"

Home from university for the summer, he'd gone upstairs to rummage around in some old things of his and come across my grandfather's trunk. I was a favourite of my grandmother, perhaps because she loved music, and she'd thought his papers might have some meaning for me. I was touched by the gift, which came to me after her death, over two decades ago, but after a cursory glance through them, they'd gone back into the trunk; I hadn't touched them since.

Now here was Alex, a big soft teddy bear of a man-child with a very earnest expression on his face, a Bell face in most ways, fleshy nose, muddy brown eyes, thick lashes and eyebrows, offering me two books. They were both slim, the same size and thickness and cheaply bound in the same black leather. They appeared identical except that one was obviously in more pristine condition than the other.

"Let's take a look. Where did they come from?" I turned my lamp up to a higher intensity and took the books into my lap.

"From Grampa's trunk. It was with his own books and his letters to Grandma."

There's something endearing about Alex's use of such familiar names for people he never knew, couldn't possibly have known. His own grandparents—my mother and father, and Beth's—all encouraged the use of their first names, so the children never had real people to call Grampa and Grandma. Somehow, in our talk of *my* grandfather and grandmother, those titles became attached. Alex, of course, is named for the eminent man, and so has always had a bit of interest in him.

It was clear the two books were in fact the same, but one had been heavily used. Its pages were dog-eared and blemished by what appeared to be coffee stains and numerous underlinings and tiny margin jottings, the black ink faded, the handwriting all but unintelligible. What appeared to be the title pages of both books were at the end, rather than the beginning, and were followed by a dark, grainy photograph of an old man, stiff in a high-collared suit and beard. Most notable, though, was that the books were not only in a strange language but an unfamiliar alphabet.

I looked up at Alex, who had settled himself on the arm of my chair. "Not Greek, surely."

Alex laughed. "No, Dad, not Greek, modern *or* ancient."

"Not Latin, either," I said amiably.

"It's Hebrew, I think."

"Hebrew? I was just about to guess Arabic."

"Why would you think that, Dad?"

"I don't know . . . it's a language a doctor might be interested in. Why would you think Hebrew?"

"That's what it looks like. See these two dots over this letter?" He pointed at the page with a stubby finger, neither a violinist's finger nor a surgeon's. Alex hasn't found himself yet, doesn't know what he wants to put his fingers to. "That's a characteristic of Hebrew, I think."

I closed the book I'd been inspecting and leaned back in my chair, studying my son with a slightly new interest. "You've become a linguist. Congratulations. You've been studying Hebrew at school and neglected to mention it?" He had, in fact, read French fluently since grade school, and taken Spanish in high school.

He smiled. "No, Dad, hardly a linguist, though I've thought about it. Not linguistics, but language. They come easily to me. I haven't studied Hebrew, but I've seen it. A guy I know at school spent the summer in Israel and he has some newspapers and magazines in Hebrew at his place. That's what this looks like."

"You're probably right, then," I said. "But why would your great-grandfather have a Hebrew book? Two of the same one?"

"I don't know, Dad. That's why I asked you."

⊗

Can you see where this is going? I couldn't. Two copies of a book in a strange language among my grandfather's possessions, one of them annotated. Was my grandmother sending me a message? Or was the message from the great man himself, the distinguished Dr. George Alexander Bell? Alex and I pored over the jottings, trying to glean some meaning from them, at least. An occasional word—"Hfx" and "Wpg," which I took to be shorthand for Halifax and Winnipeg, and "metal"—leapt out to confirm that the jottings were in English, even if the book itself was not, but other than that they told us nothing.

Alex soon grew tired of this inquiry and left me to pore, unsuccessfully, over the margin jottings, which I assumed to be in my grandfather's hand. The next day, the two books were still lying on the end table next to my reading chair. I *tsk-tsked* that Alex hadn't returned them to the trunk in the attic, but I didn't return them either. I placed them on my desk, and, within a week, I slipped the more heavily used copy into my jacket pocket when I left for the conservatory.

This should, perhaps, have been my son's errand. He could have taken the book to the university, where he'd have had no trouble finding a professor to identify it, even in summer. But if it was the hand of my grandfather orchestrating what was about to happen, as I believe, it was clearly his will that it should happen to me, not to Alex. Clear to me, I should say.

Armenstein's office is down the hall from mine on the third floor of the old building that houses the conservatory, where we both teach. Up there, the ceilings slope at uncomfortable angles, and a man as tall as I can easily bump his head. Armenstein has no such problem but he is, we both know, a far better musician at his cello than I with my violin. He's a short man with a round face who, when he plays, seems to become one with his cello, as if his body was designed for the instrument, it for him. In the orchestra, he is the principal for the cellos, while I am only one of many in the second violins. I suspect I am the better teacher, though.

None of these distinctions interferes with our friendly relationship. His son, Arthur, was a student of mine several years ago, and I always ask after him, as I did that day. "Hello, Rupert. What do you hear from that talented son of yours?"

"Ah, that boy," he said dryly in a faint, generic European accent that could have been Czech or Swiss as easily as German, where I knew he'd spent time. But he'd been born in Israel and had lived there until he was a young man and left to avoid military service. How he wound up here I have no idea. "You think he'd have time to drop a line now and then to his parents who are still paying his bills? I'm the wrong one to ask, George."

The sound of a violin could be heard from the rehearsal studio at the end of the hall. "How's your Hebrew, Rupert?" I asked.

"My Hebrew? Rusty. Even the wife doesn't like to use it, so I don't get much practice. Just at *shul,* but how often do I get there?" He shrugged, smiling, showing even, white teeth.

"But I still dream in it sometimes. And sing it in the shower." He smiled ruefully.

"Can you take a look at something for me?" I took the book from my pocket and offered it to him.

"Look? Sure. Just let me ..." He fumbled in his the pocket of his loose-fitting cardigan for a pair of glasses. "Now, what?"

"I was wondering if this was Hebrew."

"And I'm the only Jew you know, I suppose." He was smiling broadly, to indicate this was only the mildest of accusations.

"I'm afraid you're right," I admitted, my own smile sheepish.

He squinted at the book, turning it over in his hand before opening it, from the rear. He glanced at the title page and the photograph, then rifled through the pages, pausing here and there to peer closer.

"Ah," Armenstein said. He brought the book closer to his face, squinting. "Ah," he repeated. He looked up. "Where'd you get this book? It's old." He thumbed quickly back to the title page. "No date, but it's old. Published in Warsaw, see here?" He pointed to the bottom of the title page. "In Poland."

"It was my grandfather's. It was with some other stuff of his in the attic." I took the chair across from Armenstein's desk.

"Ah, the famous Dr. Bell."

I smiled. "Even you've heard of him."

"The clinic. My wife's mother ..."

"Oh, yes, I remember. So, what do you think? Did the famous Dr. Bell know Hebrew? I think maybe those notes are his."

He looked down at the book again. "Close, but no cigar." He smiled broadly at his use of the acquired expression. "This is Yiddish. Same alphabet, different language."

"Yid ..." For a moment, I was blank.

"You know, the Jewish language. *Schmuck, schmooze, chutzpah, mish-mosh* ... all Yiddish words. You're surprised, obviously."

"I guess I am," I said.

He looked at me frankly, the look of a man who's known another man for a long time, not well, but well enough for certain confidences should the occasion arise.

"I *thought* you were a Jew," he said. "Ask my wife; I told her as much. You can always tell."

⊗

To the attic I went now, to the trunk, gathering up the letters and the slim memoir, my nostrils filling with dust and the cloying smell of age and nostalgia, a mixture of pressed flowers and camphor. Along with the papers and books I'd inherited from my grandmother, the trunk had become conveniently crammed with my own and my wife's papers—letters, diplomas, yearbooks, and class photos from high school and the conservatory through university, and years' worth of Christmas and birthday cards Beth insists on keeping. All these I placed in a cardboard box, leaving only those which bore some stamp of my grandfather—"the famous Dr. Bell" indeed, although my lips turned into a half smile at the sharp memory of Armenstein's softly mocking tone. (Had he actually been mocking? I wasn't sure.)

And to my study, a thick bundle of letters fastened by a pink ribbon and a slimmer packet in a rubber band, a stack of medical journals, and the memoir positioned squarely in the centre of the otherwise clean blotter on my desk. To the side, a stack of half a dozen or so books, medical texts primarily, that had belonged to my grandfather. (I knew that other such books were in my sister's library.) I examined these for signs of annotations, and found many examples of the same cramped handwriting, the same faded ink. Clearly, then, the writing in the Yiddish book was my grandfather's.

I'm a meticulous sort of person, a *careful* person, so my examination of all this material took longer than it would have someone like my wife, who would have gotten down on the floor, the papers scattered around her, and perhaps found what she was looking for in hours. In my hands, it was days, in hours set aside evenings and minutes stolen mornings and afternoons between more pressing matters, a growing sense of—what? *Dread?* No, why would I even think such a term?—

well, whatever it was ticking in me as my licked thumb dried on the edges of dusty pages and my eyes blurred behind the assault of unfamiliar diction and syntax.

Of course, Armenstein hadn't really mocked me, but the assurance with which he leapt to his conclusion struck me as smug, self-satisfied. That bothered me, but reflecting on why it did bothered me even more.

It had surprised me that he couldn't read the language he so readily identified—"Why should I?" he'd asked. "Most of the people in my family who did know it were killed in the war, and my parents took to Hebrew as soon as they arrived in Israel." But that hadn't stopped him from quickly putting things into place.

"I'd say this was a memoir by one of your ancestors. Haven't you told me your grandfather wrote a memoir? This is probably by his father or his own grandfather, these jottings notes for his own book. So he must have been able to read it." He looked up and looked at me closely. Then his furry eyebrows rose and his expression softened. "This is all news to you, George, clearly."

"It is."

He returned his attention to the book. "A typical doctor, your grandfather, presuming these are in fact his notes. They're in English—I guess that's what it is—but I can't make heads or tails of it."

I laughed. "Me neither. And the ink's so faded..."

"But he must have been able to read the Yiddish," Armenstein said. "I mean, if he was writing notes, he must..."

"Yes." Beyond that, I could think of nothing to say.

He turned to the photograph and scrutinized it carefully, looked up and gazed thoughtfully at me, then back to the photo. "There's a resemblance, George, no doubt about it." He glanced at me again. "I'm not making this up. You're in shock, my friend."

"I believe I am," I said.

"Don't be. Being Jewish is not so bad." He chuckled softly. "As these things go, there are worse fates."

Armenstein turned again to the book, a mischievous smile flickering at the corners of his fleshy lips. "A good looking man, this ancestor of yours. Your great-grandfather, great-great-grandfather, whatever. No violin player, though—look at those hands. Belinsky, probably, or Belzberg, a tinker, maybe, or a ragman. But with aspirations..." He hefted the book, as if weighing its value. "A rabbi, maybe, who knows."

He looked at me and his smile softened. "Before the war, George, a dozen million people used Yiddish, did you know that? After, not so many. Even here, in Canada, there were plenty of Yiddish speakers, Montreal, Toronto.... A couple million in New York alone, I've heard. Now..." He gestured vaguely with his hand. "There's some fellows who could read this, old-timers I know at the synagogue. I'll give you some names if you'd like. They might enjoy the diversion."

The piece of paper with three names and phone numbers on it sat under a glass paperweight on my desk, just to the left of the blotter. I hadn't phoned any of them yet but was glad enough to have their names at hand. The book and its contents were the treasure chest at the end of my search, and I wanted to satisfy myself first, by myself, that it was a direction I wished to go.

I glanced at my grandfather's published articles, but all were technical approaches to medical questions or reports on research, and were not germane. The *Reader's Digest* article was informative and amusing, showing a lighter side to the man, but again, not relevant. I began to read the memoir, which, to tell the truth, I'd never read before, but I quickly put it aside, not because it was not engaging, but because I felt unprepared for what it might hold. Instead, I began the curious task of reading my grandfather's letters.

I say "curious" because it was both a pleasure to eavesdrop on his private conversation with his wife and children—a conversation going back more than seventy years—and a frustrating exercise. At another time, I might have felt like a guilty, slightly embarrassed voyeur, openly smiling at his displays of affection to my grandmother and stern, almost hectoring advice to my father and his siblings. But now, it was information I was seeking, clues, and I raced through the letters—handwritten to my grandmother, mostly typewritten to my father and uncle and aunts—without satisfaction.

The letters to my grandmother were written in a larger, more careful hand than that used for the jottings in the book, the letters more clearly articulated, and the ink was less faded, so I was able to understand much of what I read. They were hardly what could be called love letters. If there'd been any of those, she had discreetly removed them from the collection she bequeathed to me. These letters to her—written from a number of Canadian cities where he was attending medical conferences and the like—were chatty and affectionate—he referred to her as "my dear" and "my darling wife"—but contained no clues for me. If my grandfather had shared his secret—presuming even he actually had one—with his wife, he hadn't committed it to paper.

The letters to his children were also devoid of clues. One letter to my father, dated March 1933, when he would have been thirteen or fourteen, was particularly revealing, but of my grandfather's character, nothing else. My grandfather was then in Montreal, I gathered, doing research, and was responding to a report from his wife that their son's mid-term grades were disappointing. "It looks to me very much as if you must be starting on the toboggan of which we earlier spoke again," he wrote. "The only possible result of such laxness is heartache for your mother and a miserable summer for you." How this letter, much wrinkled, as if it had been crumpled, then smoothed out and refolded, came to be among his papers I could only imagine.

Finally, I turned again to the memoir. Most of it, of course, covers my grandfather's life as an adult, his years as a medical student and resident, experiences as a researcher and physician, including frontline work in France during the Great War, his move to Regina and establishment of a practice and the clinic which would later bear his name, involvement in civic and church affairs, his life as a husband and father. The writing is formal by the standards of a memoir, with a style and tone somewhere between that of the serious scientific writing of his journal articles and the more popular prose of the *Reader's Digest*. It is interesting, but not particularly revealing.

The chapter I read with most interest was the first, in which my grandfather recounts very briefly a history of the Bell family and some of his experiences as a child growing up in Winnipeg. He was the third child of seven, the eldest son of four, to Alexander and Rosalind Bell, who, in his depiction, were the most ordinary of parents. Rosalind, he wrote, was a daughter of homesteaders from the Rondeau district. Their last name is not given. She went no further than Grade 8 in school, and married at seventeen. No more was said of her family, and very little more about her, perhaps because she died young, when my grandfather was still in his teens. If he harboured any lasting affection for her, he failed to reveal it.

Alexander Bell received not much more attention. He was, his son wrote, a good-hearted, hard-working man, with his own small hardware store. The father's father—my grandfather's grandfather, his given name not referred to—had immigrated to Canada from Great Britain in the middle of the nineteenth century, settling first in Halifax, then in Brampton, Ontario, where he was, the memoir says obliquely, "in the metals business"—I recalled Armenstein's guess of tinker as a trade for my ancestor with a shiver—and married a woman named Esther. No more is said of her. No precise dates are given and there is no further information about the founder of the Bell family in Canada or his predecessors.

My next step was to open an envelope which, I had already ascertained, contained the manuscript of the memoir. There were, to the 150 or so pages in the book, over 300 pages in the typescript, which, according to an acknowledgment note in the book, was prepared by a Wilma Rychuk, the secretary-receptionist at my grandfather's private practice. I thumbed through the pages and saw numerous editing marks and notes in the margin, all in the same faded black ink used in the Yiddish book, all in the hand that by now was so familiar to me.

I turned with some anticipation to the first chapter, seeking references to my grandfather's father and grandfather. What I was seeking, of course, were signs of alteration—deletions, additions, crossed out sentences—anything that would indicate more had been written about his family and later removed, either by my grandfather or someone else. My heart leapt when I discovered something that pointed to that possibility exactly: a missing page.

Early in the chapter, in the section devoted to my grandfather's grandfather, the manuscript went abruptly from page 9 to page 11. It would have been easy to overlook this—the paragraph at the bottom of page 9 concludes there. A new paragraph begins at the top of page 11. The transition from page to page reads smoothly at first glance, but, on rereading, it is a bit awkward, disjointed, as if something were missing. I opened my grandfather's book and compared the two versions—they were identical.

Now I did have a mystery. Was this a simple matter of misnumbering or was there actually a missing page? If the latter, what did it say? Who removed it? Would it shed some light on the Bell family's origins—I was not yet able to put that question in blunter terms: were we, at least in part, Jewish?

There were few places to turn. My grandfather, of course, was long dead. So was my grandmother. My own parents had died a few years earlier. There was no reason to think my sister would know anything of family history that I didn't, so I saw no reason to concern her with the question. (It should go without mention that I'd spoken not a word of all this to my wife and children up to this point, brushing aside with joking mysteriousness their now repeated questions about what I was up to in my study.) I'd already ascertained that the publishing company that had produced my grandfather's book was no longer in business, and there was no indication in the book of who, if anyone, had edited it. I was sure that Wilma Rychuk, the typist, would be dead; our city is small enough that, with two telephone calls, I was able to confirm that. The only person I could think to ask was my aunt Marilyn, my father's youngest sister and the only one of his siblings still alive.

Aunt Mags lives in Toronto, widowed for more than ten years, in her seventies but still on her own and still physically active and sharp. I have never been particularly close to her, as my sister is, but visits to and from her and Uncle Jim and their three children were routine parts of my childhood. We've kept up, though, and, in fact, Beth and I had visited with Mags just the previous year when we were in Toronto on holidays.

That evening, after supper, I telephoned. She seemed delighted to hear from me, and we spent several minutes exchanging news of our children. Then, the pleasantries out of the way, I went right to the question; I had given much thought to how to approach it.

"Aunt Mags, is there something about our family I don't know?"

"What do you mean?"

"I don't know . . . anything."

Mags laughed. I've already said she is in her seventies and a widow but neglected to mention she is an exceptionally good-natured, good-hearted person, an easy laugher. "Well, George, I think there are things in any family not everybody knows. My Jim's father was in prison when he was a young man—did you know that?"

"Uncle Jim? No, I didn't."

"Well, neither did Jim, until he was your age and he discovered it by accident; I forget how exactly. But unlike you, his dad was still alive, so he could ask him. Not that it did him any good—Grandpa wouldn't talk about it. We never did find out what it was all about. Did you find out some wicked secret about that big brother of mine? Is that what this is about?" She laughed again, a full, throaty laugh.

"Not exactly." I don't know why this was so hard to get into words, but it was. Still, I managed to blurt out: "Aunt Mags, are we Jewish? Were we?"

"Oh, Lord," Mags said." Then there was a bang and the line went abruptly dead.

I stared at the phone in amazement, put the receiver in the

cradle, then put it to my ear and listened for a moment to the dial tone. I replaced it and was just about to lift it again and press the redial button when it rang.

"It's me, dear. Don't be alarmed. I didn't hang up on you, and I didn't faint from shock." Aunt Mags laughed self-consciously. "I dropped the phone, but it was just an accident. My arthritis ... sometimes my hands don't hold things too well. Now. You were asking if we're Jewish. If I may ask *you* a question, where did *that* come from?"

"Dropping the phone aside, Aunt Mags, you don't sound surprised. You've heard this before."

"Answer *my* question, George."

Briefly, I told her about the Yiddish book, Armenstein's comments, the missing page in the manuscript. When I finished, there was a long silence. I was about to say something when finally my aunt spoke.

"Well, George, I think you know as much about it as I do, probably more. Yes ..." She hesitated.

"So we are? Jewish, I mean?"

"Yes, I believe we have Jewish roots, on my father's side, a generation or two back. I'll leave it to the genealogists to say whether or not we're Jewish."

"How come I've never hard of this, Aunt Mags?"

"Oh, George, you make it sound like a plot. No one ever talked much about it, that's all. There was no conspiracy to keep it a secret. I believe we have some Black Irish in the family too, which is worse, in my view. Oh, I didn't mean that the way it sounds. It just wasn't talked about. My Jim was a regular Heinz 57, with Irish and Scottish and English and German and God only knows what else. He always thought a little Iroquois, on his mother's side. My point is, he was a mix, and no one in his family made any fuss about any particular part. The same with our family.

"You never met your grandfather, George. I don't mean this in a critical way, because I loved him dearly, but my father was not the sort of man who talked easily to children, or the sort of man who children went easily to with questions. And

I don't think our mother knew much more about it. It was our grandfather, or maybe even *his* father, who changed the family name, not my father. So it was already a *fait accomplis* by the time Mother married Father. We can't blame either of them."

"I'm not looking to apply blame, Mags."

"I just meant, whatever happened, it was long ago. And, like I said, every family has things that aren't talked about."

"Like love affairs and abortions."

"Well, yes." She laughed again. "And we've had a few of that sort of thing in our family. I could tell you about some of *them*."

"But isn't this different?"

"I don't know, is it?"

"Isn't it?"

"Why, George?"

I couldn't say. But after we had concluded the call, I knew what I had to do. I can't say exactly why this was important to me, just that it was. I sat in my study, my grandfather's well-worn Yiddish book in my lap, thumbing through the pages, trying again to decipher some of his notes. What had *he* been searching for in it? I gazed at the photograph of the man who I had now accepted, as Armenstein had been so quick to conclude, to be my great-grandfather or great-great-grandfather, though, frankly, I was still unable to see any resemblance. This unknown forefather's eyes were so dark, his expression so inscrutable—what had *he* been seeking? His hands, as Armenstein had pointed out, looked large and rough, certainly not a violinist's hands, or a surgeon's.

I couldn't say why I wanted to know more about this man, just that I did. I thought about my contented life, the satisfaction I felt about most things, and I thought about my father and his lack of satisfaction. It crossed my mind that I might be endangering my sense of satisfaction, but for one of the few times in my life, I felt no hesitation at the thought of facing a danger, if that's what it even was. "How would *you* proceed, Grandfather?" I said aloud, although I was certain I already knew the answer. I reached for the list of names

Armenstein had given me. The first name was Sid Handel, who Armenstein had said was a retired pharmacist with a collection of Yiddish books. I took a look at his number and reached for the phone.

* * *

A Young Lady from West Virginia

MY HUSBAND WAS a sailor in the war.

In the first year, April 1942, it was, I went to meet him in Eden, Virginia, for a weekend before he shipped out, travelling on this very train. He'd just finished training and we didn't know where he was going for sure, just to sea and that it might be a long time before we had a chance to see each other again, if ever, though I wouldn't allow myself to think of that. I was aching to see him.

I was twenty years old, in my final year at Walden College, in Ravenswood, West Virginia, and I'd never before been on a train, if you can imagine.

We'd only been married a few months, but we hadn't been together since the day after our wedding. We'd been planning a June wedding, right after I graduated, but Pearl Harbor changed everything. Bud joined the Navy the next day, and we got married three days later, December 11, 1941, a small ceremony, just Bud and I and our parents and a few sisters and brothers, in Judge Carter's living room. The judge and my father had been college roommates, and he couldn't say no to us. Then there was one night in the Walden Inn and the very next day Bud was off to Norfolk.

We had been expecting he would have a week or two's leave after he finished training, but it turned out to be a weekend pass and that was all. His ship would be leaving Norfolk the following Monday. He sent me a letter saying I should take the train from Ravenswood to Eden, that it got there around four in the afternoon, and that he'd be there a few hours later, a little before eight. He didn't say anything about where we should meet, so I wrote back asking, and, because he didn't get my letter till Thursday, he phoned. There wasn't anyone home at my parents', where I was still living, so he called Bob

Jackson's store, and Mr. Jackson came over with the message that evening, that Bud didn't know the names of any of the hotels in Eden, so maybe the best thing would be just to meet at the railway station, if I didn't mind waiting. Mind waiting? Oh, my! Why, I would have waited not just hours but days or weeks for Bud.

I remember it was a lovely trip, a couple of hours through rolling hills that were newly green, just as they are today, the trees filled with young leaves and blossoms swaying in the breeze like young ladies dressed up for a party or a pageant, like the one I'd been in the year before at the college. I had a novel with me that I read a bit of on the train; it was *Emma* by Miss Austen. What a lovely book that is, so gay. It was my expectation that when I got to Eden I'd find a comfortable seat in the station waiting room and lose myself in the story for a few hours. Perhaps there'd be a cafe nearby, where I could get a cup of tea.

I'll never forget the ten minutes before the train arrived at Eden. The train comes down into a valley, as you'll see, and crosses the river on what was in those days a high trestle bridge made of timbers, then it runs through the valley along the river, the river on one side, apple orchards on the other, and then, just before it comes to the station, it crosses another bridge, this one low, and made of steel. The apple trees were in bloom, a sea of pink and white, and we passed a meadow where children were playing by the river under the swaying arms of willows so green it hurt my eyes to see them. I remember being breathless, trying to look out of the windows on both sides of the train at once.

At the Eden station there was a redcap, a nice coloured man, who helped me with my bags, and he asked if someone was coming to meet me.

"I'll be meeting my husband in four hours," I said. "He's a sailor and he's coming on the train from Norfolk. Is there a place where I can sit and read?"

"Oh, ma'am," the redcap said, "I wouldn't dream of letting you do that." He had a pained expression on his face, as if he had just learned of some terrible tragedy, the death of a child, perhaps. "What would my own wife say if I told her I'd left a fine young lady like yourself on your own in a drafty old train station? She'd give me whatfor, you can be sure of that. You and your husband will be going to a hotel, won't you?"

"Well, yes, I suppose so."

"So please allow me to take you to the hotel right now. I won't hear of anything else. The very idea of you sitting here for hours!" The redcap had a beautiful smile filled with even white teeth.

"I don't know which hotel my husband would choose," I protested.

"Oh, you leave that to me," the redcap said. He took my bags and he led me out of the station and onto the main street of the town, which was unusually wide. The sidewalks on both sides, I noticed, were lined with large earthenware urns every twenty feet or so, filled with flowers, just as in the replica of Athens they had constructed at the college for the pageant. I was struck by that.

"Is there a decent hotel here?" I asked, still feeling uncertain.

"Oh, yes, ma'am. Is there a decent hotel?" The redcap laughed, showing those white teeth of his. "There's the baths here in Eden, and the gardens, and the college nearby. Tourists come here regular as clockwork. There's several good hotels, more than decent. Just leave that to old Will. I'll take you to the best we have."

We marched down the street past one hotel that looked like it would be all right, then another on the next block. The redcap didn't give them a glance. "Just one more block," he said. He walked with his back straight, his gait almost jaunty, carrying my bags as if they were filled with feathers.

Finally, we came to a hotel called the Eden Gardens and went in. It looked so much outside and in the lobby like the Walden Inn at home, where Bud and I had spent our wedding night, with pillars and baskets of flowers and lace doilies everywhere, that I loved it at once. The redcap went right up to the counter and said to the clerk, who he seemed to know,

"The best room in the house for this nice young lady from West Virginia, Earl. She'll be joined by her husband, who she hasn't seen in some time, a sailor man from Norfolk coming in on the eight o'clock train."

There certainly wasn't anything shy about the redcap. I had never seen a coloured man so forward, so sure of himself, but the desk clerk didn't seem surprised or take offence. "Welcome to the Eden Gardens," he said to me, and to the redcap, "Don't you worry none, Willie; I'll take good care of the young lady."

The clerk gave me a room on the second floor and the redcap took my luggage up to it. I gave him a nice tip, two quarters, and thanked him. "You are the kindest man," I told him. "You saved my life."

After he left, the thought came to me that perhaps I would lie down and take a nap. There was a very inviting-looking feather bed, a four-poster. I had gotten up earlier than usual to prepare for the trip, and the train ride itself had been tiring. I thought I would just stretch out, take a little nap, then in two or three hours or so I would freshen up, have a cup of tea downstairs in the little restaurant I'd noticed off the lobby, and go back down to the station and wait for my husband's train.

I took off my hat and my shoes and lay down on top of the comforter and closed my eyes. I was so excited, thinking that in just a few short hours I'd be seeing my Bud, but I willed myself calm. My mind wandered, first to the shiny teeth of the redcap, then to the puffs of smoke I'd seen rising from the train engine, then to the lovely countryside we'd passed through, the graceful trees lining the banks of the river we'd crossed, the flowerpots lining the main street of Eden, and finally, as if the redcap had taken me by the hand and led me there, to the pageant at the college the previous spring. Oh, how wonderful that had been, how lovely! The stage had been festooned with flowers, veils, and ribbons, and I and the other young ladies who played the parts of nymphs were dressed in white costumes made of paper, with wings. We sang like a heavenly choir, and there was a woman from Louisville who played the harp.

I was at my granddaughter's graduation in Richmond last week and it was very nice, but it was nothing like that pageant; I've never seen anything like it since, really. I just don't think they have them anymore, not like that.

The pageant at Walden was part of a festival to mark the hundredth anniversary of the founding of the college; the president, FDR himself, came down from Washington to see it. I was so excited to see him, but not half as excited as my mother, who thought that Mr. Roosevelt was almost up there with God because of all he'd done for the poor people—no, not just poor people, but all the people. I remember he arrived in a car, a long black limousine, with Mrs. Roosevelt, and somebody pulled out his wheelchair, and two big men lifted him out of the car and into the chair all in one fell swoop, and in one or two seconds he was up on the stage, he and Eleanor waving to the crowd. So sad, to see him in that wheelchair, but him so brave!

He said just a few words, thanking the college for inviting him and how eager he was to see the show. "So let the festivities begin," he said, and Eleanor wheeled him to the side and the men lifted the wheelchair down and brought him to a spot that had been set aside in the front row. I remember how much he applauded all during the pageant; I could see him so clearly from the stage, and later he sent a letter to the college saying how much he had enjoyed himself, that it was the most entertaining evening he had ever spent. When they printed his letter in the paper, we could hardly believe it: all the different places he must go to as president and he never had a better, more enjoyable evening of entertainment than our pageant! My, it made us all very proud.

I thought again of the garlands of flowers that had bedecked the stage, and my mind wandered to the armfuls of wildflowers my father used to bring home to my mother in the summer. He worked in a tannery, and walking home for lunch he would pass through a field where there were bushes and bushes of elderberries. When they were in season, my father would always pause to fill his cap with berries, no more than five minutes' work, or sometimes to fill a lardpail he would carry with him for that purpose when he was planning to make wine. When Momma would see the elderberries, she'd always exclaim, "More work!" as if she were annoyed, but she said it with a little smile. She made the best elderberry jelly. She could mix it with apples somehow and make it taste just like strawberry. All sorts of other flavours too, just the most wonderful elderberry jelly. But if she minded having to make the jelly, there were the wildflowers Daddy always brought, to bribe her.

Thinking about my daddy, I remembered how, sometimes when he would go out in the evening in summer, he would bring ice cream home. There was nothing he loved more than ice cream, my father. When my sisters and brothers and I were small, if we were asleep when he came home, he'd wake us up. The biggest ice cream cones he could get. He just thought an ice cream cone was the best thing there was. He always brought one for my mother too. She didn't really like ice cream, but that was all right; he ate it.

I was thinking these thoughts, letting my mind wander from one to the other, and it seemed to me it couldn't have been more than a minute or two before there was a tapping on the door. Who could that be? I leaped up and went to the door. "Who is it?" I asked.

"Why, it's Bud."

Bud! Oh, my.

I flung open the door and there was my husband, in his white uniform, big as life and looking oh so handsome.

I threw my arms around him and covered his face with kisses, the way I'd always done, and he kissed me. But then I stepped back. "But Buddy... how did you know where I was?"

"Oh, well, I knew," he said, very mysterious.

"But I fell asleep, didn't I? Your train came in and you must have come across that same redcap, and he told you where I was. I bet he was keeping an eye out for a good-looking young man in a sailor's uniform."

"No, no, I didn't see no redcap," Bud said. "Nope, I hitched a ride with a fella I know, another sailor, I didn't take no train at all. Hitched a ride with a fella, just got into town, more than three hours ahead of when I shoulda been. This fella dropped me off at the station, you weren't there, so I figured, you must have gone to a hotel..."

"But how did you find me?" I interrupted.

"I don't know." Bud laughed. "I walked through the street and I looked around and I just knew you were in this hotel. I went to the front desk and I asked, and sure enough, here you were. I came up to the room. And here you are."

"And here *you* are," I said.

"Here we are," Bud said.

"Here we are," I agreed.

And what a lovely weekend that was. Oh my! Forty-six years we were married, Bud and I, and never a lovelier weekend together than that one. Afterwards, he took the train back to Norfolk, and I didn't see him again for three years—three years, four months, two weeks, and three days, to be exact. After he came home, we were never parted again until the day he died. Forty-three years we slept in the same bed, every night for forty-three years, richer and poorer, sickness and health, just like the vows say, then one day he just didn't wake up. Oh, how that hurts to think of it, that day.

But, you know, I can't stay sad for long. I think of all the good years we had, the good times, that lovely weekend, the swaying trees by the river, the flowerpots bursting with flowers. The fields of wildflowers.

* * *

A Week Without Sun

THE LEAVES OF THE BIG LEAF maple are something to see, each lobe as large as the leaf of many trees, the whole broader and longer than a large man's hand or a young woman's face. Even here in Vancouver, where some trees stay green all through the winter, the maple leaves turn red in autumn and fall from the tree into flaming, crackling puddles. After the night's storm, which had broken soon after Mary Lou's plane arrived, the small park across Forty-first Avenue from Lindy and Bev's house was littered with leaves, the spongy grass blanketed with layers of red and brown that dried quickly in the morning sun, turning the lawn to rust. Mary Lou gave a final wave to Bev, who she could see watching her from the window, coffee cup to her lips. Her feet sank into the leaves with a crunch and smell as satisfying as those produced by breaking the crust of a fresh loaf of French bread.

There was a bench at the bus stop, but Mary Lou was enjoying walking through the leaves so much she stayed in them until she spotted the bus coming, then ran to catch it, the large portfolio bag she had slung over her shoulder banging against her hip, the strap tight against her breast. An elderly man sitting on the bench lifted his hat and nodded his head in a courtly way as she came running up, just as the bus came to a stop. "Don't worry, he won't go without you," he said in a pleasant voice. "I know all the drivers on this route and they're all gentlemen."

"Thank you," Mary Lou said, a bit breathlessly. She smiled at the man over her shoulder as she climbed into the bus, expecting he would rise from the bench and follow her, but he made no move, other than to return the hat to his head, which was bald except for a fringe of scraggly white hair around the ears. There was something about the man that struck her as a bit "off," as if he were an actor who had just stepped offstage still in the persona of the offbeat character he played so well. Then the bus door was folding closed and she was occupied with finding the correct change in her purse as the bus pulled away. She gave him no further thought.

The next day was overcast, more like what she'd been expecting. Looking out the kitchen window, coffee cup in one hand, slice of toast in the other, Mary Lou made a face and Bev laughed. "Welcome to Vancouver, Mary Loon. Better get used to it."

"Oh, I know," Mary Lou said. "Yesterday morning was so beautiful, though."

"Sometimes a beautiful hour has to sustain you for a week," Bev said.

"Or a month," Lindy said from behind his paper. Mary Lou thought it was funny that the paper in such a cloudy town was called *The Sun.*

Crossing Forty-first Avenue, she noticed the same old man sitting on the bus stop bench. He was dressed much the same as the day before: dark trousers, a nondescript grey raincoat, wide-brimmed hat, looked like a Tilley. As he had done yesterday, he tipped the hat as Mary Lou approached. "Another lovely day," he said. There was a bit of a lilt in his voice that made it hard to tell if he was being ironic.

"Grey skies don't bother you?" Mary Lou inquired amiably.

"Oh, no," the old man said. He laughed warmly. "My, no."

Just then, Mary Lou spotted the bus approaching and she busied herself getting her change ready. Again, the old man stayed put on the bench, nodding to her as she stepped up to the bus.

On Wednesday, there was no sign of the man on the bench, but Mary Lou, preoccupied with the interview she was headed to, didn't notice. She'd had two interviews each on Monday and Tuesday, all of them going well, she thought, but this morning's was the one she was most anxious about. She was an advertising writer with solid experience in Toronto, but, curiously, the creative directors who'd interviewed her so far seemed more interested in the Master's degree she'd just finished in women's studies at York than her track record. She wasn't sure if they were seeing it as a plus or a minus, but the two-year employment gap made including it on her CV necessary. The agency she was going to this morning was where she really wanted to work; she was thinking how to put the best spin she could on the MA when the bus pulled up.

Mary Lou stepped up to the door, then back and aside when she saw someone was getting off—to her surprise, it was the elderly man she'd seen the previous two mornings; at least, she thought it was. He was taller than she had realized and he had to duck his head as he stepped through the door.

"You were up early," she said with a smile.

The old man looked at her curiously, not comprehending. "Pardon?" He had a shopping bag in each hand, one of them from the Gap, which she thought was funny, so there was no question of him tipping his hat. He seemed to falter on the last step; Mary Lou reached out her hand to steady him, but the old man shot her such a dirty look she pulled it back, as if she'd been burned. "Sorry," she said. The man didn't reply.

Mary Lou had only one interview lined up for Thursday and it was for 1:30, so she slept in. Wednesday's had gone well; she had high hopes, but had been told she wouldn't hear for a few days. "Not so hopeful that I'm going to cancel the others I've got lined up," she'd told Bev, who nodded knowingly.

"I know you're going to get something wonderful, Loon."

Mary Lou and Bev had been roommates two years running during undergrad in Saskatoon and had remained close. In fact, it was Bev who'd landed Mary Lou with the affectionate nickname she still used, following one drunken night when they'd opened their dorm window and taken turns sticking their heads out into the snowy moonlight to howl.

In those days, Bev and Mary Lou had both been howlers, but now Bev was settled, with tightly focused goals—she and Lindy had bought the house and she was finally pregnant after months of trying. She was protective of her friend, who was nursing a broken heart, and was happy to ease her way into Vancouver. Before rushing off to UBC, where she was a sessional instructor in the French department, Bev made a fresh pot of coffee and chopped up a fruit salad, leaving it in a pretty serving dish on Mary Lou's place at the kitchen eating nook.

Mary Lou had her late breakfast, reading Lindy's discarded paper, did her yoga, and had a lazy shower, allowing herself, since the house was empty, the indulgence of a rare cry. It was noon when she left the house, thinking she'd walk a few blocks down Forty-first and window-shop at the Kerrisdale stores before catching the bus. The sky was solidly socked in again, the third day without a glimmer of sun, but it was mild and the air smelled fresh. After three blocks, she was surprised to see the elderly man she associated with the bus stop heading her way, the Gap shopping bag in one hand. He was dressed as before, in the shapeless raincoat and hat, black trousers, which, yesterday, she had realized were a wide-waled corduroy, and dirty white runners. He was walking with a jaunty gait, swinging his arms, and had a distracted, lopsided little smile on his bland face. Mary Lou thought he looked a bit like Alec Guinness in his later roles, once-lean face now grown a bit pudgy, but still pleasing to look at.

The man doffed his hat when he noticed her. "Good afternoon," he said as they passed. "Lovely afternoon."

"Hello," Mary Lou said in a neutral tone. She smiled faintly and walked on. She felt prickly heat between her shoulder blades and was certain the man had stopped and was watching her, but she resisted the impulse to look back herself.

On the next block, she stopped to look in the window of a shop that featured Mediterranean imports. A sea-blue brooch caught her eye and she went in to get a better look. A few minutes later, suddenly conscious of the time, she was hurrying to the bus stop on the next corner. She couldn't believe her eyes. The old man was sitting on the bench, just as she'd found him twice before at the stop across from Bev and Lindy's, except that this time he was reading a newspaper. She shook off the feeling of annoyance.

"We meet again," she said.

"Pardon?" The expression on the man's face was blank.

"Never mind," Mary Lou said. "Good afternoon."

"Yes," the man said, but he sounded skeptical.

She looked away, and, fortunately, the bus arrived in a moment. She boarded, but the old man remained seated, absorbed in his paper.

⊗

There's this weirdest man in the neighbourhood," Mary Lou said at dinner.

"Weird how?" Lindy asked, looking interested. He was a computer wonk with a passion for puzzles of all sorts. His government job didn't challenge him enough but provided a good salary and plenty of security. He was the best thing that ever happened to Bev, though once she'd laughed that he was, if anything, "too reliable." She didn't elaborate.

"Oh, nothing menacing. He's just around all the time, everywhere I look. An old man. Sometimes he's friendly as can be, 'lovely day,' that sort of thing. Other times he looks at me like I'm from Mars."

"Probably senile," Lindy said, going back to his chicken.

"He's not following you, is he?"

"Oh, nothing like that, Bev. He's not a stalker or anything. I'm probably exaggerating, anyway. I've seen him every day and today twice, so the second time spooked me."

"Poor old guy, he's probably thinking the same thing," Lindy said. "'Everywhere I turn, there's this hot babe with the Toronto look. It's really spooking me.'"

Bev gave him a scowl, but Mary Lou joined Lindy in a laugh.

They were having coffee when the phone rang; it turned out to be someone from the agency where she'd interviewed the day before, the place she'd set her sights on. Apologies for calling so late, but could she possibly come in again tomorrow? In the morning? No, Mary Lou had another appointment. After lunch? She was thrilled.

The next morning, Friday, there was no sign of the old man at the bus stop. Mary Lou was distracted all through the first interview, thinking about the other job, and she left feeling that she'd blown it, and too bad, too, as this agency was also a good one. She strolled down Georgia Street to the art gallery and sat on the steps for a few minutes, smoking a cigarette, but she was chilly, even in her pretty blue cardigan. It hadn't rained since Sunday night, but she hadn't seen the sun since Monday morning. Standing up, she had a glimpse of a shapeless grey raincoat and one white runner as someone turned the corner and out of sight. She gave her head a shake and walked purposely through throngs of people down Georgia to Hornby, turning right to Robson, where she slowed and began to look for a place to have lunch.

The second interview was great—it was more like they were selling themselves than window-shopping her—and she left with an assurance that she'd hear from them Monday morning. "I don't see any reason why you won't be working for us, Mary Lou," the creative director told her as they shook hands. He was a fat man wearing red suspenders and a black eye patch that made him look like a parody of the Smirnoff man. His uncovered eye was bright and lively, constantly in motion. "I just have to get final approval upstairs."

Coming through the glass doors onto Howe Street, she stopped cold, causing a man with a briefcase to bang into her from behind. "Oh, sorry," they both said, simultaneously. Across the street, the old man was standing with one foot in the street, the other on the curb, as if looking for a taxi. He stared right at Mary Lou, and, even at that distance, she could see the intensity of his blue-eyed gaze, feel the heat. She just gawked. After a moment, he raised his hand to his head, slowly lifted the hat to reveal the bald pate and snowy tufts, and gave her a knowing smile.

⊗

Mary Lou had never been particularly lucky with men, but she was not a codependent or a victim type by any means. She had a good relationship with her father, uncles, and an older brother. It's true, the three serious relationships she'd been through were all with older men, but she didn't think that pointed to anything more than coincidence. She had plenty of men friends her own age. One of the men she'd been in love with turned out to be married and had deliberately hidden it from her. She broke it off as soon as she found out. Another man, an investment banker who took her with him when he was transferred to England, turned out to be a bastard, but he'd started out just fine. Well, at least England was a gas, as she'd told Bev. She'd come back to Toronto two years later alone and broke, but her tail was certainly not between her legs.

For the last five years—almost as long as Bev had been with Lindy—she'd been living with Murray, an artist who was well-known in Toronto for his installations and sculptures. He had made a New York breakthrough, and it was an exciting time for both of them. It was Murray who encouraged her to go back to school and gave her financial support through the two years. Mary Lou was thirty-seven, he was fifty-three, but they were compatible as hell. She was happy with her career and was looking forward to getting back to it now that she all but had her Master's in hand, but she had daydreams of marriage and kids, one of those great old townhouses in Riverdale. Then, from out of the blue just weeks ago, Murray had called it off. There was someone else, someone he'd met in New York, but not a younger woman, not a woman at all, in fact. He was gay and it was time to admit it. It had nothing to do with her. They'd had a great run, hadn't they? He hoped they could still be friends.

Mary Lou was devastated, but she didn't feel like her life was ruined or that she would go off men. A change in scene was called for, hence the job hunt in Vancouver, where she'd always thought she'd like to wind up. She certainly didn't feel like she had a hang-up about men, as Bev seemed now to imply. She'd come back to their place in anxious tears, both exhilarated about the job possibility and distraught about the old man, not knowing what to think.

"I'm *not* imagining this," she said. She'd calmed down and they were having a drink before dinner. "This man is following me. It doesn't have anything to do with *me*."

Bev and Lindy made the appropriate noises, but she could tell Lindy didn't believe her, and even Bev seemed skeptical.

"We'll all go out for a walk later," Lindy said. "If we run into this guy, I'll have a word with him."

But there was no sign of him in the neighbourhood after dinner. "Past his bedtime, maybe," Lindy said.

Nor was he on Forty-first Avenue the next day when they set out in the car for Granville Island. It was Saturday, and they planned to make a day of it. Lindy found a parking spot miles from anything, but it didn't take too long to walk to where the shops began. The sun was struggling to break through the overcast. "Maybe we'll get a little sunshine finally before you go," Bev said hopefully. Mary Lou was finally feeling fine. They went into a pottery shop, then a glass blowers' studio. Coming out, she caught sight of the old man across the roadway. He was just standing there, the raincoat slumped over his shoulders like a cape, Gap bag in hand, the Tilley hat slouched over his eyes. She could see the flash of blue, though. "Oh, God, there he is," she exclaimed and turned to grab Lindy's arm. But when she turned back, the man was gone.

"You sure it was him?"

"He was right there, for God's sake. Right in front of that shop."

Bev held Mary Lou's hand while Lindy looked around, then went in the shop, a jeweler's. The salesgirl hadn't seen an old man in a raincoat and hat, he reported back.

They held a quick conference but decided to stay on the island. "He's not making threatening gestures or anything," Mary Lou assured them. Besides, they were all famished.

They had a fabulous lunch at Bridges. The sky was still grey, but there was one thin spot where the sun could be seen beating, like a searchlight through fog, and it was pleasant on the patio. Mary Lou had steamed mussels in an exotic broth, a lovely salad of baby greens, and most of a loaf of crusty bread—her appetite certainly wasn't affected, Bev kidded her—and they emptied a bottle of a good pinot noir, this in celebration of the job offer she was sure she'd get on Monday.

Bev made a toast. "To my best friend, Mary Loon, who'll soon be howling in Vancouver."

"Isn't it the 'cry of the loon, howl of the coyote'?" Lindy asked. Bev gave him a dirty look, but Mary Lou laughed. "It's okay. I'm not going to cry anymore. Well, not till the next time, anyway."

They were lingering over second cups of coffee when the old man came out onto the patio, following a waiter. Bev saw him first. "Mary Loon, that's not him, is it?"

She turned quickly. "Oh my God! It is."

"You sure?"

"Absolutely."

The old man was being seated just a few tables from them. He was alone, dressed as always in the raincoat and hat.

"You stay here; I'll talk to him," Lindy said.

"No way. I'm going too."

They left Bev at their table and went over.

"Let me talk to him, though," Lindy said.

The old man glanced up, and Mary Lou's heart sank. "I don't think . . ." she began, but Lindy was already talking to the man.

"Excuse me, have you been following my friend?"

"Pardon? I don't understand," the old man said. He gazed curiously at them with unmistakably brown eyes. He didn't seem distressed.

"There's been a misunderstanding," Mary Lou said. She had her hand on Lindy's arm and she gave him a quick, chagrined glance, then looked back at the seated man. He looked remarkably like the old man she'd been seeing; even the tufts of white hair peeking out from beneath the Tilley hat around the ears were the same, but the face was leaner, the eyes certainly different. "I'm so sorry."

"Please excuse us, sir," Lindy said. "We thought you were someone else."

"Quite all right," the old man said. He smiled in a patronizing way and bent his head to the menu.

"God, I'm sorry," Mary Lou said to Lindy, and again to Lindy and Bev when they'd retaken their seats.

"Forget it." Lindy's smile was indulgent, almost as patronizing as the old man's.

They made a stop at the market, where Bev bought a fresh salmon and loaded up on salad vegetables, so fresh you could still smell the earth on them. Mary Lou contributed a French bread and some irresistible-looking pastry. They stood watching and listening to a busker, a man dressed like a gypsy, complete with bandanna, who played a very decent mandolin. Mary Lou put a loonie in his instrument case.

They took their time walking back to the car, poking their heads into this shop or that. Twice Mary Lou thought she saw the old man, *her* old man—no, she *did* see him—but she didn't say anything, didn't trust herself.

As Lindy maneuvered the car out of its tight spot and onto the road under the bridge, Bev cried out: "God!" Lindy slammed on the brakes.

"What the . . ."

"There he is again. Standing right by the concrete pillar."

They all looked, but there was no one. "Jesus, Bev, it's a damned good thing there wasn't anyone behind us."

"I wasn't hallucinating," Bev said, defiantly.

"This is contagious," Mary Lou said. "It's also getting ridiculous."

"You got that right," Lindy said, clearly annoyed.

They drove home in silence. After a few minutes, Bev twisted around and reached between the seats to squeeze Mary Lou's knee.

Sunday was a quiet day, overcast again. They all slept in, and Bev made a big omelet with the remains of the salmon. The two women put on windbreakers and went for a walk in the little park while Lindy had his run. Directly overhead, the pale sun burned valiantly, but couldn't get through the cloud. There was no sign of the old man "and the hell with him if he does show up," Mary Lou said. "*Either* one of him." The big leaves of the maples crunched under their feet, and they could smell burning leaves from somewhere nearby, maybe the Musqueam reserve, which began at the southern edge of the park. They recrossed Forty-first, went up to Camosun Street and into the University Properties, past the tangles of blackberry bushes, into thick woods, where roots reached up out of the mossy forest floor to grab their ankles. In the distance they could hear a dog barking and the occasional car passing on the adjacent road, but they had the path to themselves.

"You're going to get that job, Mary Loon," Bev said.

"I know it. And if not that one, one of the others."

They walked a little further. Bev started to laugh. "Those bastards," she said.

"You know it," Mary Lou said. After a moment she added: "Oh, Lindy's okay, though."

"Some days," Bev said. They grinned at each other.

They stopped to rest for a moment, leaning against a large fallen tree. Mary Lou flexed one leg, then the other. "I'm okay now," she said. "Really."

They pushed off the tree and stood for a moment in an awkward embrace before turning back.

It rained overnight. The next morning, Monday, Bev and Lindy went to work, Bev to the campus, Lindy downtown, leaving Mary Lou by the telephone. She had a mid-afternoon flight back to Toronto, with hours to kill before she had to get ready. Bev would be home in plenty of time to take her to the airport. All the places where she'd interviewed had the number here and her number at home in Toronto. "It doesn't really matter whether it's today here or next week at home," she'd told Bev. "It would be nice to go home knowing, though."

"They'll call," Bev had assured her.

She fixed another cup of coffee, took another look at *The*

Sun. Local news on the front page, nothing really of interest. She glanced at the phone, wandered into the living room, and went to the window.

If she stood at just the right angle, she could see the bench by the bus stop. Someone was sitting there, but she couldn't tell who. The sun, she noticed with relief, had finally come out. She pressed her nose against the cool glass. Maybe there was a dark overcoat, maybe a hat. She couldn't tell. She started for the door but just as she put her hand on the knob, the phone began to ring.

* * *

Letter to a Kinsman

27 Rue de Laurence
Montreal, Quebec
August 27, 1937

Dr. Samuel I. Cohen
2300 Park Avenue
New York City, NY

MY DEAR DR. COHEN,

My name is Reuben Cahan. Reuben, of course, speaks for itself—I am the namesake, one of thousands, I'm sure, of the great biblical warrior. As for Cahan, far be it from me to instruct a learned man such as yourself on the origins and lineage of the name whose variations we share. Cohen, Cahan, Cohn, Kahn, and many others, we are all descended from the seed of Aaron, brother of great Moses himself, the first of the Jewish priests, through generations of rabbis and scholars. A book I read recently makes the bold pronouncement that all bearers of names with that "kohen" root are related; it describes that line from Aaron to you and me and our thousands of cousins as being "pure and delicate and precious as a string of pearls." A pleasant thought, wouldn't you say, cousin?

But my purpose is not to provide a discourse on genealogy, nor, I suppose, am I giving you information which is not already in your possession. I am certain that a man of your breeding, education, and standing in the community would have more than a passing interest in the rich veins from which you sprang.

So you will know that I am correct when I salute and greet you, cousin, kinsman, *landsman*.

I will not belabour this point further. Rather, with your

kind indulgence, I will go directly to the inescapable conclusion which, in fact, leads me, with somewhat trembling hand, to begin the process of putting the following sequence of words to paper, addressed to you.

And that is that I write to you not merely as a stranger, though assuredly we have never met, but as a relative—distant, yes; long-lost, most certainly; but a relative nonetheless—as one whose blood calls out to the blood of the other.

Indeed, my blood does call out to yours, for it is the same blood.

(Incidentally, so there should be no apprehension of deception, let me hasten to say at this point that while I address you personally, Dr. Cohen, I am writing similar letters to several other *mishpocheh.*)

But, and I want to make this very clear from the outset: this is not a call for help, not a plea, nor a wail, nor even a suggestion that, from the comfort and security of your Park Avenue home and offices—which, I have been told, are sumptuous and comfortable almost beyond belief in their appointments and furnishings—you should hold out a hand of support to members of your kin—your *blood*—who, through circumstances over which they had little, if any, control, have fallen into desperate straits.

No. This is merely intended as a description of those circumstances and straits, the exercise of what might charitably be perceived as a familial duty to keep one branch of a loving family abreast of the news and daily doings of another, and no more than that. If, on the other hand, after hearing my tale, you should feel a twinge of conscience, a sincere and heartfelt desire to reach out a hand of comfort, the drawing in, for example, of outcast cousins to the warmth of security in your bosom, or the proffering, to cite yet another example, of some small token, that, of course, will be a decision only you can make. I put myself—and those dependent upon me but too weak or frail or timid or voiceless to speak on their own behalf (I speak here of my beloved mother, my precious sister)—entirely at the mercy of your judgment and discretion.

⊗

My father, of blessed memory, came to North America in 1906 from Berlin as a representative of the Great Britain Life and Casualty Assurance Company, a company through which you hold a number of different policies, I am told—yet another link between us.

He was named Melush, originally, but renamed himself Emmanuel and was always called Manny. He was an extremely handsome man, as well as being a clever and charming one, and was—and, I assure you, I am not exaggerating—extremely attractive to women, a fact that he was always scrupulous to avoid exploiting, while, at the same time, unthreatening to men. In fact, he was a man who other men always felt comfortable with, looked up to, felt that they could confide in, a man, in short, who inspired not envy but admiration.

My mother was the youngest daughter of Israel and Rachel Agatestone, and a member of one of Ottawa's most prominent Jewish families. Her father, as the owner of the city's most fashionable fur and millinery shop, was quite well to do, and her mother had a reputation as an elegant hostess and a leader of the city's philanthropic causes. She was a founder of Hadassah in the city and was its president all during the years up to the war, at the same time that her husband was president of their temple.

Both of my mother's elder sisters were already married—one to the owner of a dry goods store that would later blossom into one of this country's largest retail operations, the other to a lawyer who would serve many terms, as a Liberal, in the House of Commons—and her brother, while not yet married, was already a graduate of the Harvard University School of Medicine—having been obstructed, because of being a Jew, from McGill—and was well established in his practice in the city, a practice devoted to solving the puzzles of internal disorders, just as is yours.

(As an aside, I should tell you that it was he, my uncle Benjamin—Dr. Benjamin Agatestone of Ottawa, whose death at an early age of a stroke was a blow to both the Jewish and medical communities of Ottawa as well as the family—who inspired my choice of you as one of the recipients of this letter. And I should confess too that because of actions of my father, which I will soon elaborate on, my mother has long been estranged from her sisters. It is truly tragic the indifference with which some individuals approach their family. For without family, what have we? Nothing, I say. Nothing!)

My mother's name was Dorothea, an indulgence, in a family where the other children were all named for Torah personalities, of her mother's passion for the novels of George Eliot. She was born in 1893, when my father was already a year past his *bar mitzvah*, and was just eighteen years of age on a certain day in October, in the year 1911, when my father, who was strolling down Sparks Street on his way back to his office from a luncheon at the Chateau Laurier, passed the shop of the man who would soon become his father-in-law, which he had visited on a number of occasions on business.

Now, his eye happened to fall on a display window, where a beautiful young woman—my mother, as it turned out—was arranging clothes on a mannequin. As he would tell the story later, my father found himself motionless, his feet refusing to move, as people bustled past him on the sidewalk, staring through the glass at two beautiful female forms, one naked, the other quite elegantly dressed but with her sleeves pushed up to the elbow, her hair tucked up into a fluffy bun atop her head, her lips thoughtfully pursed around a half-dozen safety pins.

"Contrary to what you would expect," my father would always say when he told this story, "my eyes went quickly to the form of the female that was clothed, and there it stayed, enchanted and transfixed."

My mother, I should say, was a great beauty, with dark, shining eyes, a severe smile, and gorgeous auburn hair that fell in a succession of ripples and triplet curls down past her pale cheeks to her shoulders. She was afflicted with a rare astigmatism that would later in her life make her quite unusually nearsighted, but, in the flowering of her youth, produced a quizzical cross-eyed glance that most people found charming, and, to many men, was irresistible.

That was exactly the effect it had on my father when, so his story continued, my mother soon looked up from her preoccupation and their eyes met, a joining of vision that must have been somewhat oblique, both from my mother's astigmatism and the thickness of the window. Not so oblique, however, that their souls were not able to travel the length of that mystical joining and mingle. They were married within weeks, shocking Ottawa society, and I was born scarcely a year later, as forces in Europe were hurtling toward the brink of the great conflagration that was soon to descend upon the world.

So it was that my own part of my family's story began.

⊗

Now that I have captured your attention, as I feel confident I have, allow me to tell you at more leisure some of the facts of my father's life, for it is he whose strengths and weaknesses conspired to bring us, his family, to this dire juncture.

I mentioned his employment with Great Britain Life, and you may well be surprised that this august company existed so long ago and that its origins are Germanic—in fact, the company was founded in 1836 in Dusseldorf by two brothers named Meinz, sons of a merchant whose business was nearly destroyed by fire, thereby setting a lesson for the all-but-impoverished family. By the turn of the century, when my father arrived in Berlin, a green but ambitious *stetl* boy from Galicia, the son of a peddler of Bibles whose own ambitions had rarely reached beyond the next farmhouse and the distant bend in the road, the company, now one of the largest of its type not only in Germany but throughout Europe, was headquartered in Berlin and had changed its name, from the original, somewhat pretentious *Meinz Frere* to Great Britain, in hopes, no doubt, of acquiring an international lustre. The president of the company was Wulther Meinz, a grandson of one of the founders and a man noted for his virulent anti-

Semitism, but, at the same time, a certain shrewdness of mind that drew a distinct line between business and personal—even political—pursuits. Great Britain Life was, at the time, one of the largest carriers of policies among the Diaspora, one of the very few companies, in fact, that specialized in tailoring policies for, and selling them to, Jews. As such, it had a large Jewish sales force, and my father, who was, as I've said, an extremely handsome and clever man, had no difficulty joining that thriving company of men, and prospering.

"Can you sell to Jews?" was what this *eminence gris* Meinz said to my father.

"Who else would I sell to?" was my father's response—this, at least, according to family lore.

I hope you will not consider me vain or gratuitous for mentioning my father's good looks. The fact is that his handsomeness, along with a remarkable facility for languages, was the key to my father's success in the business world and a central factor in his life. He was a tall man with the posture of a cavalry officer, black wavy hair that, in later life, took on a silvery lustre, and a mustache much like that worn currently by the popular film star Clark Gable. As you can imagine, such a wealth of physical attraction and an ability to put people at their ease make for a natural salesman, since every other man is eager to hear what he has to say and not in the slightest prone to disbelieve what he hears.

This talent—shall we call it that?—made my father successful beyond his and his employer's wildest dreams; by 1904 he was the leading salesman in the company's large force, and a favourite of Herr Meinz himself. This success, combined with his abilities as a linguist—he could speak English, French, and German like a native and had more than a passing familiarity with Italian, Spanish, Portuguese, and a number of the Slavic languages as well as an actual native fluency in Polish, Russian, and Yiddish—made him a natural candidate for duty abroad as the company, during the inflationary years prior to the Great War, sought to expand. Indeed, prior to his posting in New York, he was stationed in London and Paris, setting up offices and recruiting sales agents, making significant inroads into the territories of competing companies—almost exclusively among a Jewish clientele.

He was dispatched to New York in the summer of 1906 at the height of a virtual tidal wave of Jewish immigration to the New World. Like any good salesman, he was going where the customers were.

As Meinz himself put it, in a letter to my father outlining his new duties: "Go where the Jews are. Make them ours."

My father, ever gregarious, jovial, generous, and shrewd, was, once again, wildly successful, being personally responsible for selling hundreds, perhaps thousands, of policies among the immigrants—many of them *landsmen* from Galicia—who toiled in the garment trades and inhabited the teeming ghettos of Lower Broadway and Brownsville like small fish overflowing their ponds. His efforts established the company as one of the premier insurers in the eastern United States. Indeed, by 1911, when my father was dispatched to Ottawa, the company had become firmly established. But my father's continued presence, sadly to say, had become, to use the parlance of that industry, a liability.

For here, at last, it is time to touch upon a central element in the story that I am enfolding for you, my father's weakness for gambling. It was a character flaw that may seem trivial enough to the casual observer but was, in fact, as fatal as the crack that splits a diamond in two, was, in fact, the cause of his untimely undoing.

Whether it was a factor of heredity or environment, I can assure you I do not know, but there was in my father a certain fascination for danger, for the thrill that can only be achieved when much is at stake. This is hardly a unique characteristic—indeed, if the Torah is to be believed, it is one that has run rampant through the generations among us Jews, hence our frequent poor luck in the marketplaces and political arenas of the world. Some men, rarely Jews, indulge this weakness through military affiliations; others, through wandering adventures, like Marco Polo and Amerigo Vespucci, both of whom were, as you no doubt know, Jews. With my father, the weakness chose to exhibit itself through a fascination for gambling: cards, dice, horses; wherever, in fact, there was an element of chance upon which financial stakes could be wagered, the higher—as my father's personal worth grew—the better. Indeed, it was the pursuit of that thrill, when all seems to hang in the balance—life, security, happiness, and the continuance of a certain way of life on one hand, and ruin, poverty, personal danger, and flight on the other—that most drove my father and was, ironically, the inspiration for his greatest successes, though that hardly made him a charlatan, as my sister Rebeccah insists. Well, she has her reasons, of course, poor child. You may judge for yourself shortly.

Although my father had indulged his weakness in the Old Country—particularly in the casinos of London and Paris when he was stationed in those capitals—it wasn't until he reached the New World that the flaw in his character, which heretofore had appeared as little more than a charming crack in an otherwise brilliant stone, now blossomed forth into the dangerously divisive fracture it was destined to become.

As it was, my father was a trailblazer, not a man content ever to rest on his laurels or to direct, from an office high above the toiling minions in his charge, operations with which he had little actual connection. It was his destiny to open territory, to conquer, not to maintain or service, and he was more than ready to move on by 1911, when, as it happens, he found himself deeply in debt to representatives of certain social elements of which you and I, as gentlemen of the world, are aware but too discreet to mention. These elements, unable to secure payment of his debts from my father through conventional means, had taken their case to his superiors at Great Britain Life and Casualty, threatening to expose him.

There was no question, therefore, that, despite his successes in New York, despite all the company owed him, despite the high regard with which he was held by the company—or should I say because of these factors—it was deemed timely that he should move on to new territory.

"You'll find plenty of Jews in Canada, don't worry," that's what his mentor Meinz wired my father, perhaps to soften the blow of the transfer.

Ottawa was then, as it is now, a city of considerably smaller size than New York—a mere one hundred thousand souls in the census of 1910, according to a notation found in my father's papers—but, at the same time, of considerable charm. There was a vibrant social life, as one might expect of the capital of a small but thriving nation, but, for environmental and sociological reasons largely of an ethnic nature, considerably less danger of the type that my father found so attractive—though in sufficient amount to cause his ruin in years to come, as you shall see. There was a large Jewish population, and still larger ones in Montreal and Toronto, to the southeast and southwest, and my father quickly established himself as the director of an ambitious push, manned by a large sales force, to blanket the population with the kind of protection and security, suitably tailored to the needs of the individual, that Great Britain Life could provide. As such, he became a man of some social stature, and, because of his handsomeness and charm, considerable eligibility.

It was inevitable, therefore, that the paths of my father and mother should cross.

⊗

You may well pause to ask, sir, the direction in which I am leading you. That direction, and its eventual goal, will soon become clear enough. My purpose in describing the people and events that have so far encompassed the bulk of this letter, however, is twofold, and I can easily explain now.

Firstly, it has been my intention to give you, as accurately as possible, considering the brevity of time afforded us, a picture of the circumstances of my family—we, the Cahans of Ottawa and later Montreal—in our happy days, the better for you to understand the distance we travelled when we later were to fall—literally, for at least two of us—to the depths of misfortune.

Secondly, I have wanted to give you a glimpse, to merely hint at, the dark forces that, despite the sunshine we may at the moment be experiencing, are always lurking in the background, ready to rend the fabric of our lives. And here, sir, I refer to the larger family of all mankind.

The fabric of *our* lives began to unravel in the spring of 1921, just a few short years after the close of that Great War that, despite its devastation on the global theatres of the world, had left so little a mark on our happy family. (God's little joke, perhaps.)

Father was then a man of forty-one, in the prime of his life, as handsome and charming as ever, a leading citizen. Mother, still lovely and youthful, gracious and respected, had matured into a loving wife, a doting mother. We children, myself, my sister, Rebeccah, and my beloved brother, Benjamin, born in that order, were happy, healthy—at least until my brother's untimely death—bright, and promising. Together we were a family presenting to the outside world a vision of perfect domestic bliss, an idyll of the life to be pursued, the life worthy of living.

The fortunes of the Great Britain Life and Casualty Assurance Company had undergone a great turmoil during the war. Meinz, that man of despicable prejudices but shrewd business acumen who had been my father's original employer and sponsor, had been destroyed by the war, his fortune dissipated in the service of the Kaiser, his country home overrun, one of his two sons killed at the front, though the second one, a pilot, distinguished himself and now, so I see in the papers, is an important personage in the new German government, a trusted aide of that tragic-comic little fellow who calls himself Hitler. The company was completely reorganized after the war, its European division all but defunct, its North American division virtually independent. Father, older now and more stable, with the firm hand of my mother on his arm, less prone to fall into the sway of temptation, had risen to be vice president of the eastern Canadian region and served on the board of directors. It had been years since he'd succumbed to the siren call of the gaming halls.

Because of his prominence in business circles, it was only natural that Father should be pursued by political interests, and in June of 1921 he was a delegate to the convention of the Liberal Party of Canada, meeting at the Chateau Laurier. On the second day of the convention, a Friday, June 17, there was to be a reception in the afternoon, and, because Father was a considerate and generous parent, he left the hotel after lunch and returned home to fulfill a promise he had made to us children. An hour later, we were at his side, stiff in our finest attire, our hearts beating wildly in our little chests, as the prime minister, Mr. Meighan, entered one of the huge ballrooms at the chateau and made his way cheerfully down a long line of well-wishers, taking the hand of each in his own and shaking vigorously.

I, a child of only nine, was nearly overcome with excitement when the prime minister, his whiskers looking strangely like those of our Irish wolfhound, bent down and offered his hand, exclaiming what a fine little gentleman I was.

"I am most pleased to make the acquaintance of so distinguished an eminence as yourself, Mr. Prime Minister," I told Mr. Meighan, parroting a pretty speech my father had made me practice.

"My goodness, but you *are* a well-spoken little fellow," the great man replied.

It was less than fifteen minutes later that Benjy, then only four and the apple of all our eyes—Benjy, sweet Benjy with his irrepressible grin, wide almond eyes, and mop of fine hair exactly the shade of auburn of our mother's—it was then that Benjy somehow managed to wander, unnoticed, from the sight of Rebeccah, who had been charged with looking after him, and myself, charged with the supervision of both of them, down a hallway and, in a manner which was never satisfactorily explained, through the open doorway of an elevator shaft, there to fall three stories to his death.

The only consolation, such as it was, to be had in this tragedy was that, according to the physician who pronounced him dead, our darling Benjy's neck was broken and he probably felt no pain, only the intense fear—perhaps muffled by exhilaration—of his fall.

This was the beginning of our destruction. Our house on Rideau Terrace—an imposing colonial structure that father had had built for us and that for so long had been filled with happy noise and laughter—fell prey to long moody silences, reflecting the mood of my mother, who, thereafter, was often ill. To change her environment, father arranged for a transfer of his headquarters to the Montreal office, and to this most elegant city we moved, to a fine old house in Mont Royal that had once belonged to a senator. But it was here that, perhaps because of his despair, perhaps because of the proliferation of temptation, father once more began to yield to his weakness, and that his presence was brought to the attention of men allied with those elements in New York whose debts had never been paid.

He fell into their grip, a tightening hand whose squeeze would never relent, driving him *meshugge,* until, in 1929, when, like so many men whose fortunes had been ruined turned in desperation to the casting away of their own lives, he plunged from the window of his seventeenth-storey office in the Place Ville Marie, a bitter if perhaps unconscious choice of death for a man whose own precious child had so recently died in much the same manner.

⊗

It's impossible, sir, to fully convey the impact of my father's death on the surviving members of our family, but suffice to say we were devastated. I was seventeen, hardly more than a child and still in school, though soon to abruptly be out in the world earning a living, since, as it turned out, we were penniless. Rebeccah, poor Rebeccah, was only fifteen, a particularly vulnerable age for girls, when the whole world seems to revolve around popularity. She had enjoyed much; now it all seemed to dissipate, the invitations to parties ceasing to come, the telephone falling silent, heads turning in the hallways of her school.

As for my mother, it pains me to think of the terrible deterioration of body and spirit to which she succumbed, let alone to describe it. She had been moody, prone to illness, and subdued since the death of her beloved Benjy—the youngest and, as any good psychology book will tell you, always the most precious. Now, she took to her bed, shattered, not so much by my father's actual death, I believe—since terms between them had been strained for some time—but by the harsh reality of the plight his death had thrust us into. Overnight, she seemed to become an old woman. But even worse than the physical assaults were the ravages upon her intellect and spirit. She had always blamed father, I'm certain, for taking us to the Chateau that fateful day, for letting Benjy slip away from his sight; at the same time, she had, in some vague, intangible way, resented me, as if I too must share that blame—a guilt I grudgingly take upon my shoulders—as if my very life was somehow a reproach for my brother's death. Now, these feelings which hitherto had been directed at both my father and me, became focused, like an angry boil nearing its moment of explosion, on me alone, and I found myself in the ironic, bitter position of being the sole financial and emotional support of a woman whose hatred for me had become tangible.

I came home from school one day to find three stocky men in ill-fitting suits banging on the door of our home. They were sheriff's deputies armed with a foreclosure notice from the bank. Mother was upstairs, ignoring the noise, or oblivious to it, and Rebeccah, thank God, had not yet returned from school. I assured the men there'd been a mistake, a misunderstanding. I explained that my father's death had thrown the family into tumult; I pleaded. They left grudgingly, granting me two days' reprieve to make arrangements with the bank. I went directly upstairs to ask Mother what she knew of this situation. Her door was closed and she didn't respond to my knock. With trepidation, but fearing the worst, I tried the doorknob, and finding it unlocked, pushed the door open. My mother was sitting up in bed, looking more like some harridan from the ghetto than my beloved, pampered mother. The joyous auburn curls that had once been her pride, the subject of countless brushings and primpings through the day, now hung limp, lifeless, greying. Her once charming astigmatism had become a prune-faced squint, most unbecoming as she fixed her stare on me. The odour of unwashed bed linen hung in the air.

"Mother . . ." I began.

"Go to hell," she interrupted.

Shocked, I fell silent, took a step backward.

"And rot there, for all I care," she continued. "Now get out of here."

I did as instructed, though confused and broken-hearted. Standing on the upstairs landing, I heard the front door open and a moment later heard Rebeccah's cheerful call of greeting, tinkling like a bell. I made an instantaneous decision to take charge of the affairs of our household, no matter the cost to myself. The next day I visited the bank, obtained an explanation of our plight from the manager—we were, it turned out, several months in arrears, Mother having not responded to several of his letters—and wrung a brief reprieve from him. I never returned to school, not even to say goodbye to my teachers and classmates.

I am my father's son, though, and I persevered, as cheerfully as possible, considering the times through which we were living. Perhaps because of the disgrace my father had brought on the company, Great Britain Life was uncharitable (just as my mother's sisters were), refusing me a position, but a friend of my father's at a rival insurance firm made arrangements that resulted in my first job, selling policies on commission only. The market for life insurance, of course, was nil, but casualty was another matter, as I soon learned. Businesses which have property to protect respond quite favourably to even the most subtle of hints that, should they neglect to buy a policy, unforeseen acts of God could possibly result. The laying out of such a proposition requires the most delicacy and tact, skills which, as an extremely young man, I had little currency in; my first attempts—following a spectacular and surprising success which resulted from a quite innocent remark that was misunderstood—were dismal failures, resulting not only in refusals but threats of bodily harm and summonsing of the police. But I learned quickly, and I am convinced that some things are inherited. I am hardly the handsome man my father was—taking more after the smaller-boned build of the Agatestones, and bearing quite a striking resemblance, particularly around the eyes and nose, to my grandfather Israel—but I do possess a considerable amount of my father's natural charm. I put people at their ease; I instill confidence. This has been my salvation, and part of my undoing.

My career in the insurance business was hardly spectacular, but it was comfortable and proved a good training ground for a young man attempting to adapt to a changing world. I specialized in selling fire insurance to small businesses—restaurants, clothiers, wholesalers, and the like—and found I could be quite convincing, while subtle, in describing both the dangers to be faced and the advantages of my company's policies over those of its rivals. On a number of occasions, I found it necessary—making use, with an appreciated sense of irony, of several men whose acquaintance I had made earlier, when they were involved in the persecution of my father—to demonstrate to reluctant customers the dangers that I thought I had so eloquently described; but these instances of last resort were as rare as they were distasteful. At any rate, my involvement with insurance would prove to be short-lived, due to my somewhat unexpected introduction to the world of automotive retailing, which came about in a peculiar way.

I was strolling through a small park, on my way to visit a potential customer, when, passing the boating pond, I was attracted by a high musical laugh, and, looking up, noticed a young woman dressed all in white, including a broad-brimmed hat, standing up in a small rowing boat. In the moments that followed, my horrified eyes witnessed the boat teeter, the woman's arms raise gracefully into the air, like those of a ballerina executing a difficult turn, one side of the boat raise dangerously high from the water, and then, in a sudden flurry of arms and splashing water, the entire composition before me turn upside down.

I wasted no time, of course, in stripping off my jacket and plunging into the lake, which proved to be not very deep, no more than chest high, in fact, and by the time I reached the capsized boat, the woman was standing, looking about frantically, and calling out a name, "Naomi, Naomi." I dove under the boat and immediately encountered the holder of that name, a child of perhaps three or four, hair streaming, face turning blue, foot securely caught under a seat in the boat, a predicament I was able to quickly undo.

"You've saved us," the young woman in white exclaimed when I splashed to the surface, the child—her sister, as it turned out—under my arm. I didn't point out that the woman had needed no saving herself, but thrashed out of the water, the child still in my arms, and there, laying the poor, nearly drowned creature on the grass, began to apply pressure to her thin chest and blow air into her purple lips. The young woman trailed behind, murmuring incomprehensibly, but when, at last, the child gave a cry and opened her eyes, I looked up, an exultant smile on my lips, and found myself gazing into the emerald eyes of the young woman, who, I now realized, seeing her face really for the first time without benefit of contortions, distance and screaming, was younger than I, and quite attractive, lovely, in fact.

"You've saved us," she repeated, and, once again, I refrained from protesting. We knelt there together, the now crying and bubbling child between us, for a long moment, sharing a gaze that, I suppose, was somewhat like that which passed between my father and mother on that street in Ottawa so many years before, when their souls passed along the force of their gaze to mingle and a love was born. What passed between Louise—for that was her name—and me was indeed similar, but, admittedly, of somewhat lesser intensity.

I don't want to go into details of my relationship with Louise, except to say that it is enduring, that she is, at this time of my greatest calamity, my one strong staff upon which I grasp and lean. But it is she, in an indirect way, through her father, who brought me to the state in which I now find myself.

After the child was breathing comfortably and feeling better, we wrapped her in my jacket and immediately took a taxi to the two girls' nearby home, where, after explanations, I was welcomed like a champion, a hero. Part of that welcome involved the open, hairy arms of the girls' father, Anthony Alami, the owner of Montreal's largest General Motors agency and, under several corporate names, a variety of used car lots. As in those fanciful stories so beloved to readers of pulp novels, Mr. Alami took me into his business, and, despite his reservations—he almost changed his mind when he learned I was Jewish—gave me a first-class education in the automotive retail business, an education comparable, in every way, I'm sure, to what one might receive from McGill University—even Harvard.

Mr. Alami became my father-in-law, and I was with him for several years, working my way up to top salesman at his flagship dealership. I ended my association with him as manager of one of his used car lots, which operated under the name of "Farmer Jonez," two years ago when I went into business for myself, after a misunderstanding with my benefactor over certain practices, common in the industry, in which, I admit, I may have been overzealous, even careless. Louise was upset, of course, but, to her credit, she stood by me, defying her father at considerable cost.

"You, Father, are the greatest hypocrite in the world," Louise told him, most rashly. Her loyalty to me was certainly commendable but unwise, and was attributable to her youth and Mediterranean blood.

Mr. Alami responded by banishing her from his home, and it is my greatest hope that the grey cloud under which we now labour will reveal a silver lining in the form of a reconciliation between my wife and her family.

At any rate, I continued my involvement in the used automobile industry by becoming what is known as a freelancer. I buy and sell cars, but not *from* lots, rather *to* them. I acquire the cars privately, through a variety of means, and make them available to dealers. Sometimes, I purchase cars in rural areas and resell them in the city, where prices are higher. I visit homes for the aged, where automobiles can often be picked up for a song from people who no longer have use of them. Funerals are, similarly, good leads, and I'm a frequent visitor at auctions, where the goods of farmers and small businesses that have gone bankrupt can be inexpensively obtained.

And, I reluctantly admit, I steal cars.

You will express shock at this, no doubt, but it is a relatively harmless crime, completely devoid of violence and hurting no one but insurers, for whom, as you can well imagine, I have little sympathy, and dealers, most of whom, I'm sorry to say, are guilty themselves of the most flagrant crimes against their customers, in terms of faulty repairs, overcharging, and odometer adjustments.

And it is extremely profitable.

I fell into this aspect of my trade quite by accident, about a year and a half ago. I had sold a car—a 1932 De Soto—to a dealer in an arrangement that was quite satisfactory to both parties. I had acquired the car, perfectly legitimately, from the nephew of an elderly woman who had died, leaving her affairs in his hands. The day after I sold the car, I happened to meet this young man on Rue de Chappel, where he was strolling with a young lady.

"Ah, Mr. Cahan," he hallooed, introducing me to his companion. "How fortunate that we should meet. I was going through some of my aunt's personal things last night and came upon this, which I thought you should have."

It was an extra key for the De Soto, for which I thanked the young man profusely, too embarrassed to tell him the car was already beyond my control.

"Well, this is very nice of you," I said. "I was going to have another one made, just this afternoon."

"That will save you a nickel," the young man said.

We exchanged further pleasantries, and I then moved on, the key in my pocket but no larcenous thought in my head, I can assure you. That did not arise until several days later, when, driving past the dealer's lot where the De Soto was parked, the key forgotten in my weskit pocket and the plates from a 1928 Stanley I had just sold lying on the passenger seat beside me, these seemingly disparate currents suddenly crossed in my mind, creating a small turbulence.

That evening, behind the wheel of a magnificently kept 1933 Stutz I acquired at an auction some time before and couldn't bear to let go, I drove past the dealer's lot several times and took note of the DeSoto's location in relation to the street, the extent of the adjacent lighting, the numbers of people passing by, and so on. Had the situation seemed more difficult, I might have been deterred, but, in fact, what I had in mind seemed quite easy; I must admit, there was an element of risk, of danger, that appealed to me in a subtle but delicious way `I couldn't then, or now, explain. I can only tell you, Doctor, that it made me smile—smile as, shortly after midnight, I parked my Stutz several blocks away from the dealer's lot, smile as I casually strolled toward it, smile as I slid behind the wheel of the DeSoto, which was unlocked, and smile as I inserted the key, brought the engine to life, and drove away.

The second stage of my career as a criminal had begun in earnest, though I hardly thought of it in those terms.

Having performed one theft so successfully, I quickly fell into the pattern of behaviour that has led me to my present predicament. I could not, in my wildest dreams, have predicted the way it would unfold, however. I would, whenever circumstances seemed right, hold back a key or have an extra one made, so as to expedite my later "recovery" of the car following its sale. Because I dealt with so many cars, I always had a supply of licence plates and registration papers—all completely authentic—from a variety of provinces and neighbouring states. I would sell a car in Montreal, recover it the following week, sometimes actually from the dealer I'd sold it to but more often from its proud new owner, and resell it in Ottawa or Hull or Trois-Rivières. Or I would recover a car originally sold in Toronto and resell it in Niagara Falls or Buffalo, all cities which already had been on my route. At the peak of my activities this past spring and summer, when I was, perhaps, overextending myself, fully a third of my business was in "recovered" cars, some of them recovered more than once—one, a 1933 Studebaker with red leather upholstery that I took a particular liking to driving, was recovered and resold three times.

It was inevitable, I suppose, that I should be caught, although one of the many observations that I've made in recent years about the criminal mind is that such inevitability rarely occurs to the criminal. Indeed, in the exhilaration of his successes, it appears to him that he is invincible—even *invisible*—and that the forces of law and order, those petty bureaucrats and burghers so dedicated to the pedestrian, *orderly* unfolding of life, lack both the wit and the intelligence to get the better of him.

Such delusion! It is, in fact, that very dedication to order which the criminal mind so despises that makes the forces of law and order so perfectly suited to the deceitful art of laying out traps.

And so, with the inevitability I had disdained, I became entangled in just such a trap, its fierce claws closing in on me as if I were some dumb brute of a beast, its pelt inviting a profit, crashing me to ruin.

One day a few months ago, I had effortlessly recovered a shiny 1935 Buick from a lot in St. Sainte-Anne-de-Bellevue and was on my way to Longueuil, where I knew I could make a quick sale, when I happened to spot a red 1933 Chevrolet parked in an open garage but looking somehow dejected. I had developed a feel for such things, and, sure enough, when I made inquiries, I found the car was available for sale. Little did I know that this innocent-looking vehicle would be my undoing.

I should explain that my entire family was at the time living in an old but entirely presentable house on Rue de Laurence, Louise and I and the recent addition to our family, our darling son Benjamin, occupying the ground floor, my mother and Rebeccah the rooms on the upper floor. Yes, my mother and I, despite her enmity for me, continued to live under the same roof. Her resentment of me, or hatred, whatever it was, had settled into a cold but manageable pattern: she remained a part of the our family—what other choice did she have?—but participated in its life at only the most marginal level, often coming to table for meals but rarely speaking to me. I should say here too that, though my mother's condition had continued to deteriorate, Rebeccah's fortunes had improved considerably—so much more bitter, then, the sudden reversal that would be brought by my imminent arrest.

Rebeccah had grown into a handsome young woman—no match for what our mother had once been, but a beauty in her own right—but the shocks of our brother's death and then our father's suicide, and our mother's increasing dependence on her, had left her permanently damaged, and she was painfully shy. She had barely been able to finish high school, and university seemed out of the question. So too, for a long time, was employment of any sort that required meeting the public, and her inability to connect on any meaningful level with a young man was a heavy burden on my heart. But the presence of my Louise in our household had been a tonic for Rebeccah. At Louise's urging, my sister had begun to accompany her on afternoon outings; the two of them had lunched out any number of times, gone to exhibits at the museum, even taken in a few matinees. With Louise again as the instigator, Rebeccah's wardrobe had taken a giant step forward, and her hairstyle grown more becoming. Her natural beauty was allowed to shine, and at these outings, Louise reported to me, my sister was turning many a head. So when Rebeccah mentioned at dinner one night that she was thinking of applying for a job at a shop owned by a woman Louise knew, I was delighted. It was not for the sake of the income—my automobile dealings were bringing in more than enough money for our family to live on comfortably—but I was sure that being among more people on a regular basis would be excellent therapy for Rebeccah.

"You certainly have my enthusiastic approval," I said.

Rebeccah then surprised me with her next announcement: "I've been thinking too, Reuben, of taking driving lessons."

"That's an excellent idea," I said. "The streetcars are not that reliable, especially in winter. And it will give you more of a feeling of independence to be able to come and go as you please."

"Rebeccah will need a car," Louise observed.

I noticed my mother, seated in her usual silence at the end of the table, raise her head, an unusually alert expression flickering over her cloudy eyes. "Yes, a car," she said, surprising us all. Mother was far from mute, but more and more, she lived within herself, and it would often be days at a time between her pronouncements.

"A car, of course," I said. "Nothing could be easier."

"A nice red one," Louise said, and she and Rebeccah burst into a fit of giggles, which delighted me.

"Yes, red," our mother said.

That very day, I telephoned a fellow I knew who had a business teaching driving and arranged for my sister's lessons. And I began to keep my eyes open for a suitable car for her, something red, safe, as easy to drive as I could find.

Just the thing came to my attention within two weeks, the 1933 Chevrolet I mentioned earlier. It had been owned by a sporty young man who left it, in excellent condition and with low mileage, in his parents' garage when he went abroad to climb mountains in Switzerland. He was killed in a fall and his parents couldn't bear the sight of the car, which allowed me to purchase it at a favourable price. Very favourable.

I should have been satisfied with that, but the vision of the criminal grows increasingly narrow, Doctor. I should have brought the car home, given it to Rebeccah, and been done with it, but I didn't. I drove it to St. Hubert, where a dealer

I often sold to was delighted to take it off my hands. I made a profit, but so would he. Three days later, I received a telephone call from a man who works at the automobile registry office—a man who has himself profited handsomely from my transactions—to inform me of the name and address of the Chevrolet's new owners, a young couple in Saint Leonard. Two days after that, after supper, I said my goodnights to my mother and sister, kissed Louise, and took my departure from the house, ostensibly to spend an hour or two over billiards and cigars at my gentleman's club. Instead, I parked my Stutz on the corner of Rue Jean-Talon and Julien and took the streetcar to St. Michel. At Boulevard Viau, I transferred and went as far as Rue Robert, which was just three blocks from where the red Chevrolet sat parked outside a neat white house in a block of neat white houses. The windows of the house were dark. No sound or movement came from the house or those nearby as I unlocked the Chevrolet with my spare key, opened the door, slid in, closed the door, started the ignition. Within moments, the red Chevrolet, with me comfortably inside it, was blocks away. And no one, I was certain, was the wiser.

What I did not know was that all of my actions involving the Chevrolet had been observed by the police. I was watched when I bought the car and when I sold it. I was followed to Saint Leonard, and observed as I purloined the car. I could have been arrested at any point, including when I locked the recovered car in a garage I kept for just that purpose, near where I had parked my own car at Rue Jean-Talon and Julien.

But, for whatever reason, the police chose to wait until the following day, when, with new licence plates mounted on it, I drove the red Chevrolet into our driveway. I had barely alighted from the car before I was surrounded by uniformed policemen and taken into custody by two burly men in plain clothes.

"Please allow me to say goodbye to my wife, my sister, and my mother," I asked them.

One of the men, a good-natured fellow with a red mustache, laughed. "Go right ahead, Cahan. You won't get another chance for quite a while."

With my hands cuffed behind me, I was allowed to receive a kiss on the cheek first from Louise, who also briefly hugged me, and Rebeccah. "This is a monstrous mistake," I told them, although my heart felt heavy. "A misunderstanding. I'll be home shortly."

My mother didn't come downstairs to see what the commotion was about, but, as I was being led to the police car, I looked over my shoulder and was surprised to see her standing at her window, squinting in my direction.

⊗

And that, my dear Doctor Cohen, is my story. I will not insult your intelligence by suggesting a moral, or a response. No, far from it: I leave any lessons you may wish to infer, any gestures you may wish to bestow, entirely up to you. As for me, it is too late for anything you might be able to do to be of any use, regardless. I have already been convicted of my crimes—indeed, I entered a plea of guilty, augmented by a plea for mercy, for what else could I do?—and tomorrow I am to be sentenced. The minimum I could receive, according to the law, is three years in a penitentiary; the maximum twenty! Because of my relative youth, my spotless record—never before so much as a driving violation, even during the heat of my insurance sales career, though there were, admittedly, some close calls—and the circumstances of my family, there is reason to believe the judge will be predisposed to be lenient. Even, in a most delicious of ironies, the inscription on the certificate of bravery I was awarded by the Junior Chamber of Commerce following the rescue of Mr. Alami's two daughters was read to the court. But, alas, the extensiveness of my crimes, the "callous disregard and, indeed, *flaunting* of the rules of law" inherent in my behaviour, as expressed by the Crown prosecutor, and my demeanor in the courtroom, which, despite my plea for mercy, has been "lacking in proper repentance or even apparent awareness of the seriousness of the crime"—again, the observation of the prosecutor—all these things conspire against me. My own lawyer, a man most experienced in these matters, tells me to expect five years, probably no more, certainly no less, though he tells me too I am an excellent candidate for time off for good behaviour.

Five years! Even if it is only four, it is almost too long a time for the mind to grasp, to comprehend. I intend to put the time to good use, however. There is a library in the prison I am likely to be sentenced to, or so I am told, and I have every hope of continuing my education, broken off so abruptly by my father's death. I'm particularly anxious to improve my abilities in languages, another trait I seem to have inherited, for I have thought for some time that a man of my talents and inclinations may well be able to prosper in the older, more cultivated atmosphere of Europe, where our family's roots began and still are inextricably embedded. In four or five years' time, the nonsense now adrift in that part of the world will surely have faded away, and I look forward to travelling abroad.

No, my dear Doctor, waste no effort or tears on my behalf. I am the author of my own fate, and I am prepared to accept it. No, it is my mother and sister I fear for, and it is they to whom I direct your attention. My wife, estranged though she is from her parents, will surely benefit from their forgiveness and generosity, especially now that there is a grandchild in the equation, but there is no reason to expect that generosity to extend to Louise's in-laws, my mother and sister. If my story—*our* story, really—has elicited any feelings of familial responsibility, any desire to reach out a hand of assistance to kinsmen, it is *they*, poor helpless creatures, who should be your concern, not me.

My mother, despite her hatred of me, is lucid enough to realize the predicament in which my impending departure has put her. She should be in an institution, but Rebeccah and I had determined between ourselves that that was something we would not do. Now, I am not so certain. As for Rebeccah, she grows more bitter, turns more into herself, every day—grows more like our mother, in fact, though the realization of that is almost more than I can bear.

No, my dear Doctor, cousin, think not of me, but of them, members of your extended family who have fallen dangerously on the bitter shoals of life's precious coast. I have had my chance at the exercising of responsibility to them; my failure has been bitter and filled with regret. Now, I pass the key to you, place it into your hand.

But do you care? Do you reach out your trembling hand, your mouth filled with phrases of comfort and solicitude, your heart brimming with the tearful, joyful warmth of familiar welcome? Ah, why should you? We are so far away, my voice so distant and faint, our faces so blurred, even our very names unfamiliar to you. We are, after all, mere strangers, tied to you by the most fragile of threads, the rope of pearls long since broken, the pearls themselves cast to the wind.

* * *

Last Words

THE DAY AFTER HIS FATHER'S heart attack, Portman and his wife were on their hurried way to his bedside when, on the flight from Calgary to Toronto, he ran into a fellow he knew. Harris Yulin was an architect who'd been involved with a major civic redevelopment proposal Portman had covered for the paper a few years earlier, when he was still fairly new. The proposal was defeated in a referendum, and, although Portman had gotten to know Yulin fairly well, he hadn't seen him since. The project was a big one, and had become controversial, a renewal of four square blocks around the old city hall, with renovation of that sandstone building, a new civic hall, a hotel, stores, an arts centre, the works. It would have cost a third of a billion dollars, with the city putting up half.

At the paper, it was generally acknowledged that Portman's reporting had been the decisive factor in the vote, and it had cemented his reputation as a digger, a rising star. There were too many discrepancies in the project, too many unanswered questions, too many benefits accruing to the developers, all thoroughly explored in his stories, which ran almost daily in the weeks leading up to the vote. Even the paper's editorial board, which had first supported the proposal, as did the mayor and most of city council, had been influenced by Portman's stories, and the editorials grew increasingly skeptical, the support lukewarm, eventually dissolving altogether. After the vote, his colleagues took Portman out for a drink, toasting him.

As for Yulin, his business hadn't suffered unduly as far as Portman knew, but he certainly didn't make the big fee he would have, or get the boost to his reputation, and he hadn't been involved with anything nearly as big since. At any rate, although Portman was still covering city hall, Yulin wasn't mixed up with anything that had to come to planning commission or council, where he and Portman would have again crossed paths.

Yulin was a big affable sort of man, slope-shouldered, with a five o'clock shadow that usually began around three. During the months when the civic project had been on the front burner and they'd seen each other frequently at meetings and had become friendly, he had suggested Portman and his wife come to his house for dinner sometime, but he'd never followed through with an actual invitation.

Now Yulin was sitting three seats behind Portman and Donna on the wide-bodied Air Canada jet, in economy rather than first class or business class, where Portman would have expected him to be. Portman had noticed him during boarding, but their eyes didn't connect and he wasn't sure if Yulin had seen him. After the seatbelt lights went off, he told Donna he was going to say hello to someone he knew. The stewardess was just starting her round with the liquor cart at the head of the aisle and he had a few minutes.

Yulin was in the aisle seat, reading a report propped up on the briefcase in his lap, a music headset over his ears. A man and a woman who looked to be a couple were in the other two seats, the woman by the window. They were engaged in conversation. Across the aisle, all three seats were filled as well, so there was nothing for Portman to do but stand in the aisle and lean in toward Yulin. The motion caught his attention and he raised his eyes, deep-set brown eyes that seemed both cruel and intelligent. He recognized Portman immediately.

"Dan," he said, noncommittally, with neither warmth, enmity, nor even surprise.

"Hi, Harris. I noticed you when we were boarding and thought I'd come back and say hello." Portman smiled. "Surprised to see you back here with the masses."

He meant it only as an innocent joke, but perhaps business was bad and he'd hit a nerve. "Fuck you," Yulin said. The man and woman beside him looked up simultaneously, mild surprise on their faces. Yulin turned toward them and, seeming to address himself to the woman, who wore her lustreless brown hair in an unflattering short cut, said, "Pardon my language."

"No big deal," the man said, although his companion didn't seem convinced. She looked at Yulin, then up at Portman, as if trying to determine the source of an irritation.

Stung, Portman stood immobile for a moment, watching this exchange between the seatmates. Then, without saying anything more, he turned on his heel and went back to his seat. The colour had drained from his face, and as soon as he sat down, Donna leaned toward him.

"Something wrong, honey?"

"No, nothing."

She gave him a close look but didn't press. A minute later, the stewardess was there and they were engaged in the business of getting their drinks. Portman wasn't a good flyer and he usually liked to have several drinks on a flight. He asked for a double Scotch, reaching into his wallet for a twenty-dollar bill for himself and Donna, who had ordered her usual glass of white wine. The stewardess also gave him a close look but then handed over the extra little bottle without comment, just a neutral, "Here you are, sir."

"There's something," Donna said. "Who was that?"

"Just some guy I know from work. It's nothing, honest."

She made a sour face but didn't say anything more. After a minute, she reached over and squeezed Portman's hand.

By the time they arrived in Toronto, he'd had four drinks, the initial double and three regular ones. He felt fine, but had a relentless craving for a cigarette, although he hadn't smoked for over a year. He stayed in his seat until Yulin had filed past, and in the terminal they had to move fast to get to their Montreal connection, so there was little chance of running into him again. The couple who'd been Yulin's seatmates were on that flight too, though, and, lining up to board, Portman noticed the woman looking at him. He gave her a weak smile, and she looked away.

They got to Montreal around midnight, and Portman's mother was waving a greeting from behind the glass partition, looking haggard and years older than the last time he'd seen her, just a few months earlier, when he'd gone home for his father's sixty-fifth birthday. She had the expected brave face on, though.

"Daniel, Donna, over here," she called, although she already had their attention.

"How's he doing?" Portman asked as they walked to the car through the almost empty, tomblike airport.

"He'll be glad to see you," was all she said.

He gave her shoulder a squeeze, and, just for a moment, her stride faltered. He thought she was going to collapse against him, but she caught herself and walked on as if nothing had happened. Nothing *had* happened.

They drove in silence along the still busy 520 and down the 15 to Westmount, stopping at a convenience store on Sherbrooke so Portman could buy cigarettes, over Donna's objections. It was past one in the morning when they got to the house, the hedge-lined crescent where Portman and his father had played catch deserted and silent. His mother parked in the driveway, not bothering with the garage, and Donna and Portman carried their suitcases into the house, where the dog, an ancient, grey-muzzled Bouvier, greeted them with noisy joy. She had been the family pet, Portman's really, since he was in high school.

"Daisy, get down," Portman's mother said, irritated.

"It's okay," Donna said, giving the dog a pat, and Portman leaned over and buried his face in the familiar smell of her fur, let her bathe him with her tongue. "You two," Donna said. Her voice was lighter than it had been all evening on the planes. She gave her short blonde curls a shake.She took her bag to the room she and Portman always stayed in, his old bedroom, then disappeared into the bathroom, leaving Portman and his mother alone in the kitchen, lit only by the small light over the counter. He put his hand on his mother's arm and this time she did collapse, allowing herself to crumble against his chest, as if this were the moment she had been waiting for all day, the moment in which she could finally let go.

"It'll be all right," Portman said. It sounded lame even to his ears."I don't think so," she said. "Not this time."

They stood that way in the semi-darkness for a minute, her weight pressing on him like an unmet obligation, but the acceptance of that obligation was itself a payment, and when she pulled herself back and straightened, she had arranged a smile on her face, not just a brave smile. For the first time since they'd arrived, she seemed to fully recognize her son, to be glad to see him. "Your father really will be happy to see you," she said. "I know he has something he wants to tell you."

In the morning, they had the simplest of breakfasts, juice and toast and coffee. Portman brought the still-unopened package of cigarettes to the table and placed it next to his coffee cup, as if challenging his mother or wife to protest, but neither made a comment. Then, with Portman driving, they headed back into the city. He hadn't slept well, but he felt comfortable behind the wheel of the old sea-green Volvo, the same car he had learned to drive in over a dozen years earlier. The car had been new then, but Portman's father seemed to trust nothing untoward would come to it, and he'd been right; Portman had been a fine driver right from the beginning. The Volvo had held up, and although his parents could certainly have afforded a new car, they'd stuck with it. "The old beast still handles well," Portman said by way of conversation, but his mother, who sat beside him, with Donna in the back, gave him a puzzled look. "The car," he added. "Still drives fine."

"Oh, yes," his mother said absently.

At the hospital, Portman dropped the two women off at the main entrance. Walking back from the parking lot through the bright August sunshine, he could feel his chest tightening, a not altogether unpleasant feeling, and he paused for a moment to take a deep breath and will his heart to slow. He reached for the cigarettes in his jacket pocket, tore off the cellophane and aluminum foil, and tapped a cigarette out, the first one he'd held in his fingers in many months.

It wasn't just in driving that his father had shown his trust in Portman. Even as a teenager, young Dan had felt he was treated as an adult, with respect, and allowed to make his own decisions. "Make your own mistakes—God knows, I made plenty of my own," his father told him more than once. "Make your own mistakes, and you'll get all the credit for your successes." But the elder Portman had been disappointed when his son chose journalism school rather than following him into law, been disappointed when he'd moved west, been disappointed even with Donna, who was a student nurse when they met. He'd never expressed any of this disappointment, though, showing pride over his son's successes and genuine affection for Donna eventually. Portman really only knew of his father's feelings through intuition. There was something in his father's eye, some hesitation, something unsaid between them that troubled Portman but he felt incapable of dealing with head-on.

Still, he knew he retained his father's love and trust. This slender bond of confidence made the arguments the two men had had in the last few years all the more hard to understand for Portman, all the more frustrating. They were petty arguments over trivial things, politics and sports, the objects of the disagreements clearly not their true source. They'd even argued, the last time he'd been home, over the dog—Portman liked to give her treats; his father disapproved. Portman and Donna had discussed the possibility of his father suffering from the early stages of dementia, perhaps even Alzheimer's disease; whatever it was had perhaps been brought on by a mild stroke a few years earlier that had seemed to leave no lasting damage, or the pair of mild heart attacks, clearly warnings of something more serious to come. At his father's birthday party, he recalled now, Portman's innocent question at the dinner table about his father's health had led to a long diatribe from the older man about the state of health care in the country. Portman, again innocently enough, replied that it was Father's own beloved Liberals who were largely to blame.

"That attitude would please your own beloved Stockwell Day, I suppose," his father shot back, giving Portman a penetrating glance, then turning back to his plate.

"I have no more idea what would or wouldn't please

Stockwell Day than you do, and you know it," Portman retorted.

He would have said more, but he could feel Donna gently kicking him under the table, and when he glanced at her he saw her milk-chocolate eyes narrowed in what he knew was a secret smile.

Thinking of all that again, Portman put the cigarette to his lips, picturing himself lighting it and drawing smoke greedily into his lungs, feeling the satisfied tightness, then realized with an embarrassed start that he had forgotten to get matches. He crumpled the cigarette in exasperation and threw it away. As he approached the hospital entrance, he noticed a tramp in a ragged overcoat patrolling outside the main doors and gave him the package. The urgent need had passed.

He found his mother and Donna in the gift shop near the elevators, buying a copy of *The Gazette*. "He likes me to read the headlines to him," his mother explained.

"I could do that," Portman said.

They took the elevator to the cardiac unit in silence, sharing it with an elderly East Indian couple who stared resolutely at the floor. Portman found himself gazing with intensity at the swirls and folds of the design of the woman's chartreuse sari, losing himself. When the door opened on the third floor, the couple seemed confused, getting out of the elevator but then immediately spinning around and re-entering it, bumping into the Portmans as they attempted to exit. Portman felt an odd sensation in reaction, a mixture of irritation and amusement.

His mother led the way down the hall and around a corner. At the nursing station, a stout woman in a faded pink pantsuit uniform gave them a cheery greeting. Turning to Portman, she announced in a hearty voice: "And this must be the prodigal son."

Portman smiled weakly and followed his mother into the room. Donna held his hand tightly. He had the folded newspaper in his other hand.

His father's eyes were closed and his breathing was so shallow as to be all but imperceptible. Portman's mother went right up to the bed and took her husband's hand in hers, reassuring herself. When she looked up, there was a glimmer of light in her eyes. "He looks a little better today."

Portman took up a position on the other side of the bed, with Donna slightly behind him. "Hello, Dad," he said, although it seemed unlikely his father could hear him. For several minutes they all stood there, their heads bowed as if in prayer, but their thoughts were directed downward, not up. Portman's father lay motionless, but, as Portman's eyes grew accustomed to the intense artificial light, he gradually was able to make out the feeble rise and fall of the older man's chest.

"Donna, dear, let's have a cup of coffee," Portman's mother said, and, before he could protest, Donna gave his hand a good-bye squeeze and the two women retreated from the room. Portman continued his standing vigil for another minute or two, then looked around for a chair. There was only one in the room, squatting stiffly against the opposite wall like a silent observer. It was heavy bottomed and upholstered with worn, thinly padded green plastic.

He pulled it over, seated himself as comfortably as he could, and reached over to hold his father's dry, whispery-skinned hand, brushing aside the tangle of electric wires in which his father was enmeshed. The hand was cool, but not cold. He looked again at his father's chest to reassure himself. The elder Portman had always been vigorous; now he seemed to be possessed by an odd fusion of robustness and fragility.

After a few minutes, the stout nurse in pink came in and checked the readings on the electrocardiograph. She gave Portman a distant smile but said nothing. She made a notation in the chart.

"He's not in a coma, is he?" Portman asked.

"No, no, he's just sleepy today. He was awake a lot yesterday. He had a little broth for breakfast, then he went back to sleep. He was asking about you before. He'll be around in his own good time." The last sentence was pronounced in a slightly severe tone, as if the nurse was accusing Portman of wanting things to happen on *his* schedule.

"Good," he said. "Thanks."

He sat in silence for several minutes, his thoughts familiar and predictable. A family trip to Disneyland, another, just he and his father, to a northern lake for fishing. The ivory-handled razor his father had presented him with on his thirteenth birthday. A cheese sandwich the two of them shared one summer evening, when Portman was sixteen or seventeen and had crept into the house way past his curfew to find his father up and waiting, but not angry—inexplicably, he could taste that cheese on his tongue now. Then his mind wandered and he found himself thinking of Harris Yulin, of possibly getting in touch, but he wasn't sure which one of them owed the other an apology. The craving for a cigarette—that sweet sharp needle in the lungs—surged through him again, then just as quickly subsided.

He thought of his mother's comment that his father had something to say to him. Advice? Apology? Or something small but practical, like the location of a safety deposit key. Portman had no idea.

He had laid the folded newspaper on the foot of the bed when they entered. Now, he unfolded it and arranged it on his lap, scanning the front page. The doomed Russian submarine, the Toronto doctor who'd leaped in front of a train with her baby, rising gasoline prices. "Hope fades for submariners," he read aloud, immediately regretting it. He skipped over the story on the subway woman. "Gasoline prices continue upward creep. Ottawa insists it's not to blame."

He opened the paper to page 2. His mother had said the headlines, but what harm would it do to go further? "Here's today's bright spot," he said, and he read the brief item of a dog that had made a long journey to be reunited with its owner. There was a photo of two children feeding a hippopotamus at the Montreal Zoo. He described the photo and read the caption. On page 3 there was a story, which he read in its entirety, about the retirement of a judge he was sure his father knew. On the next page, there was a piece from Calgary about a toddler abandoned in a supermarket, a story some of

Portman's colleagues had been working on. The mother had been identified and it looked like the story was heading toward a happy ending. "Here's one from my town, Dad," Portman said, and he read the whole thing, annotating it with insider commentary. For the first time since his mother's phone call, more than forty hours earlier, Portman felt himself relaxing slightly, as if he'd had the cigarette after all and it had done its trick.

By the time his mother and Donna returned, Portman was onto the sports page, reading the blow-by-blow account of last night's Expos game. If his father were conscious and sitting up in bed, they'd probably be arguing by this point, but he hadn't stirred. And it had already dawned on Portman that his father might not stir, that he might never get to hear his father's message, that he might go back out West without ever knowing what his father wanted to say, what might have been said.

"Oh, Dear," Portman's mother said. She stood uncertainly in the doorway, seemingly holding her breath. Portman strained his ears for his father's breathing but it had become so quiet now as to be all but beyond hearing. Just a small, almost indiscernible movement of his chest betrayed the elusive breath, a flutter.

* * *

A NOTE ON THE TEXT

This book has been set in two classic American typefaces, Century Schoolbook and Trade Gothic, which reinforce the everyday character of Dave Margoshes's stories.

ABOUT THE AUTHOR

The author of twelve books, including three novels, Dave Margoshes has had his work published in numerous magazines and anthologies throughout North America, including six times in the *Best Canadian Stories* volumes. Margoshes worked as a newspaper reporter in the US and Canada, and has taught journalism and creative writing. His writing has won a number of awards, including the City of Regina Writing Award, the John V. Hicks Award for Fiction, and the Stephen Leacock Prize for Poetry. He lives in Regina.